# DANDELION

by

## GAVIN HOFFEN

**Eloquent Books**

Eloquent Books
An imprint of Strategic Book Group
P.O. Box 333
Durham CT 06422
www.StrategicBookGroup.com

ISBN: 978-1-60911-698-9

Printed in the United States of America

Book Design: Bonita S. Watson

# *Acknowledgements*

The story told within this book is based on some true events, but I do not claim that the historical accounts are all based upon facts or are chronologically correct. My expertise is in estate agency and I know very little about spies, MI5 or wires. Any accuracy within the book has been stumbled upon more than likely by accident. The characters within the story are purely a figment of my imagination; the names have been plucked out of thin air (apologies if you can see yourself in any given character).

Writing this book has been harder than I ever imagined, and as a result I have had to accept help from a number of kind people. I would like to express my thanks to my friend, Tony, who helped me edit the book and whose father, then a Group Captain in the RAF, really was booked to fly back from Gibraltar in Sikorski's aircraft. Your help and advice has been nothing short of priceless. To the late Warrick Forrester, who invited me into his home to give me a valuable insight as to what South Marston was like during those darker days of Word War Two. A big thank you to Laura Tweedle and Amanda Jones, without your initial enthusiasm for the novel this book would probably not have been written. Bob, and Barbara at the Carpenters arms in South

Marston deserve a mention. Thank you for feeding me such great meals and giving me inspiration to set some of the book in their lovely pub. Julian Knops provided much inspiration, your enthusiasm for the property market was a great source of insight, thank you also for being a great boss – it truly was a pleasure to have worked with you. To Serena, my girlfriend, thank you for putting up with me over the years that it took to finish this work, you have been fantastic. Last but not least my parents, you have been superb, without your loyal support this would have not have been possible. Thank you.

# Winston Churchill speech in the Commons

## *7th July 1943*

"We learned yesterday that the cause of the United Nations had suffered a most grievous loss. It is my duty to express the feelings of the House, and to pay tribute to the memory of a great Polish patriot and staunch ally General Sikorski. His death in the air crash at Gibraltar was one of the heaviest strokes we have sustained......

.......I was often brought into contact with General Sikorski in those years of war. I had a high regard for him, and admired his poise and calm dignity amid so many trials and baffling problems. He was a man of remarkable pre-eminence, both as a statesman and a soldier. His agreement with Marshal Stalin of July 30th, 1941 was an outstanding example of his political wisdom. Until the moment of his death he lived in the conviction that all else must be subordinated to the needs of the common struggle and in the faith that a better Europe will arise in which a great and independent Poland will pay an honourable part. We the British here and throughout the Commonwealth and Empire, who declared war on Germany because of Hitler's invasion of Poland and in fulfilment of our guarantee, feel deeply for our Polish allies in their new loss.

We express our sympathy to them, we express our confidence in their immortal qualities, and we proclaim our resolve that General Sikorski's work as Prime Minister and Commander-in-Chief shall not have been in vein. This house would, I am sure, wish also that its sympathy should be conveyed to Madame Sikorski who dwells here in England, and whose husband and daughter have been simultaneously killed on duty.

# Chapter 1

# Swindon

*Monday 2<sup>nd</sup> August 2008*

Becoming an estate agent was never part of my grand master plan, but it had become a job that I loved in so many different ways: the company car that you could abuse as much as you liked (and often had to when running late for appointments), the variation of properties and people and the immense feeling of ecstasy when negotiating a sale or putting a property on the market amongst fierce opposition. However, I loved my job mostly because I worked with a good bunch of people who were completely dedicated to their jobs despite the unsociable hours. The property industry however was not all fun and games, as estate agency is, without doubt, one of the most stressful jobs out there, especially working for a large company as I did. The pressure to achieve targets for sales, mortgage leads and listing properties was difficult to take and was definitely not for the faint-hearted. My colleagues dealt with the stress of day- to-day life in their own personal ways, but my escape often was alcohol.

The digital clock in the corner of the room displayed the time as eight forty-five a.m., giving off a gentle and warming red glow. Hailstones pounded a nearby window as thunder erupted from the distant heavens above. A bitterly chilling draught on my face had woken me from a deep sleep, moments before a furious, overweight man had come bounding in screaming in a foreign tongue. I jumped up in a frenzied panic trying desperately to take in my unfamiliar surroundings as I was barraged with what I can only assume was every single swear word in this strange man's native language. Wearing only a pair of boxer shorts and a grubby white vest my host for the night furiously screamed at me in either Greek or Turkish as he repeatedly pointed to a door in the corner of the dark, musty living room. I glanced down at myself to take stock of what clothes I was wearing: creased navy jeans and an unfamiliar red t-shirt made suitable attire for my rapid escape.

My head ached in colossal proportions. I was so dehydrated that my mouth was as dry as the Sahara desert but I needed to keep my wits about me as I tried to establish where the hell I was. I made every effort not to make eye contact with my not-so-welcome host as I tried to piece together fragments of memory from the previous evening. I had found myself in a small, dark and damp living room. Everything was alien to me: the dog-chewed sofa that had been my bed for the night, the ironing board laden with a pile of unfamiliar clothes and the revolting wet dog and stale smoke smell.

I needed to get out of there before my stomach decided to empty its contents over this already unimpressed man's floor. Without giving a second thought to my absent footwear, I made a sudden dive for the door that my new friend had been vigorously pointing at; my heart raced pumping adrenalin throughout my entire body as I launched myself through the door. In doing so, my shoulder smashed into the door frame knocking me off balance as I plummeted to the floor in the narrow hallway, the tiled floor cold against my arms and cheek. Momentarily gazing up to re-establish my bearings, I could hear the full force of the storm outside as heavy rain hammered on the glass-panelled front door. Without any further hesitation, I was up on my feet and shutting the door firmly behind me.

In only seconds, the rain had drenched me from head to toe as I stood in the street looking at the door that had been my exit route, while flowing water on the pavement covered my freezing cold bare feet. Pepe's kebab shop was positioned directly next to the door that I had escaped from; I shook my head in utter disbelief as realisation dawned on me of the schoolboy error that I had made the previous evening as it unravelled in front of my eyes. With a skin full of alcohol and a probable overwhelming desire for a greasy kebab, I had evidently got myself into such a state that I was unable to locate the correct door to the fast food shop.

*This behaviour would have to stop*, I warned myself as I started the ten-minute walk to my parents' house to have a quick shower and ready myself for another week at work.

Arriving at the office thirty-five minutes late and smelling of stale alcohol was not one of the wisest moves I had made in my young career. It definitely didn't add any weight to any future prospects of promotion. My Manager, Ralph, was furious. It had taken Ralph approximately ten seconds to intercept me as I subtlety tried to sneak into the office undetected, my aching head not prepared for the bollocking that was to follow. With the both of us stood in the cramped kitchen located at the rear of the office, I felt like a naughty schoolboy as I tried as hard as I could not to exhale with too much force over Ralph as he vocally reminded me of my responsibilities as Assistant Branch Manager. I could feel myself break into a sticky sweat as the room filled with the smell of smoke and stale alcohol; Ralph's words were now starting to sail over my head. I understood all too well that he had to be seen by the others to be making a stance against my inappropriate behaviour, but we both knew deep down that I was far too gifted at my job to be subject to any serious form of punishment.

"Hammy, if this happens again I will personally drop-kick your sorry arse from here to Head Office." Veins appeared on his rosy cheeks as he continued. "As penance for your disappointing behaviour, you may now have the pleasure of showing Mr. and Mrs. Bamber around Twenty-two Lansdown Close at ten a.m.

I could feel my already fragile condition deteriorate further as I contemplated my punishment: a morning with the biggest pair of arseholes I had ever met. Number Twenty-two Lansdown Close was a property that I had never seen before, so with a large bunch of keys and half a packet of headache tablets, I left fifteen minutes early in order for me to take a look around before the Bambers arrived. Lansdown Close was a highly popular location. Its tree-lined street and the large and imposing bay-windowed Victorian terraced homes made it an area that buyers flocked to. It certainly was a pleasure seeing these properties for the first time. Number Twenty-two stood tall and proud as it nestled behind a well-groomed hedgerow set back off the road. Something caught my eye as I approached the large oak front door. Positioned to the centre of the door, directly underneath a gothic brass knocker was an A4 sized stained glass window; the rich array of colours and painstakingly detailed characters were hard not to admire as I closely examined the scene depicting what I can only imagine was from the Last Supper. The religious theme seemed to continue when I had turned the lock and forced the door open to a chorus of creeks and scrapings. As I entered through into the grand entrance hall, I found photographs of Jean Paul the Second mingled on a wall with framed family portraits and scenic paintings.

*What a treat!* I thought, as I noticed the two crystal chandeliers that hung beneath wonderfully crafted plaster ceiling roses and the original Victorian Welsh quarry floor below that was still in place; the current vendors had presented their property exquisitely. Glancing at my watch, I still had ten minutes before my beloved guests were due to arrive - enough time to explore the spacious living accommodation and prepare my sales pitch.

My stomach had changed from a volatile sick sensation to an empty, starving, bottomless pit. My head felt like it was experiencing a regiment of drummers performing their routine inside it, but my mouth was crying out for an urgent intake of liquid or food. The kitchen was located at the far end of the hallway towards the rear of the property. My initial thoughts on seeing the house were that the four hundred and fifty thousand pound price tag was on the optimistic side, but seeing this home's magnificent pièce de résistance for the first time made every single penny worthwhile. The kitchen measured twenty feet long and fifteen feet wide, the room having a pitched roof that was home to three velux skylight windows and two rows of sunken ceiling spotlights. From the slate flooring to the granite work surfaces and the sunken plasma screen in the wall, this place oozed quality. I imagined the parties one could have in a place like this as I rifled through the vendor's cupboards looking for a quick bite to eat. The cupboards were down to the bare essentials, so with what little semi-skimmed milk there was left, I poured myself a bowl of cornflakes; I really had forgotten how good they taste. With my bowl of cereal, I wondered back through to the hallway to take a peep through the stained glass window to see whether the Bambers had arrived yet. As I moved through into the hallway admiring the different pieces of artwork hanging on the walls, a note caught my eye that sat on a polished side table:

Dear Mary,

    I hope all is well with you. If you could be kind enough to put plenty of food out today and tomorrow for Puddles as we will be back tomorrow evening (food in kitchen cupboard next to the sink). Please can you check that all windows and doors are locked as we are expecting the estate agents round (can't trust these agents!)? See you on our return.

Many thanks<br>Alison & Geoff

*Who and what was Puddles?* I thought, as I placed the note back exactly where I had found it. I hadn't run into any pet on my earlier brief look at the house but figured that it was more than likely that a cat was gallivanting outside somewhere. I couldn't see any sign of the Bambers as I strained to see through the stained glass window in the front door.

"They probably won't even turn up", I mumbled to myself as I turned back towards the direction of the kitchen. Making very sure I hadn't spilt any milk on the lovely floor as I retraced my steps, something on the stairs caught my attention. Sat invitingly, half way up the stair case, was a stair lift. Stair lifts were one of those funny contraptions that I would come across on a regular basis in my day-to-day life without having actually tried one out; with no sign of my guests, it seemed a good idea at the time to have my first experience of hassle-free stair climbing.

With my bowl of cornflakes sitting safely on my lap, I settled down into the comfortable chair laying my arms on the rests provided. A small control panel was positioned on the end of an arm rest with an 'up' and 'down' button. Without a moment's hesitation, I pressed the 'up' button. As if woken by a huge heard of elephants, the chair suddenly sprang into life making its way slowly and gently up the staircase.

*This is the life!* I thought to myself as the chair slowed slightly as it came to the bend towards the top of the staircase. As the chair made the left hand turn on the stairs, I could sense that my arms were slowly moving inwards towards my torso. Before I could comprehend what was moving, I felt the arm rests apply pressure to both of my sides; the stair lift had stopped three stairs short of the top. I tried to shuffle my body forward but to no avail; I was pinned in. Taking care not to spill my cornflakes, I tried to twist my body slightly to narrow its width but the grip of the arm rests was too firm. My blood pressure was rising as my mind raced on how to get the hell out of this thing. I repeatedly hit the buttons on the control panel but nothing happened. I sat there for a moment listening to my heart beating away when a creak of a door on the landing grabbed my attention.

*Was that a creak or just the noise from the old hot water pipes?* I was considering this when the answer revealed itself in front of my very eyes: I had just met Puddles.

Saliva oozed out of its mouth as it growled louder by the second; I was almost at eye level with what I can only describe as the most ferocious-looking Alsatian dog I have ever seen, his back arched as if about to launch an attack on me. Without giving a second's thought, I threw the cornflakes towards its direction spraying milk and cereal all over the vendor's cream stair carpet. Puddles leaped at the bowl and began to lick it dry.

*That will keep it occupied for all of ten seconds*, I thought, as I made another desperate attempt to struggle my way free.

"Ding Dong, Ding Dong."

Shit, the Bambers were here! With Puddles' attention now firmly back on me, I examined as clearly as I could the limited options that I had to play with. I could remain deadly silent, pretend that nobody was in and pray that Puddles would keep its slobbering mouth shut. Or I could call out: "It's not locked; come in!" The latter option had its flaws. Firstly, I would have to expose myself as a complete incompetent fool who managed to get himself held captive by a chair lift whilst tucking into the vendor's food supplies. Secondly, the door may not have been unlocked at all which would have added salt into an already deepening self-inflicted wound.

"Ding, Dong."

Puddles started to growl more loudly - any moment now he would erupt into a chorus of barking. I remained as silent as I humanly could, afraid that even breathing would expose my position. As I sat trapped in my chair, I contemplated the phone call that I would very likely have to make to my office, asking for assistance. Ralph was going to murder me!

I waited for approximately twenty minutes until I found the courage to pull my mobile from out of my pocket. Even Puddles had lost interest by now and sat with his back to me. Within seconds of the line connecting to my office, one of my colleagues had rapidly explained how a trainee this morning had locked himself out of a house and that Ralph was in a foul mood as a result. My arm holding my mobile shook as I started to explain my slight problem. My colleague listened in silence as I explained;

she ended the call with very few words. I feared that this time I was about to push my Manager's patience to the absolute limit. During what seemed to be an entire lifetime, I waited in silence with genuine fear inside me; for once my cock-sure attitude had been knocked. I prayed that Ralph would be in a forgiving mood and wouldn't decide that I had become expendable.

After a forty- five minute wait, the remains of the Last Supper all over the front door mat and one hefty bill for a stained glass window heading my way, I was free.

# Chapter 2

# Gibraltar

*March 1943*

Some forty years prior to my birth, a twenty-something Albert Davies sat in the sweltering afternoon sun, blowing smoke rings into the airfield's heat haze rising up from the baking tarmac. Sweat gathered on the brow of his forehead dropping beads onto his cigarette, while his pale-blue uniform shirt clung to his back displaying no dry patches whatsoever.

The afternoon now seemed quiet and restful compared with the hive of activity that was the morning; security at the airfield had been tightened with the arrival of a B-24 Liberator aircraft and its important entourage. Although nothing out of the ordinary for such an active RAF base like Gibraltar, what was unusual, thought

Albert Davies as he sucked the last drag out of his cigarette, was the early arrival in the day of a large multiple-engined Russian aircraft alongside which the Liberator had parked.

*Whoever had been on board the Liberator would have been of the utmost importance*, pondered Davies since the crew and passengers had been collected by an escort of unmarked Governor's limos and taken to an unknown destination. Although curious of the Russian aircraft's arrival, Corporal Davies's task in hand was not to lose sight of the British B-24 Liberator that sat about twenty metres in front of him, and the cargo, that was currently being employed as a seat for its guard. He had been given strict orders not to load the cargo onto the aircraft until told to do so. The B-24 was due for departure later that evening so he started to fear that he would be on guard duty for a further five or six hours. It was becoming easy for him to slip into daydreams with the Mediterranean sun beating down on him. Memories of his young wife, Victoria, back in England were never far from his thoughts and he counted every minute that passed before his eighteen month tour of duty came to an end.

As the sun started to tighten Davies's already tanned face and neck, the unmistakable sound of a military jeep could be heard coming towards him through the afternoon's thin air. A slight cloud of grey smoke could be seen behind the vehicle as it raced towards the Corporal's position. Davies glanced down at his watch as the olive-green jeep pulled up alongside the pile of crates and the young guard sitting on them. The time was approaching close to five p.m. A tall and rigid man stepped out of the jeep; he was wearing a perfectly-ironed summer-issue Royal Air Force uniform with sleeves on his shirt meticulously rolled up to just above the elbow. The four stripes of a Group Captain sat on each of his shoulders. Davies was quick to his feet dispelling his grogginess; he offered a salute that was smartly returned. The officer had a gentle manner about him. He appeared confident but yet reserved, *someone who you would want fighting next to you in the trenches*, the young Corporal thought. His skin was a dark brown which meant that he had probably been here on this rock for as long as, or even longer, than himself.

"No need to load those crates on board anymore young chap," said the officer who was wiping beads of sweat away from his brow. "Orders from the very top. Another aircraft will be flying in early morning to take them back to London where they will be reunited with their owners."

*Nothing unusual*, thought Davies. *If the passengers on this flight already had a pile of luggage, and with a full compliment of fuel to get them back to England, they were obviously paying great attention to keep the aircraft as light as possible*, he argued to himself.

"The problem we have, Corporal, is that those eight crates need accompanying back to England." The Group Captain looked deep into Albert Davies's blue eyes trying to find the slightest of reactions, but before Davies could utter his first words, the Officer continued: "What I'm trying to say is that if you felt confident that, to the best of your abilities, you could personally oversee that this cargo reached its destination, then I don't see why you shouldn't have a few well-earned days leave in England as a just reward."

Albert Davies could not believe his good fortune; a couple of stolen days with Victoria would be a godsend and all for babysitting a few wooden crates. He could feel a sense of importance and responsibility surge through his veins; after all it was he who was selected for this special task above all other servicemen on the Rock. For the first time in months Albert Davies was a proud man.

"It would be an honour and a privilege, Sir," he replied, trying desperately to subdue his feelings of excitement. The Officer nodded his head and, sporting a friendly and brotherly smile, he patted Davies on the shoulder.

"Jolly good, that's the plan then." The Group Captain handed the young guard a cigarette from the silver case in his breast pocket. "Stay here, Corporal with the cargo and await further instructions. I will speak with your CO to ascertain if the 'Black Tails' will be with you and to arrange your leave." By now the officer had jumped back into the jeep and was about to awaken the engine.

"Wait," Davies shouted inappropriately, slightly forgetting who he was addressing. "The what tails will be with me, Sir?"

The officer smiled like a mother would when first asked about Father Christmas by her child. "The Black Tails," he paused momentarily. "They are a squadron of Polish Mark 1 Spitfires stationed at Lyon-Born in France. They are used mainly for escort duties; the pilots paint the tails black with a small skull and crossbones, painted in white, at the tip of the tail. I suppose they do this to look more intimidating, but at the moment they don't seem to be so forthcoming in committing their beloved squadron." With this, a raw from underneath the jeep's bonnet erupted and a plume of grey smoke rose from the back of the vehicle. Within seconds, the olive-green jeep was just a black spec far off in the distance.

Two heavily-armed Military Police Officers stood side-by-side only yards from the front of the converted Liberator of RAF Transport Command, their fully-loaded machine guns resting in their hands ready for the quickest of responses. A couple of groundcrew went through their checklists attending to different parts of the aircraft.

*These two groundcrew were like a couple of bumble bees*, thought Davies, as they darted from place to place on different sections of the fuselage. Security at Gibraltar was not always so visible, but with the visit of the Polish Commander- in-Chief, General Vladimir Sikorski and his daughter, security was stepped up for all to see. As the early evening sun started to ease its grip on the back of Davies neck, a jeep containing more groundcrew arrived quickly jumping into the flight of the bumble bees, weaving in and out underneath the aircraft's belly. The Corporal flicked away his cigarette and got up to straighten his legs and to get the blood pumping around his toes again. Although it was not his place to ask questions, Albert Davies did have a curiosity about what he had been sitting on for what had been the best part of the day. The two guards in front of him did not look the friendliest of human beings but the curiosity to know what was in the boxes was growing stronger. Gingerly he approached the guards.

"Excuse me, Sirs," said Davies trying to project his voice as deeply as he could. The guards did not acknowledge the young Corporal. "I don't suppose you gents know what I have been sat on all afternoon?" One of the burley guards turned. "A bloody wooden box," he said in a thick Sheffield accent. The other guard started to snigger.

"He's only jesting with you," said the other guard, also in a Sheffield accent.

"Whatever it is, it's bloody important," continued the guard. "That lot was unloaded off Sikorski's aircraft last night. They are under his personal protection. Whatever they are, he treasures them so much he didn't want to risk them breaking when taking them to the Governor's residence where they stayed last night."

*Maybe he would find out what he had escorted back with him once he arrived in England,* Davies thought. *Maybe their owners would show him?* Whatever they were, Davies was soon to see Victoria again and that's all that mattered.

Early evening turned into late evening and the suffocating heat had transformed itself into a bitterly cold and biting wind, while the once gentle lapping sea could now be heard thundering against the rocks all around the airfield. Davies wished he had brought a coat or blanket to keep him warm. The time was quarter to eleven and Davies was fast becoming in desperate need of sleep, his eyes squinting to keep out the cold and not to make them feel so droopy. From the corner of his eye he registered the two eyes of a truck coming towards him from the distance, the headlights becoming brighter the closer it came. Eventually the groaning noise of the diesel engine could be heard above the roaring waves and the stiff wind as it approached further. As the lorry pulled to a grinding halt only yards away from Albert Davies's feet, he could make out the outlines of three men in the cab, cast in shadow. Both the driver's and passenger's doors opened at the same time and an instantly recognisable face stepped out of the driver's side.

"Hello again, Corporal," said the Group Captain with a familiar smile as he closed the door behind him and strode towards Davies.

"You look cold. Here put this on," he said as he slipped out of his standard issue coat, the four bars of a Group Captain sewn on towards the bottom of the sleeves. If it wasn't for being so damn cold, Davies would have declined the offer, but survival instinct took over and he eagerly took the coat from the Senior Officer and thanked him courteously.

"Corporal, I would like you to meet Flight Lieutenant Prchal," said the Group Captain. Davies could sense a level of pride in the Group Captains voice. "He is the pilot who will be flying the Liberator out tonight. He is the Czech's finest pilot who comes personally requested by Sikorski himself."

Davies saluted and shook his hand firmly. "Pleased to meet you, Sir."

Flt Lt Prchal looked like a pilot, Davies thought, with his brown leather flying jacket, the thickly waxed hair and arrogant air about him.

"It might be an idea, Sir, to introduce the Fight Lieutenant to those gun-wielding snowdrops before he starts climbing into the plane or he might be met by a round of bullets from them instead of a salute!"

The Group Captain and the pilot chuckled to themselves.

"Good idea, Corporal," said the Group Captain as he started to turn away from Davies and head towards the Military Policemen. He looked back.

"Sikorski and the rest of the entourage and crew will be arriving shortly, so just hang fire for a short while and we will have you back in the warmth in no time."

The time was seven minutes past eleven. The four huge Pratt and Witney engines roared as Eduard Prchal opened up the throttle whilst still holding the brakes; the B-24 that had taxied to the end of the runway crept forward slightly as the engines desperately tried to pull the aircraft forward against the brakes. The Liberator with General Sikorski and his entourage that included his daughter, lurched forwards as Prchal released the brakes. From where Davies and the Group Captain were standing they could just make out the RAF roundels and the

Registration Number, AL 523, on the tail of the fuselage as the B-24 started to race forward from the end of the runway. Locally, the only source of light was from two high voltage lamps that hung overhead on poles while the runway had limited lights that gave off just enough light for the pilot to establish the sides of the runway. The aircraft raced passed them still gathering speed, Davies and the Group Captain waved as the Liberator started to climb into the night sky. The noise of its four engines nearly deafening them as the aircraft gained height. The Group Captain turned to Davies with an almost regretful look in his eyes.

"Thank you so much for all of your...." He abruptly stopped and suddenly turned back in the direction of the Liberator. "Can you hear that?" he said holding his finger to his lips.

Davies listened; he could hear the engines whining, then they seemed to cut out and then spark into life again. He was just about to say something when, from out into the distant sky, the awful noise of propellers racing as they rushed towards the ground could be heard by all on the base, the haunting sound of a crippled plane diving hopelessly towards its end. Within just a few seconds of the gut-wrenching scream of the doomed aircraft, a colossal splash occurred out at sea maybe just less than a mile away from the runway. Davies fell back onto the wooden crates that had been his seat all day. Dumbstruck, he looked up towards the Group Captain, whose head was tilted forwards, motionless.

# Chapter 3

# Swindon

*Monday 2nd August 2008*

I had not noticed that the mood of the office was glum and sombre when I returned from my excursion with the Bambers. I was too pre-occupied with the notion that I was in for the biggest bollocking of my life from Ralph. As I placed my folder and keys down on my desk, I could see a sad and distant look in Ralph's eyes as he sat behind his computer screen at his desk directly behind me. I could tell that the morning's events had pissed him off in colossal proportions. I strolled to the back of the office where the key cupboard was located to put the Lansdown Close keys away. In doing so I passed four of my colleagues, two desks either side of the office, but not one acknowledgement was made. My usually jovial colleagues now just sat gazing aimlessly into their plasma screens.

*Surely my morning's antics had not caused such a foul atmosphere?* I thought to myself, as I struggled to get the big bunch of keys safely on its loop. In what was normally such a happy office, I knew that something had to be wrong.

Ralph was a simple man to get on with, not easy, but simple. He was what I would call from the old school variety, believing in good old fashioned values; a man's word was his honour. Although Ralph knew that each and every one of his staff was a gifted salesman, he disliked our 'Cartier and Rolls Royce' image. He liked his negotiators to have a willingness to get down and dirty; if a sale depended on trudging through a muddy field, knee high in God knows what, just to secure a sale, then that is what he would expect. A colleague once told me that a few years ago, in order to achieve the maximum selling price of a bungalow, Ralph had spent four of his Sundays retiling a little old lady's bathroom. Ralph had not mentioned this to anyone, I guess because he did it for reasons other than praise, but I knew and respected him fully ever since I had heard this tale. I turned to head towards the kitchen to get a glass of water from the tap.

"Hammy!" It was Ralph's voice. I quickly turned to face him. "I need you to do the twelve o'clock valuation at Clarence Road, then I want words with you as soon as you are back!"

With Ralph in a mood like this, I could understand why my colleagues were being so sheepish; maybe it was a blessing in disguise being sent out on one of Ralph's valuations. At least it would keep me out of this environment for an hour or so. I also did not mind going to Clarence Road which is a typical late Victorian street with bay windows, red brick, two reception rooms and two bedrooms usually. It was the one road in Old Town where Knight Allen's sold boards hung in abundance. You could not walk down the street without passing one of our boards within an interval of about twenty steps. With only fifteen minutes until twelve o'clock, I hastily gathered up the camera and laser measurer. Two bollockings for being late in one day was not going to happen.

I gave two firm knocks to the wooden front door of Seventy-eight Clarence Road. Sold boards hung either side from numbers

Seventy-seven and Seventy-nine, so *a hat trick would stick two fingers up to all of the other agents*, I pondered, as the door suddenly swung open. A short, well-dressed Asian man stood in the doorway wearing a beautifully white smile. He was dressed exquisitely. Dark brown polished shoes accompanied his perfectly fitting stone wash jeans; he wore a brown suit jacket unbuttoned to reveal a light pink open neck shirt - clearly a man of property, I presumed, as I returned his firm handshake.

"I see you guys know a thing or two about selling property," he said in a heavy Birmingham accent as he motioned me to come in.

"We do our best Mr. Singh," I cheerfully replied as I stepped into his living room. The property smelt heavily of damp. In fact, there was so much damp that the seventies-style wallpaper was having tough times trying to stick onto the walls; portions of the decayed carpet had been pulled out to reveal large sections of exposed wooden floor boards.

*This property was not in keeping with Mr. Singh's dress code*, I thought to myself, for he was, after all, definitely a man of many properties.

"Forgive me for being presumptuous, Mr. Singh, but I am guessing that this is not your main residence," I said, treading very carefully, as he may well have decided to live in a shit hole like this. But Mr. Singh's over enthusiastic laugh told me that he did not live here.

"I see that you have sold the two properties next door to this one," he said as he scratched his inner calf.

*Just what I need, a splodge of flea bites*, I thought, as I tried to formulate my response.

"Yes," I replied knowing exactly what his next question was going to be. "We sold your neighbour's property for one hundred and fifty one thousand, and Seventy-nine went for one hundred and forty eight thousand pounds."

Mr. Singh looked impressed, but I needed to bring him back down to reality.

"Those two particular properties were, however, in excellent decorative order and your property does appear to require a programme of modernisation."

He nodded reluctantly and gestured with his hand for me to take a look around.

"Let me know what you honestly think of this."

The property was truly in a terrible state; the kitchen was almost non-descript with just a sink and an ancient looking cooker that stood solitarily in the corner. From the rear of the kitchen, through the disintegrated timber-framed windows, I could see that the narrow rear garden had received no attention in what must have been years.

"Did you manage to rent this out Mr. Singh?" I asked, as I carefully made my way upstairs.

"It's been unable to be rented for the last eighteen months and before that I was gifted by a long term tenant, an elderly lady who stayed here for eleven years."

*That would explain the condition of the property*, I thought, as I went to examine the two double bedrooms upstairs. A gas boiler hung on a wall in the back bedroom, with dark smoky stains covering the front panel. *This place is a death trap*, I noted down, as I carefully came back down the creaky stairs. Mr. Singh watched in trepidation as I approached him, for he anticipated that the news was not going to be good.

"Mr. Singh, I will get straight to the point," I said as I looked him straight in the eye. "With all this work involved I don't think you're looking at more than one hundred and fifteen thousand pounds."

His whole face dropped, he put his hand across his mouth and then ran his hand through his gelled hair; he clearly looked shocked.

"But you said you achieved one fifty next door."

I had to be careful not to lose my composure.

"You have to realise, Mr. Singh, that next door is beautifully presented. It has double glazing, a modern kitchen and a trendy games room in the converted cellar. This property however, Mr. Singh, requires a programme of modernisation that could set you back twenty five thousand pounds."

He looked confused. "The properties next door have cellars?"

I was amazed; I had got the impression that everything I was saying was going in one ear and out the other.

"Yes, Mr. Singh, they have."

I turned and made the few steps to the nearest wall in the lounge. Wooden tongue and groove panels covered half the wall.

"You see, Mr. Singh, where your stairs go up on the other side of this wall, your neighbour's property has stairs going down underneath their staircase that you access from here at this point."

I pointed to the wooden panels. Mr. Singh looked confused and not particularly interested.

"So you're telling me that if I pull these planks away I may have stairs going down to a cellar?"

Again, it was not hard to read his thought process.

"Yes, more than likely. In fact, I would be amazed if it didn't have one, but converting cellars usually takes up more time and money than they are worth."

Before I could get the last remaining words out of my mouth, Mr. Singh had placed his keys and phone down on the floor and proceeded to yank away at the wooden panels.

Within minutes we were both standing before a stone staircase that led downwards into unwelcoming pitch blackness.

"You have no idea what breeds of spiders are going to be down there!" I joked, praying that he was not going to ask me to go down and take a look. I really didn't want Mr. Singh to be getting grand ideas about fitting out what was sure to be a soaking wet dungeon as cheaply as possible in order to get a top whack selling price. I wanted to get his business straight away. I crouched down and opened my brief case; I pulled out my camera and laser measurer.

"Shall I get this up and running for you now Mr. Singh?" I said in a quest to try and speed things along a little. "I say we stick it on for one hundred and twenty thousand and see what happens."

I had already started to make notes for my sales particulars. After a brief pause, Mr. Singh nodded.

"I work abroad all of the time so you will only be able to contact me by e-mail. I'll give you the keys now, and, if I could ask you to keep checking on it as I don't plan on coming back up to Swindon for a while."

It was this kind of vendor that I loved to deal with; there would be no hassle from having to try and book viewings, no constant phone calls hounding us for updates and hopefully a handful of his other properties coming our way too. What made this property even more attractive to me was that it was exactly what my best friend Ben was looking for; it would be an all-round easy sale. It took me twenty minutes or so to measure up the property and draw my floor plans; I didn't see the point in taking photographs as the condition of the property was far from photogenic. I offered Mr. Singh my lowest sale fee of 1.25% which was gratefully accepted (I wasn't in the mood to get bogged down in a negotiation showdown). With the house measured and my terms of business signed, my work here was done.

Ralph had swooped on me like a bird of prey the second I walked back through the office doors; like an eagle to its victim there was no escape. He gave me enough time to put down my folder and brief case on my desk before gesturing with his hand for me to accompany him outside. The pavement outside our office was busy with people hurriedly going about their business, shoppers, retired folk and smartly dressed professionals en route for lunch. Ralph, however, walked slowly, his head tilted downwards towards the pavement apparently not seeing the human traffic around him.

"I've decided to leave, Hammy. I am sorry you had to hear it last as I wanted you to be the first to know."

I heard the words coming out of my Manager's mouth but I just couldn't process them in the way that I thought I should be.

"What? You're, you want to leave?" I struggled to keep my mounting questions coming out all at once. "Why? Who are you going to work for? Is it because of me? Since when?"

Ralph just carried on walking, his head not moving from its tilted position.

"I feel that it is time to move on Edward. I came here many years ago in search of something that has proved to be just too illusive. With the recent loss of my grandmother who lived fairly locally, I feel there is very little to keep me here in Wiltshire."

I had learned soon after meeting Ralph that he liked to speak sometimes in riddles and I had now acquired the knowledge not to question them. If he wanted to translate them, then he would do so in his own time.

Drops of rain started to fall from beneath the dark forming clouds; pedestrians looked up and started to hurry towards shelter. I had stopped walking to see if Ralph would stop, but he had simply carried on.

"What are you looking for, Ralph?" I shouted down the street towards his back, the rain now starting to come down heavily. He stopped, realising I wasn't next to him, and abruptly turned and strolled back towards me.

"I'm going to work my notice period of four weeks, so I will still be around for the next month."

He tried to look upbeat and enthusiastic but I could tell that he was emotional inside. He placed his hand on my shoulder.

"If I was going to another estate agent, then you know that I would take you with me as my second in command, don't you Hammy?"

I knew that Ralph had a lot of respect for me, as I did for him, but seeing him have such a hard time in telling me that he was leaving really hit home hard for me. We had been through great times, and really devilish hard times, together. Over the last two years the two of us had built such a reputation for our company that other agents simply could not dream of competing. I could feel a tear welling up in the corner of my eye.

"You're the best Manager I have ever worked for and I know that you know what is best for you."

I could see a tear in the corner of his eye form, even though the rain had drenched us from head to toe. He shook my hand before we briskly marched back to the office.

Ralph was not married; he had no children and talked very little about the existence of any friends. I had always thought that he liked it this way as he was so committed to his job. On the rarest of occasions when I had turned up for work half an hour early, Ralph would already be seated working away on his computer. We all spent unhealthily long hours at the office but Ralph, I think, if given the chance, would have spent his entire life working away at his desk. Over the years he had learnt how I worked. He would know when to hold me back and when I needed restraining, and he knew the times when to push me to the very limits. It was probably a selfish reaction I had experienced when he had told me that he was leaving, selfish because, unless I became the Branch Manager, which I didn't particularly fancy, I would have to mould into somebody else's leadership. It was safe to say that I was going to miss my friend Ralph.

# Chapter 4

# A field over Southern England

*March 1943*

Albert Davies did not feel particularly honoured or privileged as the B-17 Flying Fortress he had hitched a ride with descended from the brilliant blue sky into thick grey clouds. Sat directly behind the pilot, strapped into the small jump seat on the flight deck, Davies held his stomach tightly as the turbulence threw him from side to side violently. The pilots, cool as you could imagine, chatted away to each other as they pushed buttons and pulled levers making preparations for their final approach. Through the large cockpit windows, Davies could see rolling hills and a network of hedges, stone walls and fences that separated the differently coloured fields below. He held onto the pilot's armour plated chair trying desperately to keep his stomach contents down.

Hours after the air disaster in Gibraltar earlier that morning, the Group Captain had described this flight to the young Corporal as a "once in a life time opportunity"! It had been by pure coincidence that this American B-17 Flying Fortress of the 3181$^{st}$ Bomber Group had landed at Gibraltar a few days earlier in desperate need of mechanical and medical attention. Davies had no idea how the Group Captain had persuaded the American pilot to take him and the crates back with them on their way back to base, but however he managed to do it, he wished he hadn't. Although the Group Captain had told him that the aircraft had been in a scrap with a couple of German Messerschmitt 109 fighter aircraft, he had left out graphic details and had certainly not informed him of the shear extent of the damage done to this war machine. When Albert Davies had climbed through the crew's entrance hatch back on the tarmac in the early hours of the morning, he could instantly see the reality of the damage done by the German fighters. The crew's hatch was located at the rear of the aircraft and in getting to his position on the flight deck, Davies had had to step through the cramped Radio Operator's compartment, or what was left of it. The small confined space was riddled with hundreds of bullet holes, large sections of the plane's sides had simply been blown away as the aircraft had flown through fields of flak and anti-aircraft fire. The small window to the side of the Radio Operator's table had shattered into tiny segments and it was covered in blood. He followed a line of bullet holes with his eyes from the Radio Operator's station all the way back to the Waist Gunners' positions. *Pure carnage*, he thought to himself as he noticed the two dried-up puddles of blood on each gun position. This bird had taken heavy casualties.

It had only been eight or so hours ago since he witnessed the tragic event of the Liberator going down in the sea off Gibraltar, but seeing the place of work, first hand, of these incredibly brave airmen made the previous evening's events seem somehow irrelevant. He had slept for most of the flight but was now firmly awake as the tired bomber was aggressively buffeted up and down as it descended further into English airspace.

"You're not looking well, if you don't mind me saying?" said the young American pilot peering back over his right shoulder. Davies did not feel well and he knew that he looked like death warmed up, but he desperately didn't want to appear weak in front of these courageous young allies.

"I'll be fine," he said trying not to be sick all over the back of the pilot's leather bomber jacket. "I'm probably feeling a touch better than your plane!" mumbled the young Corporal. The cockpit descended into polite laughter.

"Point taken", said the co-pilot in a sorrowful tone. "We lost five crew members on the last mission. We were on a raid over North Africa aiming to knock out an advancing German tank division. That's before our group ran into a pair of prowling Me 109's. Our electrics are almost frazzled, the radio is being held together by a medley of bullets and God only knows how her engines are still running, but she keeps plodding on."

The co-pilot swivelled his body ninety degrees to his left to face the pale Davies.

"So, my English friend," he said in a cool southern American accent, "what is so important that a cargo needs a personal escort back to what can only be described as a secret airfield in Southern England?"

The pilot also turned to face Davies. "Whatever is in those crates is cherished and loved by somebody."

Davies could hardly muster enough energy to keep himself awake. He figured that the two pilots would not buy into the fact that he had no idea what he had been guarding for the best part of a day and certainly had no clue as to where they were heading for, so he remained in silence.

Breathing in slowly and then exhaling slowly, Davies pushed his nose up against the square window to his left hand side. From the pilot's window, he could see that the aircraft was extremely low, maybe only a few hundred feet from the ground. He watched a picturesque church with quaint little cottages surrounding it as the pilot put the aircraft into a steep bank to its left; people on a narrow windy lane were visible as they stopped to look up at the unusual sight of this wounded American bomber. Light drizzle made streaky patterns on the cockpit windscreens as the pilot pulled a lever above his head to summon the undercarriage. With a tiresome grinding noise and a short click the two large wheels were down and secure.

"That's a relief," said the pilot quietly to his second in command.

Davies did not need to ask what he meant. He had already wondered to himself whether the undercarriage had escaped injury and he was mightily relieved to hear the clicking sound of the wheels locking into place. The aircraft was descending quite steeply now; it was leaving the young Corporal's stomach in knots. Still with his nose against the Perspex window, he was able to pick up tiny details of the cottages as they raced by below. Beautiful red roses were visible climbing the walls of the thatched cottages as the roofs levelled in height with the B-17. He could see people coming out of their front doors to investigate the bellowing engine noise overhead. Albert Davies was just about to open his mouth to inquire if the pilot planned to land on top of a village, when suddenly a sprinkling of large aircraft hangers raced into his narrow field of vision; Davies leaned forward to take in more of the unfolding view ahead. Four hangers were clustered together with a slightly smaller hanger isolated on its own towards the right hand corner of the airfield. Several had their huge iron doors slid open to reveal their contents of different types of aircraft.

"Get that runway cleared," said the pilot in a slightly anxious manner.

Davies, at first glance, could see no sign of any runway; in fact the harder he looked the more nervous he became.

A group of ten or eleven young men who worked at the Wiltshire airfield had heard the distant gargling sound of the Flying Fortress's engines; with much haste they had rushed from the 'paint shop' hanger to the long concrete runway to perform their task. On top of the runway sat camouflage netting that was positioned underneath row upon row of synthetic hedges that were fixed to small wheels. These were arranged in such a way that from the sky, any enemy aircrew would simply believe that they were looking at fields upon fields, a clever way to disguise a couple of large and unmistakable concrete runways. It took the young civilians about thirty seconds to remove all hedgerows from the runway; it must have been a practice that looked very much like the Wimbledon ball-boys of today bringing on the huge covers to protect the court in times of rain.

Albert Davies had seen the runway slowly appear before his eyes only seconds before the injured bomber touched down on English soil.

"What the hell is this place?" gasped Davies in complete amazement as he tried to count the Spitfires and Stirling Bombers that were scattered around the airfield randomly.

"That I can't help you with, my friend," said the pilot as he turned the aircraft around to come back slowly down the runway in the direction he came from. "Whatever this place is, it's not on any of my maps. I've even got a military map of all the bases in Wiltshire and this place sure as hell is not on it - which tells me they are very keen for the Germans not to find it!"

A young man wearing civilian clothes and ear protectors gestured with his outstretched arm for the pilot to turn off the runway and come to a stop; the pilot cut the throttle and stepped on the rudder pedal to commence his turn.

"So what happens to you now?" said the pilot as he brought the aircraft to a standstill.

Davies had not been given clear instructions by the Group Captain back in Gibraltar; he had been told that once he arrived at his destination, he would wait until somebody came and requested the cargo. For security, the young Corporal had been given the password 'Dandelion'. Once the person collecting the cargo gave Davies this password, he would be safe in the knowledge that it was being handed over to the correct person.

"I just wait here for somebody to collect the eight crates I guess," said Davies as he wrestled with his safety harness.

The pilot took off his headset and slid open his side window; he turned his entire body round to face his passenger.

"Don't you mean seven crates Corporal?" Davies was confused; he had sat with them long enough to know that the full complement of crates was eight.

"I don't understand", said the young Corporal feeling rather alarmed. The pilot chuckled to himself; he pulled out a folded piece of paper from inside his jacket and handed it to the Corporal.

"I thought that Group Captain of yours would forget to tell you."

Davies unfolded the paper and proceeded to read the note that was on official Royal Air Force headed paper.

> I, Group Captain Jack Williams of Royal Air Force Fighter Command, hereby surrender x1 (one) case of undisclosed content to 1st Lieutenant Danny Hudson of the 3181st Bomber Group, for reward of his assistance towards the allied war effort that went beyond the call of duty.
>
> Jack Williams

*So that's how the Group Captain persuaded the American pilot to take him back to the UK. He bribed him,* Davies thought to himself as he digested the words in front of him.

"Well that seems to be jolly conclusive," he said as he handed back the piece of paper to the pilot. "But how do you know the cases are not full of sand?" asked Davies.

The pilot smiled.

"I don't my friend; I just trust your Senior Officer that it will be worth my while, like he said."

By now, a handful of locals had gathered round to take a closer inspection of the unusual visitor. "You got any injured on board?" shouted out a rather plump, rosy-faced, middle- aged man in a heavy Wiltshire accent. The pilot shook his head through the cockpit window. "No, they were unloaded in Gibraltar. We do have some cargo that needs to come off if you're feeling strong," shouted back the pilot.

The three men wearily lifted themselves up from their seats and exhaustedly made their way back through the belly of the aircraft towards the crew hatch. Davies was desperate to get his feet onto solid ground; he could not wait for the fresh country air to replace the oily petrol smell that he had been inhaling for the last God knows how many hours.

Davies watched as the locals eagerly unloaded the cases from the smouldering aircraft. He desperately hoped that whoever was coming to collect the cargo would not be long as he was exhausted and, quite frankly, he was sick of the sight of these wooden crates. As it started to sink in that he was actually somewhere in the South of England, thoughts of his wife came flooding back to him. He felt a surge of guilt come across him that over the last twenty four hours he had hardly thought about his wife, Victoria, something he was sure he would be able to forgive himself for, considering his recent ordeals. Davies could not wait to see her again, to hold her, to kiss her and to snuggle up to her in bed again. Whatever he had been through over the last twenty four hours was going to be worth every single second with her. Davies and his wife lived in a small village just outside Bracknell in Berkshire, so if he was in Wiltshire, he could be thankful that at least it would not be a terribly long final leg of his journey. Albert Davies had orders that once the crates had safely been handed over, he was to return again to Wiltshire in three days time to RAF Lyneham, where he would catch a return flight to Gibraltar.

The crates were placed onto the back of a flat bed lorry where they were taken, along with Davies and the American airmen to a nearby building close to the aircraft hangers. The two pilots had decided to stay at the field overnight in order to get some rest and to sample the local ale. Davies wished he could join them at the local pub but he had not yet fulfilled his task, and although he would have loved to spend more time with his new friends, he did not want to be away from Victoria any longer than necessary. Davies said his goodbyes as the pilots wondered off in the direction of the village in search of a public house leaving Davies alone sat on the seven wooden crates. Davies took a moment to take in his new surroundings. He was thankful of a few minutes to himself. He felt in his pockets for his cigarettes; he was out of luck. He must have smoked them all on the tarmac in Gibraltar. Two men in their mid twenties, wearing civilian clothes, walked by, pulling large trolleys behind them.

"Do you gents have a cigarette I could have?" asked Davies.

The two young men dropped the handles to their trolleys and strode over to the Corporal's position.

"Blimey, a Group Captain! You must be the new test pilot," said one of the men.

Davies looked down to take stock of what he was wearing. He still had Jack William's coat on - he would be in no hurry to explain that he did not hold this rank.

"What is this place? Where are we? Why are you not dressed in uniform?" Davies struggled to hold back the questions. From behind him, he could hear a straining tractor engine. He looked back to see a Police motor-bike turn into the gates of the airfield perimeter closely followed by an old Ferguson tractor towing something that towered above the tractor driver's head. As the tractor turned in, the trailer followed carrying a fuselage of a Stirling bomber. With the tail gun turret leading the way, the heavy straps strained to keep the beast of the machine in position on the seemingly nimble trailer.

"What in God's name is this place?"

The two young men smiled with a certain pride as one of them put a cigarette in his mouth and handed Davies one.

"Not many people know about this place," said one of the men as he dragged on his cigarette. "We are a shadow factory to the Woodley Works, near Reading. The Ministry of Aircraft Production thought that it would be a wise move to build a shadow site just in case the Nazis blitzed Woodley."

*That would explain why this place was not on any of Lieutenant Danny Hudson's flight maps*, thought Davies as he watched a newly-assembled shining silver Spitfire being pushed out of an aircraft hangar to the left of where he stood.

"You make Spitfires here?" asked Davies in amazement as another unpainted Spitfire rolled out of the hangar.

"He learns quick don't he, Harry," said the youngest looking man in a manner that irritated Davies. Before Davies could muster a reply, the two young men returned to their trolleys and proceeded to walk off in the direction of the far end of the runway. Once again the young Corporal was left alone.

# Chapter 5

# Swindon

*Tuesday, 3rd August 2008*

I had sent Ben a text message the previous evening to let him know that I had just taken onto the market a property that suited all of his requirements. I had not quite expected the barrage of texts messages throughout the night pestering me to make an appointment for him to see it as soon as possible.

Ben had been looking for a property for the last six months or so, but was becoming increasingly frustrated with properties selling before he even had the chance to arrange a viewing appointment. He was determined that he was not going to miss out on this opportunity. Although I loathed doing early morning appointments, Ben had persuaded me to arrange for him to see it at quarter past nine in the morning. It was the least I could do in light of his unsuccessful property search.

It was the Tuesday morning, and, after waiting only a few minutes on the door step of Seventy Eight Clarence Road in the fresh morning air, I could see my best friend briskly walk up the road towards me. Wearing his usual attire of trainers, jeans and surf t-shirt, he excitedly put his face up against the window to try and steal a sneak preview. My fingers were cold; I had difficulty in selecting the correct key and sliding it into the lock. I could sense that Ben was fidgety behind me eager to get in and take a look inside.

"Come on old bean I'm freezing my nuts off here,", he said, as the Yale lock turned and the door opened with the help of the full force of my shoulder.

"Hello," I shouted as I stepped through the front door, picking up a pile of junk mail on my way in.

I wanted to make sure that the property was vacant. I hastily checked in every room to make sure that Mr. Singh had not decided to stay the night in Swindon. The house was empty. The property seemed to require a lot more work on second inspection than it did the previous day, but Ben seemed to be engrossed in the property. As I carefully made my way back down the creaking stairs, I could hear loud tapping on walls. Unfortunately my best friend had recently acquired the typical developer's trait of banging and tapping away at walls. Within minutes he managed to pull up the remainder of the carpet in the living room to reveal the original wooden floorboards.

"This place is a dream," he uttered to himself as he submerged his head up the chimney breast. I tried to turn on a light but nothing happened; the electrics were probably turned off at the mains. I always carried a torch in my folder just in case a potential purchaser wanted to take a look in a loft, or the back of a dark cupboard etc.

Ben had moved on into the kitchen, where he carefully measured the width and length of the room with his tape measure. "Mate, this can be made into such a lush place."

I hadn't seen Ben like this for a long time. He almost seemed to slip back into childhood as he tried to lap up the information all at once with unreserved excitement. Impatiently, he tugged on the back door wanting to explore further.

"Go and have a look at the rest of the house and I will try and find the back door key in this bunch," I said as I fumbled with the back door lock trying out every key. Ben had already gone to explore upstairs. By the time I had opened the back door, Ben was already coming back down the stairs.

"It's going to need a new boiler and…." he stopped. I turned to look back from where I stood in the kitchen to see Ben pulling away at the wooden panelled wall in the lounge.

"Hello, hello, what have we here?" he said in a strangely reserved manner. I was going to tell him about the cellar only when we were ready to leave but Ben had already found it. Within just a few moments the entire original doorway was exposed. Making mimicking ghost gestures, he turned to me.

"Are you coming down with me, old bean?" Ben knew all too well that I had a fear of spiders and that there was more chance of him finding a pirate ship down there than me going down in a dark, wet, spider-invested, dirt-ridden dungeon. I handed him my torch from my folder.

"Be my guest buddy and I'll wait up here," and with that Ben ducked his head and started his dark descent down the stone staircase.

I pulled my cigarette packet from out of my packet and took the last cigarette out; I headed towards the back garden quickly to have a sly fag, which was not normal practice but I figured that Ben would not mind. The garden was massively overgrown and I struggled to find a suitable place to stand without ruining my shoes or suit. I settled for a rusty drain cover to stand on as I tried to shelter my flame as I attempted to light my cigarette.

"Hello there," came a voice from behind my position; I turned to see an old man peering over from his side of the fence, his hair white, greasy and untidy. "You selling Penney's place then? I aint seen her in a long time – is she dead?"

Slightly knocked back by this seventy-something year-old man's bluntness, I took a deep drag of my cigarette and inhaled it into the depths of my lungs.

"I've no idea my friend," choosing my words carefully. I didn't want to get dragged into a deep and meaningful conversation with a nosey neighbour. "She only rented the place," I continued with his full attention focused on me. "It will probably get snapped up by a first time buyer or an investor looking to modernise it."

He was just going to open his mouth when I saw Ben in the kitchen doorway waving for me to come over towards him. He looked excited and impatient. The old man was still peering over the fence.

"No rest for the wicked eh?" I said as I carefully made my way back towards the house flicking my cigarette somewhere in the jungle behind me.

As I approached Ben, he stepped back into the house to hide himself from the neighbour; I could tell that he had something behind his back.

"Mate, you are not going to believe what I found down there."

His excitement was getting contagious and my heart rate started to speed up in anticipation.

"Show me, you bastard," I said, unable to imagine what he was holding. Slowly he pulled his arm from behind his back, milking the situation as much as he could; I arched my neck around his body to try and see what treasures he had found. My face dropped with disappointment as soon as I caught a glimpse of what my best friend was holding. I looked up at him, my eyebrows raised.

"What's so exciting about this?" I said as Ben handed me the object.

I moved through into the living room to stand in front of the front window to give me some more light and more privacy from any potential prying eyes. I held the object up to the window, but the glass let no light through whatsoever. Gently shaking it, I could feel the bottle had its contents of liquid still inside.

"There's more," said Ben as he peered over my shoulder. My attention now very much on the neck of the bottle; I held it closer to the window pulling aside the net curtain to let more daylight through the window. The top and the neck of the bottle appeared to be covered in some sort of wax covering that was stamped with something; I brought the bottle close up to my eyes to inspect in greater detail.

"It's an owl, or a bird of some sort." I mumbled.

I couldn't put my finger on it, but I had seen the image before. I could just about make out a bird of some variety with outstretched wings, its beaky head pointing ninety degrees to the right. It was difficult to make out every detail as the wax stamp had deteriorated over what must have been years. Clutched in its claws appeared to be a garland with something etched into the centre.

"You say there's more of these, matey?" I said not taking my eyes off the bottle. I looked up. Ben had already vanished underground. With the bottle still in hand, I walked through into the kitchen and popped my head through the back door; I could hear the old man next door banging pots and pans in his kitchen. Now satisfied he was not spying on us, I shut the back door and headed back into the lounge. Peering down the dark hole that was the cellar entrance, I could hear Ben clambering around beneath. The moist air was heavy on my lungs.

"Coming, old bean," garbled Ben as he followed the light coming from the torch hanging out of his mouth. Step by step I could see my friend appear from out of the darkness carrying a large wooden crate. Nearly barging me over, he rushed passed me and hurriedly placed the seemingly heavy crate in the centre of the living room. Pushing the lid off, Ben revealed a box made to contain twenty bottles, split up into five rows containing four bottles per row. One of the centre bottles was different from all of the others. I placed the bottle I had in my hand carefully back into the vacant compartment; gently I lifted the odd bottle out of the crate. This bottle was exactly the same in weight, colour and size, but was wearing some sort of paper wrapped around the neck. As if holding an unexploded bomb, I slowly put the bottle down on the floor and knelt down beside it. The paper looked ancient and ever so fragile; I was unsure whether it would disintegrate if I pulled at it too hard. Focusing my attention on a corner of the paper, I painstakingly manoeuvred my finger and thumb so that the corner was positioned centrally between the two. Terrified of tearing the paper, I pulled it upwards as carefully as I could inch by inch.

"Isn't this exciting?" said Ben as he bent over blocking most of my light.

I gave the piece of paper one last pull and it was free. I stood up and gathered close to Ben so we could both see at the same time what, if anything, was on the paper. Gently I straightened it. The paper was very thin, the edges were frayed and it was a dirty coffee colour.

"What the hell is that?" There was confusion in Ben's voice.

I too had no idea what I was looking at; the image in front of us had been hand drawn and, by the looks of it, probably in a rush. There was a series of small squares with a squiggle weaving in and out of them; a thick straight line ran diagonally across with a smaller thick line dissecting it such that it almost appeared like a cross. At the end of the thick diagonal line was another square that had been circled several times.

"It looks like something my sister drew when she was two years old!" said Ben; his attention was now back to the twenty bottles that probably contained alcohol. I rotated the image ninety degrees, examined it, and then rotated it another ninety degrees. At whatever angle I looked at it, it still made no sense whatsoever. Frustrated, I threw the small piece of paper into the crate and picked up another bottle.

"We should really get somebody who knows what they are talking about to take a look at these before we crack them open."

I could see Ben eyeing them up. I knew exactly what he was thinking. I didn't want to leave the bottles at the property; I knew that removing them would effectively be theft, but I couldn't take the risk of any other potential purchaser finding them. If Mr. Singh had been aware of their existence, then it would have been a completely different matter, but as he had no idea at all that they were down in the cellar, I had no problem with taking them. My car was parked only a few meters away from the front door so it would be no problem at all to get the crate into my boot without raising too much suspicion.

"What are you up to now?" said Ben.

I could tell that he didn't want to miss out on any potential excitement. I looked at my watch; we had been at the property for a good fifty five minutes.

"I should really be getting back to the office, but there is Champers wine shop just a few doors away from my office. Fancy popping in there with one of these puppies before I go back in?"

Ben nodded his head in excitement. He had already started to place the wooden panels back to the wall to conceal the cellar entrance; it didn't take me long to lock up and make sure that all lights were off.

# Chapter 6

# Swindon

With exotic drinks from all corners of the earth, Champers was a wine connoisseur's dream. If there was a tipple that took your fancy and they didn't stock it, then rest assured they would have it in shop by the end of the week. I often used the shop to purchase cigarettes and chewing gum; I frequently felt inadequate that I was only spending a few pounds as opposed to hundreds on a single bottle of wine, but they didn't seem to mind. If they did, they soon wouldn't.

I had kept a single bottle back from my boot so that I didn't have to take the whole crate in with us; the small scrap of paper with the strange image was safely in my pocket. Risking the ever increasing swarms of traffic wardens, I decided to park directly outside the shop as I only expected to be in there for a few moments. It had only been open twenty minutes so I was hopeful that there might not already be a large number of customers in there. With the ringing of a bell above my head, the door opened. To my relief there was nobody on the shop floor apart from Lawrence and Nigel who were the owners. Lawrence originated from Glastonbury and made every effort that his shop had that unique festival flavour. The shop floor was lined with straw around open boxes of various wines and spirits; quite often he would be seen handing out small glasses of local ale to get his customers in the buying mood. Aged in his mid forties, he went out of his way to try and keep up with the latest music trends and fashions; Nigel was older and more reserved.

"What can we do for you today Hammy?" said Lawrence as he looked up from rolling a cigarette. He looked deep into Bens face.

"Something tells me your not here for twenty Marlborough Lights."

We made our way to the long counter that was positioned at the back of the shop where Nigel and Lawrence were stood behind.

"I was wondering if you could tell me what this is?" I looked behind me to make sure that the four of us were alone.

"This sounds interesting," said Nigel; he did not seem to be in the best of moods.

With great care I pulled the bottle from out from under my suit jacket and gently placed it onto the counter. Lawrence sparked up his rollie and picked the bottle up, peering over the top of his glasses. He examined it meticulously. After several minutes he started to look uneasy, almost uncomfortable, and without saying a word he handed it to the older man. Nigel shook his head slowly.

"This can't be it, just cannot be!"

Lawrence hastily made his way to the front door to switch the open sign in the window to closed. I glanced at Ben. He was wearing the same confused look that I must have had on my face.

"Can this be real?" said Nigel as he held the bottle up to the light, his right hand shaking ever so slightly.

Lawrence positioned himself behind the older man.

"I think this is the real deal," he said not taking his eyes off the object.

Cautiously he took the bottle off his partner and turned it over to expose the bottom of the bottle.

"Christ! Look at this!"

He held the bottle up close to Nigel's face, but Nigel looked pale and rather unwell at this point.

"Can you gents offer any explanation as to where the bloody hell you found this?" said Lawrence, an uneasy smile forming over his face to try and lighten the situation.

"I can't do that my friends," I responded, "but I can tell you that I have nineteen more bottles tucked away!"

As I held my hand out to take back the bottle, Lawrence reluctantly handed it over. I examined the underneath of the bottle, something I had not done back at the house. On the base of the bottle were the initials, 'A.H', etched beautifully into the dark glass, a detail that had escaped us before.

"How come you became very excited when you both saw these initials?" I asked Lawrence, who now looked to be in a state of shock.

"Where the Hell do I begin?"

I could tell that Lawrence was struggling to maintain his composure.

"Could I possibly take that off you for a moment?"

Lawrence held out his hands as if he was about to receive a new born baby, as I handed it back to him.

"Is it wine?" said Ben respectfully.

"Oh good God no!" Nigel responded. "It is the finest port that is said to have ever been made." He leaned on the counter.

"People have devoted their entire lives to these bottles including the most celebrated scholars." It started to dawn on me that we had discovered something rather special. "So much speculation surrounds them as to their existence." Lawrence placed the bottle on the table. "If this bottle and the others you have are not clever fakes then it is the find of the century." He looked up at us both.

"Do either of you have any idea what this could be?" I looked at Ben who was shaking his head. "The 'A.H' on the base of this bottle are somebody's initials from our colourful past." Lawrence smiled; he was clearly enjoying the situation.

"Anthony Hopkins?" blurted Ben.

"Not bad, but think more famous and powerful."

I looked at the bottle and the bird like image pressed into the wax seal.

"Of course," I replied. "Adolf Hitler!"

Using the invaluable power of hindsight, by looking back at my best friend and myself standing on that shop floor, I realise now that that moment in time was the point of no return. What we should have done was leave the crate of port with what would have been the most grateful of recipients and walk away from them forever, but this did not happen. I wish that a public school education would have sown enough moral fibre into my conscience to have left the crate safely where we found it in the cellar, but it did not. I often wonder how different things would now be if the two wine experts hadn't known anything about the bottle in front of them, but they did know, all too well.

Nigel nodded his head thoughtfully.

"I need to pinch myself. I am going to wake up in a moment and this will have been just a dream."

Lawrence took over.

"What you gents are evidently looking at is a personal gift from the Polish wartime Prime Minister, Vladimir Sikorski, to the leader of the Third Reich and Nazi Party, Adolf Hitler."

"What the fuck? I don't understand," said Ben.

"I couldn't have put it better myself." Lawrence continued: "Legend has it that in nineteen thirty-nine when the Third Reich was in the process of building up their armed forces, speculation was rife that Germany was going to invade Poland. In order to stop any possible hostile attack, Sikorski personally sent these bottles of fine port as an offering of friendship."

I was engrossed; I felt a hunger for more knowledge that had to be fed.

"But Hitler did invade Poland," I said trying to remember my A-level history lessons.

"Did he not like port then?"

The two gentlemen erupted into heavy laughter.

"History tells us that Hitler had a rather large soft spot for fine vintage port," said Nigel as he wiped away his tears from his eyes. Clearly, he could tell that I was confused. "There is huge doubt amongst scholars and historians alike that these bottles actually did exist, or ever did." Ben and I hung on Nigel's every word. "Nobody has ever claimed to have caught sight of them, which makes it just impossible to verify the myth."

Lawrence picked up the bottle and with his little finger pointed to the bird pressed into the wax seal. "It is believed by some that Sikorski thought it to be a nice touch to seal all of the bottles with the eagle emblem of the Third Reich and to engrave every bottle with the German leader's initials." Lawrence watched us closely like a teacher making sure that his pupils were paying attention.

"Well that sounds fair enough. So why did Hitler still invade?" asked Ben instinctively.

With his index finger Lawrence pointed to the eagles head. "If you can just make it out, the eagles head is turned ninety degrees to the right." I moved closer to the bottle to study the intricate details.

"And?" I said feeling still rather in the dark; Lawrence smiled.

"Did you pay no attention at all in history?"

My blank look provided him with the answer. "The eagles head should in fact be pointing ninety degrees to the left! Sikorski made a careless schoolboy error that may have been the catalyst for World War Two!"

A thud on the front door broke the silence in the shop, followed by tapping on the front window. I was dumbstruck; I turned to Ben who looked like he had just seen a ghost.

"We will be open shortly," shouted Lawrence from behind his counter, for he clearly had more important things on his mind than the sale of a ten pound something bottle of plonk.

"Hammy is that you?"

The voice was distant through the glass but was familiar. Snapping out of my state of shock, I turned to see my colleague Jess peering through the window. I looked at my watch.

"Christ it's nearly eleven!"

I had been out on a viewing appointment for nearly two hours; Ralph will kill me. I rushed over to the front door.

"Jess, I'm just helping a mate out. I'll be back in a moment."

She looked confused but nodded. "I need some fags, you dick. Trust you to get the shop shut."

Nigel had heard that my fellow colleague was after some cigarettes. "Hammy, catch these." Nigel tossed a pack of unopened Benson and Hedges over to me and I slipped them through the letter box; Jess looked even more confused.

"I'll catch up with you back at the office," I said, trying to get rid of her as quickly as I could. With that I turned and headed back towards Ben and the two wine shop owners.

"Where were we?" said Nigel, who was obviously keen to get back to the topic of port.

"I don't understand." Questions started to fly into my mind. "If this bottle and all the others were a gift from Skorki, or whatever his name was, to Hitler, then how the hell have they come into our possession?" The second I heard the words leave my mouth, I realised that this was one question they would not be able to answer.

"Well Hammy." Lawrence folded his arms, "If you would give us the slightest idea as to where you stumbled upon these delights, we may be able to shed some light on that question."

Not all the tea in China was going to make me disclose the location as to where we found the crate, but I did want to give them as much information as I possibly could. I was just about to open my mouth and produce a blatant lie when Ben whispered in my ear: "your pocket mate."

In all the excitement of learning about these bottles prestigious history, I had completely forgotten about the strange diagram that I had found wrapped round a bottle neck. Paying great attention not to tear the frail piece of paper, I carefully pulled it out of my jacket inner pocket.

"This was in the crate when we found it." I handed it to Lawrence. With great patience he unrolled it and studied the image; he turned the paper clockwise so he could study the picture from every angle.

"Looks like some sort of circuit board or something."

He handed it to Nigel. The older man exhaled deeply and set his eyes upon the image.

"That's not a circuit board you idiot. I would say that's more likely to be a drawing of an airfield."

Instinctively I screwed up my face to show that I was not convinced. Nigel continued.

"If you look at these squares surely they represent aircraft hangars, and look at this long thick line. That's a runway if ever I have seen one and these squiggles must be access roads." Nigel handed it back to me for me to see for myself. He was right, it was an airfield.

"Now I am no expert in military history," Lawrence pulled out a cigarette paper from his pocket and started to role another cigarette, "but I do have a very close friend who is a fine wine collector and comes with an overwhelming knowledge of wartime history. If you like, I'm sure he will be happy for you to have his number."

The one thing I least wanted to do was let any other outside party into our little secret, but I knew that we would need further professional help.

"Do you think he would mind us ringing him?" I asked rather naively.

The two men behind the counter erupted into laughter again.

"I think you would make his year let alone his day. Also he is the only person I know with that level of money, if you guys wanted to sell." Lawrence started to flick hastily through an address book.

*Wanted to sell?* I thought. It had not crossed my mind until now that we could actually sell the bottles. Myself, and, I'm sure Ben included, had planned on drinking every single last one. "Sell?" I uttered, the thought still going round my head.

Nigel stood up straight.

"Yes, I think if our friend verifies that these are the real deal, then I would imagine these bottles would break the record for the highest amount ever paid for one bottle."

I started to feel a little unsteady on my feet. I turned to look at Ben; he looked hypnotised.

"What was the highest amount ever paid for a bottle?" I asked totally having no idea what levels of money we were talking here.

It was Lawrence who continued.

"In December nineteen eighty-five, at Christies auction rooms in London, a gentleman by the name of Christopher Forbes outbid a Marvin Shanken for a bottle of wine that is believed to date back to the Thomas Jefferson estate."

Lawrence fumbled around for a lighter that seemed to take an eternity.

"Well?" shrieked Ben; he was clearly as eager as me to get that sale price.

"Well, that particular bottle went for one hundred and fifty six."

My heart sank, after all that build up. "For just one hundred and fifty-six quid?"

Lawrence smiled. "That's one hundred and fifty six thousand, four hundred and fifty dollars to be precise."

I was speechless. I had lost the ability to talk. My best friend clearly hadn't.

"You reckon these puppies could go for more?"

Both Lawrence and Nigel nodded in complete synchronisation. "You have something here that is so historically significant, the world has seen nothing like this before. The sky's the limit for something like this."

Lawrence scribbled down a name and number from his address book and handed it to Ben. It bothered me that we knew nothing about this man but I did trust Lawrence and Nigel inexplicitly. I was confident that they wouldn't put us in contact with somebody who would turn out to be untrustworthy. I thanked the two gentlemen for their assistance and promised to keep them updated with any progress that was made. Out of instinct, and seeing how much Nigel and Lawrence appreciated seeing the bottle, I suggested that they may like to keep this bottle for a time, but they refused on the grounds that it was not their place to be keepers of something so staggeringly significant. Again we thanked them for their help and time then headed for the door, returning the closed sign to open as we left.

A quick phone call to work claiming I was feeling too sick to carry on freed my day ahead, a move that Ralph was probably expecting anyway. In my six years of estate agency I had never claimed a day off sick, but being in the knowledge that I had what was likely to be over one million pounds worth of the best port money could buy in the boot of my car, I wasn't going to lose any sleep over it. Ben and I headed straight for our local pub to take stock of what had just happened and to make a phone call to a Julian Knapp.

# Chapter 7

# Swindon

*Wednesday 4ᵗʰ August 2008*

Even though we had been greeted with an international ring tone on Julian's mobile phone the previous afternoon, he had insisted on meeting us the following day. He had been called by Lawrence as soon as we had left the shop, a call that had woken him in the middle of the night but he hadn't minded in the slightest. As soon as he had heard what the subject of the phone call was, he had started to pack his suitcase, immediately aborting his important business trip in Cairo. It was suggested by Julian that the three of us meet up in a quiet country pub close to where Ben and myself lived the following evening; we settled on the Black Horse in Wanborough.

Although it is situated only a few miles out of Swindon, I had only visited the village of Wanborough on a couple of occasions. The Black Horse sat on the fringes of the village; it was a true village inn for the locals. Positioned on the top of a rather steep hill, the pub enjoyed marvellous panoramic views across the beautiful Wiltshire countryside. On arrival, the large car park was empty apart from three cars, one of which was a black Bentley Continental.

"Looks like somebody wealthy is here," said Ben as he admired the prestigious vehicle through the windscreen of my car. We had arrived at a quarter to six, fifteen minutes early to make sure that we found the meeting point on time; I was unsure whether to take a bottle in with me straight away but decided that one would be OK tucked away in the brief case I used for work. Anticipating a slightly curious welcome from the pub, I had persuaded Ben to wear his best suit and tie, so that at least any curious locals would figure that we were just businessmen crunching figures or doing whatever businessmen do.

We entered through the main door that led straight from the car park into the main bar area. Tables set up for dinner were positioned in an equally sized room through archways just off the bar area. A large open fireplace separated the two rooms and a gambling machine flashed an assortment of coloured lights in the corner of the room. Before the attractive bar lady behind the bar could take our order, a tall well-dressed man swiftly approached us with an outstretched hand, "You must be Hammy and Ben," he said as he shook my hand firmly. "I'm Julian Knapp. It's an absolute pleasure to meet you." He was well spoken with no particular accent. "Please let me get you gentlemen a drink." Without a moment's hesitation, he proceeded to pull a wad of twenty pound notes out of his suit pocket and handed it to the barmaid. "Keep these gentlemen in drinks all evening if you don't mind, and, have whatever tickles your fancy too." She looked impressed. It was hard not to be; Julian Knapp had a certain presence about him that was difficult not to admire. After ordering our drinks, Julian invited us to his table in the corner of the bar with an outstretched arm. It was fair to say that I liked Julian from the moment that I first met him. As we sat down to the table, I struggled to place his age; his hair showed very few signs of greying and his tanned skin showed very little evidence of ageing, so I settled for early fifties. "Before we start gentleman, I must thank you sincerely for meeting me at such short notice, since I am sure that you gentlemen have far better things to do than spend an evening with an old codger like me." I actually couldn't think of anything I would rather be doing. Julian looked out of the large window to his side. "What a wonderful corner of the world you live in," he said as he took in the beautiful sweeping countryside before him. He turned back to face us, looking sincere. "Apart from Lawrence and Nigel, have either of you told anybody else about your miraculous find?" Ben immediately started to shake his head frantically whilst he cleared his throat of lager. "Fantastic, that's great news," he said as he poured himself another glass of wine.

Moments after Julian had asked if we had brought an example for him to examine, two young men in their late teens waltzed in and planted themselves at the bar. "Two Stellas please, love and change for the fruit machine," one said in a broad Wiltshire accent. The hoody-wearing locals paid us no attention whatsoever. I figured that this must be a regular haunt for suited professionals going about their business. Either way, I didn't consider them to be a security risk. I pulled my brief case up from the side of my chair and placed it on the table, while Julian was clearly having difficulty in containing his excitement as he slowly rocked forwards and back in anticipation. Enjoying the suspense, I momentarily delayed in clicking open the small brass locks on my leather case, Julian didn't take his eyes off my hands. Without any further hesitation, I popped open the locks and slowly opened the case. Maintaining eye contact with Julian, I carefully took hold of our bottle and gently placed it on the table. Julian gasped aloud, "Je dois rever; ca c'est trop bon pour etre vrai." I was never my french teacher's pride and joy back at boarding school during my A-levels, but somehow enough had stayed with me to able to roughly translate as "I must be dreaming; this is too good to be true." I instantly knew that Julian was educated in this subject matter. As if handling the Holy Grail, Julian very respectfully lifted the bottle up from the table and examined it closely. "Gentlemen," he announced, "you have succeeded where so many have failed before you." I turned to look at Ben, who was hanging on every word that came out of Julian's mouth. "I can think of numerous historians who have dedicated the best part of their lives trying to ascertain if this casement ever existed, and now to have what appears to be the genuine article placed safely in my hands is truly remarkable." Julian pointed with his little finger to the eagle that was pressed into the wax seal, as I had a funny feeling that I knew what he was about to say. "Knowing Lawrence and Nigel like I do, I'm sure that they spared no detail in explaining to you both these bottles' colourful past and the historical significance of your marvellous find." I nodded my head slowly, paying great attention not to come across impatient in any way. Julian continued: "I'm certainly not foolish enough to believe that you gentlemen will tell me where you discovered this gem, but would you mind telling me how many others there are of these?"

I swallowed down the last of my pint, cleared my throat and replied: "twenty bottles in all, sitting very snugly in a wooden crate." Julian looked surprised. At that moment I remembered the scrappy piece of paper that was wrapped around one of the bottle necks, but I didn't expect him to know anything about it or what it was meant to symbolise but it would be silly not to ask. I reached into my suit inner pocket and placed it onto the table.

"Lawrence and Nigel said you were a fountain of knowledge when it comes to history," I said as I slid the map towards Julian.

"They are too kind," he said as he placed the bottle down and unfolded the map. "Well, well, well, what do you have here?" Julian reached into his breast pocket and pulled out a pair of glasses and put them on. "Incredible," he said as he looked up to myself and Ben. "What a peculiar coincidence this is, that I should be sat here in beautiful Wiltshire with you two gentlemen and with this object you have brought for me to see." Rain had started to fall outside that created streaky patterns on the pub's old sash windows. Julian's attention was momentarily distracted by the change in the weather. He briefly looked out of the window and then turned back to us. "Gentlemen. Missing out the intricate details, could you tell me if you came across this sketch and fine port in Wiltshire?" It was quite obvious that Julian had some kind of knowledge of what this sketch symbolised, so it seemed fairly safe to tell him.

"Yes," I said, wanting to give him as much information as possible without putting him on the scent of where they were discovered.

"That's very interesting indeed." Julian took his glasses off, placed them on the table and continued: "Now I have to confess that World War Two airfields are not my particular area of expertise, but I am in a position to be able to tell you where this is." Ben placed his glass on the table and leaned forward. Without realising it, I had mirrored him exactly. "I see I have your undivided attentions." Julian seemed to be enjoying the moment. "This is what appears to be a hurried sketch of an airfield not five miles from here." Nigel was correct, it was a bloody airfield. Momentarily I processed the thought of an airfield, something didn't add up.

"But there isn't a former wartime airfield within five miles of here," I mumbled. Ben must have agreed. "The nearest military, or ex military airfield is Wroughton, and that's got to be at least ten miles from here." I knew that there was a sprinkling of grass airstrips in this region but certainly nothing as substantial as having runways and clusters of aircraft hangars.

Julian topped up his glass of wine and continued: "It may be the case that your port and this airfield are somewhat linked. I have to admit that the core of my interest is with these bottles, which we will discuss in greater detail in a moment." That seemed like a good idea to me, for I too was keen to get back to the subject of the port and more in particular, how much revenue it could raise.

"This is unmistakably, although drawn rather crudely, South Marston airfield."

I was about to interrupt but Julian continued with his speech. "Because they were so rich with metal workers from the Great Western Railway Works at the outbreak of World War Two, Swindon and the surrounding villages became the hub of a rapidly assembled aircraft industry." I couldn't keep my silence for any longer, I had to interrupt.

"My ex girlfriend Emily who I went out with for nearly two years lived in South Marston, and in all that time of visiting her I never saw an airfield in that small village."

Julian politely chuckled to himself. "At any stage, were you actually looking for an airfield in South Marston?" I had to concede that I had not, for I had never set out searching for an airfield, but surely, I thought, if one was there, I would have noticed it before.

"I take it that both of you have seen the gigantic Honda car factory on the fringes of South Marston?" Julian smiled. "That is your airfield, and, when you drive into South Marston, on your right hand side before you enter into the heart of the village you will see big factories that I think are currently being used by haulage companies." Of course, I thought to myself, thinking about it they did look like aircraft hangars.

"So all of that land was some big airfield?" asked Ben instinctively.

"Yes indeed," replied Julian, "and a very important and significant one at that. During the war the site was used to produce the legendary Supermarine Spitfire and the now extinct Shorts Stirling bombers amongst other things."

"Will you be eating with us tonight boys?" We hadn't noticed the attractive barmaid approach our table. She didn't seem to take any notice of the alien bottle of port sat on the table. If she knew how much a bottle like this would cost, I thought to myself, she would have given it a little more attention. "I haven't eaten since on the plane this morning," announced Julian, "absolutely dreadful food; I'll have the pie of the week and include whatever my young colleagues are having." Food was the last thing on my mind as I had butterflies in my stomach with constrained excitement; both Ben and I shook our heads. "Another two pints would be good, however" and with that the barmaid walked back to behind the bar. Julian spread out his knife and fork to make way for the arrival of his pie. "The only other bit of information I can give you about this airfield that may be of some significance to you and this map is the absolute dreadful nightmare that Honda had when purchasing a large area of the airfield." I could tell that the conversation was digressing away from the subject of our port, but Julian had come along way to speak to us today so I patiently listened to what he had to say. "I was reliably informed some years back by one of my solicitor friends that when Honda was in negotiations to buy the land, there was a huge four year conveyancing battle." Being an estate agent, I knew all too well the process of conveyancing, the procedure solicitors would go through to make sure that the land was not contaminated, built on a waste tip or over a coal mine etc.

"What was so complicated that it took four years to sort out?" I asked, now becoming more interested in this old airfield.

"Well you see, all Honda were interested in was purchasing the land to build a stonking big car works factory on top of it and to use the old tarmac runway as a test track for their new cars. However, during the early stages of the conveyancing, it came to light that there was a significant amount of underground space, in the form of bunkers, tunnels or even hangars." This was starting to become very interesting indeed. "Because the airfield would have been a prime target for the Luftwaffe bombers, very little paperwork, plans and documentation ever existed."

Ben was clearly following word for word. "Well, how did they resolve it? Did they discover what was underground?"

Julian shook his head. "No, the solicitors had accounts from local villagers that there was indeed an underground hangar and a series of bunkers but none was ever discovered. In the end it was agreed that the car manufacturer would legally be allowed to purchase the land above ground and whatever was left undetected

underground would remain the Ministry of Defence's property."
I was surprised that I hadn't heard this story before, because it
was so fascinating to me.

"Your pie sir," said the barmaid as she bent over the table to
put the hot plate down, in doing so revealing her cleavage that
I'm sure the other two noticed as well. "Would you like any sauce
with that?" She asked as she cleared the empty glasses away.
Julian declined her offer. Taking a big mouth full of steaming
hot pie he continued. "What would be very interesting would be
to ascertain the link between South Marston and your casement
of port." I had no idea in the slightest and I was pretty sure Ben
would have no idea either. "Legend had it that if the casement
of Sikorski's port did exist then the likelihood was that it went
down with his Liberator in Gibraltar; however clearly that can't
be the case. Somehow it has ended up in the same county that
it more than likely arrived in over sixty years ago." Julian took
another mouthful of his dinner. "My guess is that it was flown
to South Marston after the crash and never strayed far from the
airfield." Julian was correct; it never strayed far at all, in fact we
had found it about six miles away from the old airfield in nearby
Swindon. Julian wiped his mouth with his serviette and pushed
his half-eaten meal to the side; he took a sip of wine and leaned
forward picking up the bottle of port. "A historical find like this
would create an absolute storm if these were to appear on the
black market, so I fear that if you two gentlemen were to attempt
to auction them off or sell them privately, then God knows who
may lay claim to the ownership of this casement." Julian had just
hit the nail on the head; how the bloody hell would we go about
selling them without causing a stir or even getting arrested for
the theft of such an amazing piece of history.

"How do we flog them then?" asked Ben cutting straight to
the point, "eBay?" Julian erupted into laughter.

"Dear God no. For a start you can't sell alcohol or tobacco
on eBay. Secondly if you did, you would have every government
organisation after you, and God knows how many vigilantes after
your blood." I hadn't thought about this properly; of course we

wouldn't be able to sell them because then it might be discovered that we actually took them from a house that did not belong to us, effectively making us thieves.

"Well what can we do with them? Drink them?" I asked trying to think rapidly of every option.

Julian looked mortified. "To drink these bottles would be the crime of the century; you really mustn't attempt to open any of the bottles."

Julian turned on his laptop and waited for it to load up. "It is nearly impossible to put a monetary value on these bottles of port of yours, but, if you were to follow my advice and guidance in this matter, then I think I would be happy to make you gents an offer."

This was more like it I thought as Ben asked: "What sort of advice and guidance do you mean?"

Julian smiled politely. "Well my friends, the shear amount of money we are talking about is going to mean that you two are going to need to come up with a believable story as to how you came by such large sums of money." Working in estate agency, I was all too familiar with the money laundering act and that any large amount of cash had to be justified. If there was any doubt as to the source of the cash, then it would have to be trailed back to where it originated from.

"What sort of money are we talking here?" I asked, wondering how much of a problem the money laundering act could be. Julian turned his computer to face Ben and I. With utter disbelief I read the figures on his screen. £2,000,000 was sat staring back at us.

"Fuck me. Is that two hundred thousand pounds?" asked Ben. I couldn't muster the words to correct him. Julian quietly leaned forwards with a calming and friendly look. "No my friend, that is two million pounds. I'm presuming that you two would divide it between the two of you, so my calculations make that a cool million a piece."

"Holy Fuck," gasped Ben rather loudly, "you're going to give us a million pounds each for these bottles?" In a sudden attack of paranoia, I quickly scanned around the bar to make sure that no prying ears had caught the tail end of our conversation; I was satisfied that nobody had listened in.

"How on earth are we going to pretend that we just came by a million pounds each?" asked Ben. I could sense a slight panic in the tone of his voice. However the perfect solution was not far away.

About two years ago, in an attempt to make our fortune, Ben and I had set up a surf wear label called Boulette Boarding. With a five thousand pound loan from Northern Rock, we had ordered one thousand, four hundred T-shirts from Spain and had them printed with funky surf designs at a local printing firm. With a state of the art website designed by one of my colleague's brothers we were convinced that our small surf wear label would take the world by storm. After a good number of initial sales we thought that we were on the right track, but eventually pressures from work and limited free time resulted in our company taking a back seat. It soon became a constant irritation with people inquiring how the young entrepreneurs were getting on. With our website getting checked maybe once every three months for any potential custom, all that remained of Boulette Boarding was about six hundred T-shirts collecting dust in my parent's garage. I turned to face Ben. "Boulette my friend."

Ben looked confused, then it dawned on him, smiling from ear to ear. "You clever bastard."

Julian looked absolutely lost. "Bou what?" He inquired as he leaned back in his chair. After Ben had explained what Boulette was, Julian agreed that it was a wonderful idea to hide a couple of million pounds behind our already trading business, and, all the finer details could be discussed at a later time.

The door to the bar opened to the chorus of laughter as three gentlemen in more mature years merrily entered the building. Clearly close friends and familiar to the pub, they strode over to the bar. "Usual please, Sophie, and whatever these two clowns are having," said the oldest looking one in a broad West Country accent.

"You had a pay rise Soph?" said another of the men stopping the young barmaid in her tracks, but she looked confused. The eldest looking man who I aged somewhere in his mid sixties and dressed like a typical farmer put her out of her confusion.

"You got a pay rise as in you got that nice Bentley outside." I could see Julian slightly blush as I struggled to hear her say that it was somebody from our table.

"Anyway, where were we?" said Julian who was clearly trying to avoid having to talk cars to village locals. "I'm so excited about our meeting and hope that we can do business together that is beneficial to us all."

I supported his trail of thinking whole heartedly but I did harbour a few concerns as to the logistics of receiving such a vast amount of money without raising any valid suspicion. I needed to address my worries. Making sure that there was no prying ears homing in on our conversation from any nosey locals I leaned forward and spoke quietly: "How are we going to be able to blag that our small T-shirt company has just turned over the sum of a couple of million pounds?" I didn't expect Julian to have the answer but needed to ask the question, but his super quick thinking amazed us both. Mirroring myself he leaned forward and spoke very quietly.

"Use every T-shirt you have and sell them for peanuts or even give them away. You guys don't have to do this for a long period of time but make sure that your brand is getting out there – and quickly." He knocked back the remainder of his glass of wine and continued. "If you feel you don't have enough garments to do this then I will provide you with the funds to do another print but your label must be recognisable locally so that people close to you will know that you guys are doing very well indeed." This sounded like a great idea but failed to make crystal clear how we just managed to rake in two million pounds profit in a couple of weeks, but we were not kept in the dark for long. "Once you are happy that your product is out there and people are seeing your shirts, you tell everybody that your company has been bought out by one of these famous Australian brands to nip you in the bud and stop you trading so that you don't make a dent in their annual sales." I sat back and digested the thought.

"That's fucking brilliant," announced Ben. I had to agree.

"In reality, if you find yourselves in the unenviable position of being investigated for the source of your wealth, it will be traced back to myself who simply will demonstrate that I wanted to own an up and coming surf wear company to add to my portfolio." I had to concede that Julian seemed to hold all of the answers and it was certainly fair to say that I was happy to place my faith in him; after all Julian would want to keep the purchase as close to his chest as possible.

It was agreed that Julian would contact us in a couple of weeks to see how things were going with offloading our clothes and to arrange the transfer of funds. Only then would Julian be able to take possession of the crate that he had not even seen; he had been willing to take our word. Our meeting was concluded by Julian insisting that he contacted us tomorrow to gather up our business bank account details, an account that was opened at the beginning of our venture that currently lay dormant. He absolutely insisted on forwarding us the security of one hundred thousand pounds, fifty thousand each as a form of deposit, so that we would give him exclusive rights to this casement in order that nobody else would have a look in. He would contact his solicitor the second he had all of our details and would arrange the telegraphic transfer into our account. On that day, he wouldn't hear us complain.

# Chapter 8

# Wiltshire

*March 1943*

Albert Davies had not gone unnoticed as he paced forwards and back in front of the seven crates that were in his custody. Colin Logan had been watching the young Corporal for the last fifteen minutes from inside one of the huge aircraft hangers as he tried to gather as much warmth as he could. With ten minutes still remaining of his break, Logan decided to go and introduce himself to the seemingly agitated serviceman who looked like he could do with a friendly face.

Colin Logan was thirty-four years of age; he had worked at the site for nearly two years fitting the forward gun turrets to Stirling bombers, a job that he thoroughly enjoyed and did so for a pittance of a wage. Even with a genuine love of aviation, Logan seemed to wholeheartedly dislike the popular Supermarine Spitfire fighter plane. "The Hurricane is winning us this war", he would constantly preach down the local pub of an evening. For Colin Logan and his colleagues, other tasks at the airfield also included amongst other things, the repairs of aircraft. He loathed seeing bombers they had painstakingly put together return to their place of birth for life saving surgery, which was alarmingly common for his beloved Stirling bombers. With the countless design faults of the Stirling, and the frighteningly high fatality rate of the crews on board them, production of the Stirling started to diminish much to Logan's sadness. More and more men were being assigned to the production of the Spitfire, the Mark 21 now being the flavour of the month; he hoped that he too was not assigned to this aircraft in the following months.

"It's a good day for the Jerries," announced Logan as he strode up to Albert Davies. The young Corporal looked confused but pleased to see somebody.

"Is there ever a bad day for those wretched Jerries?" Davies inquired as he still struggled to take in his new surroundings. Logan pulled a packet of cigarettes from his oily shirt pocket and offered the Corporal one.

"You must have come in on that American monstrosity," said Logan as he lit Davies's cigarette. "American rubbish - if that had been a Stirling bomber it probably wouldn't have a mark on it" bragged Logan. Davies, although serving in the Royal Air Force didn't share Logan's apparent passion for aircraft; if a plane had got him down on solid ground in one piece then that was good enough for him. Over the distant humming of an aircraft's engines far off in the distance, a tractor towing a long trailer approached on their positions.

"Here comes the Foreman; best behaviour," warned Logan as the tractor grinded to a halt just yards from Davies's feet. The tractor engine gurgled into lifelessness. The short, podgy Foreman dismounted the archaic agricultural machine.

"If I catch the person responsible for writing obscenities about me on the hanger walls, they will wish they had never been born," grumbled the ageing man as he stopped to look up across the airfield. Davies and Logan both turned in the direction of the noise of engines getting ever increasingly closer across the far end of the airfield, while a black silhouette suddenly pounced from out of the low lying clouds. "That doesn't look like one of ours," The Foreman seemed to be in a state of confusion. "All aircraft are back and accounted for, who the hell is this?" The three men watched as the aircraft descended into a deep dive. It was Logan who was first to react; grabbing Davies by the arm of his coat, he pulled the corporal towards the direction of the aircraft hanger he had come from. "That's not ours, that's the bloody Luftwaffe." The sound of heavy machine guns opened up from the heavens above, Davies could clearly hear bullets ricocheting off the tarmac and hanger walls. "They are going for FS2," screamed Logan as they dived into the depths of a hanger. The two men hit the floor hard as bullets sliced through the wafer thin roof penetrating anything in their path. Within five harrowing seconds, the machine gun fire had stopped and the noise of the enemy aircraft's engines had faded into the distant skies.

"What in God's name is FS2?" yelped Davies as he spread himself out on the cold, dusty concrete floor. Logan was up on his feet and dusting himself off, a procedure he was clearly familiar with.

"This whole complex of aircraft hangers is called FS2," explained Logan as he offered Davies his hand to pull him up. "These four large hangars are the assembly sheds, or Flight Shed 2." He looked up to the skies. "We get a lot of that," said Logan as he helped the young Corporal to his feet. "I figure they spot us on their way back from a bombing mission and take the opportunity to give us all a jolly good fright." Suddenly the unmistakeable sound of Merlin engines bellowed out from the far end of one of the runways. Within seconds a pair of fully armed, combat ready Spitfires had raced across the runway and launched themselves into the air in hot pursuit of the German visitor. "That'll teach them" commented Logan as he pulled his cigarette packet from his shirt pocket.

"Where did they come from?" asked Davies in amazement as he rushed to the hanger doors to try and get a glimpse of the allied fighters. Logan walked over to the hanger doors.

"There's always a flight of three Spitfires that sit, fully fuelled and fully armed at the end of the main runway." By now the Spitfires were just dots on the horizon. Exhaling a plume of blue cigarette smoke Logan continued: "they came here from somewhere in France last summer needing complete engine rebuilds, not an easy task when they are the fiddly Mark 1 Spits, horrible things." He flicked his butt on the floor and squashed it with the toe of his boot. "Nice pilots, however; they are Poles from some special squadron, or so they like to think," Logan chuckled to himself. A hazy memory from the airfield in Gibraltar came flooding back to the young Corporal, something the Group Captain had said; Davies closed his eyes in concentration.

"Black Tails," announced Davies, "do those Spitfires have black tails?" he asked, rather taking Logan by surprise.

"Good God, you have heard of them? I'd presumed that the Polish Air Force had simply forgotten about those three whilst the pilots lorded it up on holiday." Logan pointed to somewhere beyond two aircraft hangars in front of us. "The three of them are staying in the Manor House that's sat just beyond that tree line; lucky buggers if you ask me." Davies seemed to agree.

A woman's shriek broke the silence, "Help, somebody get help." Davies and Logan turned and ran in the direction of the distress call; the young lady was crouched down in front of the old tractor that the Foreman had arrived on. "Christ, the Foreman has been hit," panicked Logan as he threw himself to the floor to examine the lifeless over weight man. Davies arrived soon after and bent over the young lady and Logan, but he couldn't see any signs of blood or bullet holes.

"I don't think he has been hit," said Davies slightly out of breath. "He has probably suffered a heart attack in all of the excitement with that German bomber." He leant right down and placed a finger on the side of his neck, and after a few moments, he announced that the man was dead. With his other hand he gently closed the Foreman's eyes in a slow sweeping movement. "We will need to get ..." Davies suddenly stopped what he was saying and dropped to his knees.

"What is it? What's wrong?" asked the young woman as she wiped a tear away from her cheek. Davies didn't look well; he appeared to be paralysed as he stared down at the hands of the deceased Foreman.

"You're starting to scare me now, kid" said Logan. "You look like you have just seen a ghost." Davies respectfully gripped the wrist of the deceased man and lifted it closer to his face. He shook his head sorrowfully and laid it back down on the Foreman's chest. "This is terrible" announced Davies. "What am I supposed to do now?" Logan and the young lady looked at each other in a state confusion.

"Did you know this man?" inquired Logan in a gentle manner. Instinctively Albert shook his head.

"No, he was a complete stranger, but I fear that destiny had intended that the two of us were to meet." Davies once again gently lifted up the wrist of the lifeless man lying on the floor and moved it closer to Logan's position. In capital letters, written in ink on the back of his hand was the word 'DANDELION'.

A group of a dozen or so workers had gathered round the ill-fated Foreman to pay their lasts respects and a grave silence had descended that was only broken by the thundering sound of two Merlin engines overhead as the Spitfires victoriously returned to base. As Davies stood up, he could feel himself rapidly lose his composure. "If I don't hand these blasted crates over to the appropriate person then I'm never going to get out of this place to see Victoria." Logan got onto his feet and moved close to Davies. He could sense that the Corporal was working himself into a state of panic.

"If these crates are so important I suggest that we don't leave them hanging around here." Logan put a supportive arm around Davies's shoulder. "I'll go and find some keys to a truck and we will take these crates somewhere safe for the time being, and then you can get on your way." Davies was exhausted. He couldn't remember the last time he had a good night's sleep. He had seen the deaths of the Polish Prime Minister and all on board his stricken aircraft, and, he had been one of the last people the Foreman had seen before his death. Davies couldn't believe the bad luck that was surrounding him during the last couple of days. Before he could ponder his misfortune any further, an old olive green flat bed lorry approached in front of a dark cloud of smoke. Davies instantly recognised the driver to be Colin Logan.

It was a mystery to Albert Davies how he summoned up the energy to load up all of the crates onto the back of the truck; his body ached like he had never experienced before but he knew that he had to keep going for just a little longer.

"We won't take them far," reassured Logan as Davies wearily clambered into the warm cab. "I say we leave them in the sub hanger with those Polish Spit pilots. They tend to keep themselves to themselves, so I think they will be fairly safe with them." Davies wondered to himself what a sub hanger was but he really couldn't handle a tedious, lengthy explanation. Instead he closed his eyes and remained in a state of silence; he was sure that he would find out soon enough. Logan slammed the truck into gear spinning the front wheels as the truck hastily pulled away.

"This place is amazing," said Davies under his breath as Logan steered the truck out of the main entrance gates and onto the narrow village road.

"It's quicker if we take the village road" shouted Logan above the sound of the noisy diesel engine. "This small road dissects FS2 and the runways, or 'airside' as we like to call it, there's a little gate at the bottom of this road that will lead us straight onto the main runway." Davies pinned his nose against the cold side window. A group of five or so children, who had jumped onto the grass verge to avoid the approaching lorry, waved enthusiastically at the truck; Davies did not have the energy even to return a brief wave in acknowledgement. The old lorry made its way past a series of old stone farm cottages and stone barns with thatched roofs before it made a sharp right hand turn and proceeded through a small gate. Logan had entered "airside" only a few hundred yards away from the American B-17 that sat smouldering on its own. "Horrible thing," muttered Logan as he steered the vehicle in the direction of the runways end.

"Did you say that those Polish pilots came from this end of the runway?" asked Davies as he strained to see every detail in front of him through the dirty and muddy windscreen. Logan chuckled to himself without replying. Davies could see a structure in the distance that appeared to look like a large cowshed. It certainly wasn't large enough to house any aircraft, no matter how small. The lorry proceeded to travel down a narrow concrete track that ran parallel to the main runway until the concrete faded into rough, unattended grass. Once the lorry was parallel with the runway end, Logan leaned heavily on the steering wheel making the truck turn violently to its right and the small structure that Davies had spotted moments earlier now appeared to look like a small grassy hill with a small indentation at the front.

"You're kidding me," gasped the young Corporal as the truck approached closer. "You hide a flight of Spitfires in there?"

Piotr Bednarczyk and Hainrich Karczmarz sat in deck chairs at the base of the grassy hill smoking large Cuban cigars as they jovially relived their last kill. "Colin Logan," shouted out a pilot in a thick Eastern European accent, as the two men lowered themselves from the cab. "You see that Nazi bastard? We splat him all over the floor." With that, the pilots broke into a loud sing song in their native tongue. Davies struggled to smile as he sheepishly made his way with Logan to the vocal pilots who were still in verse.

"Where are their aircraft?" whispered Davies as he looked around the airfield for the killing machines. Logan, with an outstretched finger, pointed to the front of the hill. Out of the corner of Hainrich's eye he noticed the rank on Davies's coat sleeve, so without a second's hesitation he jumped to his feet and offered Albert Davies a stern salute.

"Group captain, we are honoured by your presence."

Davies returned the salute. "At ease, gentlemen. I am a Corporal, and this coat was given to me by a Group Captain back in Gibraltar." The pilots looked at each in shock, and it dawned on Davies that the subject of Gibraltar should probably have been avoided in front of these Polish airmen.

"Did you leave there yesterday?" asked Piotr, an avid Sikorski loyalist. "We can't believe he has gone." The loss was clearly visible in Piotr's face. Davies was all too well aware that he had gone. He was having great difficulty in getting the graphic scene out of his head but he didn't think that it would benefit these airmen in hearing all about it.

"I'm afraid I arrived at the base after the terrible event had happened."

The two pilots didn't seem to want to dwell on it further. "Would either of you like a drink?" Hainrich walked round to the front of the grass hill and jumped; everything but the top of his head had disappeared under the ground. Davies quickly walked up to the point where the pilot had dropped down. The Corporal was amazed to see that the front of the hill had two large iron doors that opened outwards. A grassy slope of about six feet deep led from the entrance of the hanger to the verge of the tarmac runway, which is what Logan meant by a sub hanger, thought Davies, as he dropped down to see where Hainrich had got to. Davies felt like a schoolboy as he laid eyes on the three Spitfires that rested in tandem, perfectly sheltered from the outside world. Davies couldn't help but admire the beautiful lines and angles of these pieces of artwork.

"Incredible aren't they?" Hainrich returned from the depths of the dark shelter carrying a bottle of Scotch. "Logan out there despises these machines; he is crazy. They are like angels that dance in the heavens above." The pilot reverently patted his Spitfire on its wing tip. Even through the darkness, the outlines of a skull and cross bones were visible on each aircraft.

"Why the black tails and pirate's sign on your tails?" asked the Corporal as he took the bottle of Scotch from Hainrich. The Polish pilot looked almost frustrated to have been asked the question.

"I am forever telling this story." He climbed up onto the inner wing and sat down on the leading edge with his legs dangling down. "In France, back in Lyon-Born we had small aircraft shelters that would house one Spitfire each, but they were useless things." Davies handed back the Scotch. "Our tails used to stick out so we painted them black to try and brake up the shape. One day one of our pilot's tail got shot up with many bullet holes. The top of the tail resembled a skull with two eyes, so he used some paint to make it look like a skull and cross bones, not a glamorous story like I'm sure you suspected. " Taking a big swig of drink he wiped his mouth and looked at Albert Davies, "Really we shouldn't be here; this is not an active military airfield. We should have been back in Lyon-Born last summer with the rest of our squadron." He looked sad and regretful but he continued. "After our engines had been rebuilt we were all set to head back but orders came through that we were to wait here until further orders."

Davies knew all too well about waiting around for further orders. "So do you think that they may have forgotten about you guys?" he asked gently.

Hainrich shrugged his shoulders. "We don't know. We perform tasks like you have seen today and in return we have board and lodgings in the most generous of surroundings. We get fuel for the Spits and general repairs, so if my Government hasn't forgotten about us then they know we are doing a great job for the war effort."

"So you found the Spitfires then?" Logan's voice came from behind Davies's position. The Corporal turned to see Logan and Piotr Bednarczyk standing in the hangar entrance.

"Hainrich here was just telling me how they found themselves to end up here."

Logan smiled. "Sounds to me like they have forgotten you, but what do I know?" He stepped forwards and put his arm onto one of the three huge propellers. "I have spoken to Piotr about your minor problem and he has offered to keep them safely here until you are able to contact your Commanding Officer to get further instructions." Davies knew that he had very few other options; he could have attempted to have taken them back home and then transport them all the way back again, but nowhere could be safer than a military airfield under the protection of armed fighter pilots.

"If you could keep them here for the next couple of days, and in the meantime I shall contact base and find out what I am supposed to do with them." Piotr smiled and nodded in agreement, but Hainrich looked utterly confused.

"There is a canteen back over at FS2. I bet you could do with some food before you get on your way?" asked Logan as he sampled the Scotch. It would be a good three or four hours before Davies would get home, so he wanted to leave as soon as possible but couldn't turn down the offer of a good meal. Heavy rain started to plummet to the ground with no warning whatsoever, the four men watched the dancing rain drops as they hit the grass and bounced back up into the air for a short distance. Logan stepped forward so the rain could just about hit him. "It always bloody rains in South Marston."

# Chapter 9

# Swindon

*Thursday 5ᵗʰ August 2008*

At the age of fourteen, in the fourth year at boarding school, I decided that my God-given wealth was not going to come from studying to become a rocket scientist or a heart surgeon, but my unimaginable fortunes were going to blossom from a newly founded T-shirt company. Under what can only be described as unimaginable resistance from my academic teachers, and legal guardians, I had elected to name my new pet project 'Red Seal,' and for my upmarket range, 'Gold Seal.' At first I had everybody's patronising support, parents and teachers alike, probably because it seemed incredible to them that at the time somebody so young, and with what can only be described as a fondness for the odd spliff could be self motivated enough to plot the birth of a new born company. It didn't take long for word to spread around fellow school mates and eventually the entire staff, what Red Seal was named after. Before long the whole establishment was aware that Red Seal was a name for a certain type of cannabis, an oily, squidgy and potent form of the drug, and Gold Seal - even stronger. Before the origins of the name of Red Seal were public knowledge, my sales were pretty good, my first month turning in around three hundred pounds profit, and the second, pretty much the same. When people realised Red Seal was named after a form of drug, sales went ballistic. Much to my English teacher's disgust I spent most of his double lessons at the printers desperately trying to hurry them along and quicken production of my garments. Before I was rudely and abruptly shut down I had nearly accumulated one and a half thousand pounds worth of profit, an embarrassment to my economics teacher. I had learned that any monkey could find a bundle of T-shirts and engage a trustworthy and reliable printing company, a recipe which, if served well, could produce a lot of money, and quickly. Eleven years had passed, with a lot of academic studying behind me and a wealth of knowledge absorbed. The seeds of My T-shirt Company were still very much inside of me, and still growing.

Some of my colleagues at work who had served with the company for two years or over would remember when myself and Ben were launching Boulette Boarding, my most recent attempt at making a successful T-shirt company. This time I decided to make it a surf wear label with all the pictures containing a surfing theme, but the label would still have a smoking flavour as the name Boulette translates from French into 'meat ball' or French slang 'hot rock,' i.e. the hot ash that falls out of a spliff. In the honeymoon period of the first three months we had sold close to seven hundred T-shirts, all at ten pounds each. We could have cleared our loan, but decided to plough whatever profits we made into printing more T-shirts. As well as T-shirts we also sourced some high quality hooded jumpers and produced one hundred limited edition hoodies; at fifty-five pounds each they all sold like hot cakes. It was a venture that should have never been allowed to slip away. Looking back at those early months, I now understand why so many people expressed such an interest in our attempt at fortunes, because they could all see the potential of our young company. Estate agency is an enjoyable industry to be in but it is also an industry that will take over your body and soul; the hours estate agents put in have destroyed many a relationship, including marriages. In my time with Knight Allen Estate Agents I had seen many a long lasting relationship break up and I often feared the countless Saturdays I worked would jeopardise my relationship with my girlfriend Serena. It was these sorts of pressures on my time that eventually put Boulette onto the backburner and into non-existence. However the backbone was still there. I could resurrect the website and start pushing the Boulette brand easier than ever, for it was almost a dark cloud over my shoulder that needed to be lifted.

I had woken up early on the Thursday morning and had been greeted with bright blue skies and brilliant sunshine; I felt a massive sense of excitement as I prepared myself for the day ahead. With the gift of a glorious morning, I decided to seize the opportunity to try and offload a bundle of T-shirts to my colleagues at work, so I found an old Walkers crisp box and loaded it full with approximately fifty garments of all different colours and sizes. I felt as if I didn't have a care in the world as I waltzed through my office doors armed with my box packed to the top with T-shirts, skilfully balancing my suitcase, mobile phone and keys on top of the cardboard box. I had failed to notice my Area Manager and Chief Executive Officer standing at the back of the office quietly drinking coffee. I was surprised that my usually late colleagues were already sat perched on their desks when they suddenly decided to erupt into loud applause. It took me a moment to realise that the applause was aimed at me. Panic set in as my mind raced to try and ascertain how my fellow estate agents had found out about our discovery of vintage port. Without thinking, I dropped my box and everything balancing on top of it and put my finger to my lips in an attempt to down play their evident excitement. Simon Robson, my Chief Executive Officer, withdrew from the shadows at the back of the office and proceeded to walk up to me. I was shocked by his presence as he very rarely ventured to Swindon, so I knew that this had to be serious. I could feel my heart thump inside of my chest as he extended his hand in a gesture of a handshake. "It's good to see you Hammy. Planning on doing some car booting?" he jested as he looked at the pile of belongings on the floor. His handshake was firm and oozed authority. I looked around me and could see my colleagues grinning back at me like cheshire cats; before I could piece together my response to Simon Robson he continued to talk. "I've been studying your figures young man and it is very obvious that you are doing very well indeed." The feeling of relief was immense as it became obvious that he was here to talk shop and not a certain discovery of port. Robson walked over to my colleague Justin's desk. "Justin here tells me that you took on thirty-eight houses last month and personally sold nineteen of them." At any other point in my career I would by now have been bathing in my own ego. I would have been lapping up the praise and applauds, but not today. Today I was fed up to the back teeth of lining other people's pockets, including those of Simon Robson's. Today and from now on, I had decided that it was time for me to make some serious money and to do it without having to put in so many horribly long hours.

A loud tap at the window was closely followed by the office front doors flying open under great force. I did not need to turn around to investigate who it was, for I was familiar with Mr. Stephens's method of entering properties. "What's going on here? More Chiefs than Indians?" Members of my team subtly tried to retreat into the safety of the shadows at the back of the office, but I was like a rabbit caught in the headlights with nowhere to run, "Is that Hammy, the reprobate, I see before me?" Mr. Stephen's was a character in every sense of the word; at eighty-three, he was by far my oldest vendor and certainly the most demanding. During his retirement he had accumulated a very healthy property portfolio all funded from what I can only imagine was from a very significant military pension. With far too much free time on his hands he employed many of his days of leisure interrogating us as to why we had not sold one of his chosen properties yet.

"Hello my friend." I cheerfully said as I turned to face the old age pensioner with his customary outstretched walking stick. I obligingly shook the end of his walking aid.

"Ralph informed me that I would have one of your ghastly For Sale boards up in no time at all. Well I have to inform you, if you would be as kind as to pardon the pun, there is no sign of your sign at all."

"I apologise Mr. Stephens, but our board man seems to be somewhat preoccupied these days." What I really wanted to say was *'speak to one of my colleagues who actually gives a shit you fussy old git'* but I managed to keep hold of my thoughts. Mr. Stephens I'm sure was convinced that he alone was our only vendor and the delight in his face was clear for all to see when somebody who was evidently in senior management addressed him.

"I hope young Edward here is treating you admirably" inquired my Chief Executive Officer as he shook the end of Mr. Stephen's walking stick. I didn't pay attention to the old man's response, as I had managed to learn just to let his waffle wash over my head.

What was grabbing my attention, however, was why all of my fellow colleagues were still grinning at me as if I was the last one to get the joke. "What?" I mouthed back to them in an attempt to establish the reason for the unusually jovial mood in the office. It all became crystal clear when I caught a few words coming from my Chief Executive Officer.

"Well I'm sure your new Sales Manager will continue to provide you a top notch service." Bloody hell I thought, is he talking about me? I didn't have any desire to become a fully-fledged Manager. If I had my way, I would have handed in my notice there and then, but had to continue as normal until all the finer details were in place.

"You look somewhat surprised," said Mr. Stephens, but I wished some of his enthusiasm could have rubbed off on me; if he had known that I was soon to fulfil my lifetime's dream of becoming a millionaire I'm sure he would have understood my apparent ambivalence. Simon Robson offered his hand in congratulations which I hastily returned.

"I don't know what to say. I'm extremely flattered," and with that the office erupted into loud applause; it was good to know I had my colleagues' full support.

My Chief Executive Officer had proceeded to bend down and pull one of my T-shirts from the box beside my feet, unfolded it and held it out with outstretched arms. "Doing a touch of moonlighting Edward?" I could hear sniggers coming from a couple of my colleagues sat hiding behind their computer screens. "Did you do these yourself? They are really very good."

Before I could respond by singing my own praises, Mr. Stephens who seemed to be thoroughly enjoying his morning's outing interrupted. "That boy would sell his own grandmother if there was a bob in it for him." He probably wasn't too far off the mark as anything can be sold, I thought to myself. I should have felt awkward about colleagues, vendors and senior management gaining knowledge of my out-of-office activities but it actually served a valuable purpose; I needed to start laying down some foundation blocks to justify my inevitable success in my business. Robson didn't seem to be particularly worried or bothered about it, if not even pleasantly surprised, but I welcomed the distraction of an incoming telephone call for me. The caller had identified himself to Justin as Mr. Knapp, and I was taken aback that Julian Knapp had wanted to call me at work. He sounded extremely apologetic when I picked up the headset.

"I'm terribly sorry to call you at your place of work Hammy, but I couldn't seem to get through on your mobile." I instantly checked my mobile phone that was in my pocket, but there were no missed calls and I had a full signal so I instantly put it down to the fact that he just wanted security in the knowledge that I did work where I had said I did. True to his word, he wanted my business's bank details that I had taken into work with me that morning; he agreed I could call him back on my mobile when I was in private, which I did allowing the details to change hands.

Ben and I had discussed the previous evening what we would do with our share of the one hundred thousand pounds. We both understood the importance of not flashing the cash so that we would not raise any suspicion but we both could not resist the opportunity to treat ourselves just a few times. It was decided that we would treat ourselves to a fairly newish car each and would provide a holiday for ourselves and girlfriends to an exotic destination somewhere hot. I had always fancied a Porsche 911 Carrera and at about thirty thousand pounds for a good tidy example with relatively low mileage they were now easily within my grasp, so I itched for the day when I could waltz into a second hand show room dressed as scruffily as I could only to drive away in a flashy Porsche 911. Ben would plan on steering towards Italy with the Ferrari 456 GT, a stunning piece of machinery that he could normally only dream about; the world was soon to know that the two of us had arrived. To make our new found success even more credible I planned on contacting Laura, an old colleague of mine who had jumped ship to go and work for the local newspaper, whom I had little doubts would be delighted to run a story in the rag about how two local entrepreneurs had sold their thriving young company to a large undisclosed surf wear label. We would be the toast of Swindon.

# Chapter 10

# Swindon

*Friday 6<sup>th</sup> August 2008*

Having been given the curious pleasure of being made to work the forthcoming Saturday, I was gifted the day off much to my relief. Ben had volunteered to help his stepfather do some DIY around the house so would not be about for the day which left me at a slight loose end. The only thing I needed to do with my free time was to go to a hole in the wall and check our business bank balance for any new arrivals. Even by England's standards, it was a wet summer's day with rain beating at the windows ferociously. As I lay in my bed, I pondered on which country to take Serena to, in order to escape this miserable weather; I had always liked the Canary Islands and if I could overcome my silly fear of flying, that would make a most welcome break for us both. As I watched a green light blink slowly on my laptop as it rested on my bedroom floor amongst dirty pairs of socks and car magazines, I suddenly thought about something that had been tickling my curiosity now for several days. So as not to lose any precious warmth from under my bed covers, I quickly darted out of bed and grabbed my laptop, yanking the machine away from the battery charger that was plugged into a nearby socket. Returning quickly to the warmth of my bed, I flicked open the screen and turned it on.

Multimap was a website that I used frequently during working hours; it allowed me to look at a particular Postcode or area from the sky either in the form of a map or an aerial photograph and had become invaluable as a tool to look at houses and gardens etc before I went on a valuation. *What an incredible invention!* I thought to myself as I tapped in the words: South Marston. I selected the aerial photograph option and within seconds the screen was full of lush green fields separated by wild hedgerows and countless housing estates. It didn't take me long to pinpoint my ex-girlfriend Emily's house. Knowing where the gigantic Honda factory is located, I scrolled the scenery a couple of frames to the left to reveal a mass of huge cream factories and an abundance of neatly arranged brand new cars sitting on the many acres of concrete within the works' boundaries. It seemed a shame that what was once upon a time a quiet and picturesque little village now sat in the shadows of this monstrous car factory that towered above the ancient cottages and houses. Just like the old sketch map we had found, I could make out a number of large rectangular shapes on the perimeters of Honda that would almost certainly have been aircraft hangars during the airfield's life. Now, as Julian had said, they were being used by a removal firm with their big red vans and lorries parked neatly outside. Very few other signs of the airfield's existence were evident that day apart from one of the large concrete runways that I imagined was being used by the car manufacturer as a test track for their new cars. It was extremely long and would have made the very best test bed for the new vehicles, I thought, as I followed the runway with my eyes from the factory to the runway's end. I had committed the old map that we found to memory and I found myself rotating the laptop ninety degrees until it was at the same angle as the sketch. Bringing the screen closer to my eyes, a shot of adrenalin pulsed through my body.

If I hadn't known exactly where to look, I would have easily missed it. In fact, I had to blink and look at the image several times to make sure that I was seeing it correctly but after several moments I was satisfied that there was something there. At the end of the runway or test track there was a large area of long grass and trees that looked to have been cared for very rarely. A small road looped around the track's end clearly designed for the large lorries delivering to the site and just behind that road was a very faint rectangular shape that was a slightly deeper green than the surrounding grass. Without a doubt it looked as if the rectangular shape was raised ever so slightly and for a few moments I allowed my imagination to run wild trying to guess what could have been inside it at some point in the past. I carefully thought back to our first meeting with Julian at the Black Horse in Wanborough. *What was it he had said?* 'Honda had been involved in a four year conveyancing battle and that it had finally been decided that Honda would purchase the land above ground and the Ministry of Defence would retain the ownership of anything below ground'. It would be a fair assumption, I pondered, that if indeed there was anything down there then it would have been discovered by the workmen who laid the roads or the groundsmen who maintained the entire site.

Back in my school days, I had learnt of an urban myth that went along the lines that there was vast a number of wartime German Tiger tanks dumped and enclosed in a tomb underneath a major German international airport; the name currently escapes me. Tanks are not my thing but even I could understand that such a discovery would be a colossal historic find. Not so glamorous, I have heard many accounts and stories here in Swindon regarding the railway. Swindon being a major railway town and had been ever since the Victorian times, many locals, it seems, believe that with the introduction of the diesel engine many of the original steam engines were just driven into massive underground tunnels which had all the entrances bricked up to be forgotten about and never to see daylight again. I had always rejected the idea, thinking this would be a silly thing to do but apparently at the time it was far cheaper just to ditch them as opposed to paying hefty prices to get them scrapped.

I stared at the small rectangular shape on my screen, but I knew that there could be nothing there but the map bugged me; we had found it amongst bottles that evidently send historians into wild ecstasy, so *what was it doing there, with them?* I thought to myself. It had already been identified as South Marston airfield which I had to admit was the case. South Marston was only six or seven miles away from where I lived, so it would have been foolish not to at least go and have a quick look and see if I could get close enough to ascertain if this was worthy of further investigation. I thought about giving Ben a quick call to see if he wanted to go and have a look at the circled thing on the map we had found but I figured he had better things to do than look at a big car factory that was more than likely laden with security staff. I didn't need Multimap to tell me how to get there as I had been to South Marston countless times and knew the way very well; I shut down the computer and tossed it to the other side of the bed.

The torrential morning rain was not motivating me to step outside but I didn't want to lose any more precious time of this sacred day off. I jumped out of bed and started rifling through the piles of clothes on my bedroom floor looking for something that vaguely resembled being clean. I would aim to spend the rest of the morning checking our bank balance, nipping into a couple of travel agents to grab some brochures and then I would be free to go and look at South Marston in my own leisurely time. I sat back down on my bed dressed only in boxer shorts. The last few days had not really had a chance to sink in with me properly but as I sat there with my head in my hands gathering my thoughts; the sheer weight of the situation was starting to register. I had second thoughts about not ringing Ben to see if he wanted to come with me to South Marston, not only because I would have quite liked the company but also if we were going to run into a spot of bother snooping around Honda then the moral support would have been greatly appreciated. I glanced around my dimly lit room looking for the landing site of my mobile phone from when I had discarded it the previous evening. As if aware of my search, the chorus of 'only fools and horses' filled my room accompanied by a blue flashing glow from the corner of my room. I didn't recognise the number displayed on my screen but it was a local landline so I decided to answer the call. "Hello is that Mr. Hamilton?" The female voice on the other end of the line sounded soft and gracious whilst still maintaining an air of authority. "Just a courtesy call Mr. Hamilton", the young lady explained. "My name is Jenny and I am calling on behalf of the Royal Bank of Scotland." I stood to attention and bolted for my window to make sure that I did not lose any reception; the bank very rarely called me so I knew this was not a routine call. "We just wanted to bring to your attention, Mr. Hamilton, that your business account held with us has just received one hundred thousand pounds via a telegraphic transfer from an offshore account." I found it impossible to hold back a broad grin as I listened carefully to everything she said; Julian had been true to his word and in such good time as well.

"Excellent." I quickly responded. "We were expecting it, but we weren't exactly sure when it would get to us so thank you for letting me know."

She explained that she had to touch base with us to make sure that it had not been sent in error, but I suspected that they were fishing for the reason and origin of such a large cash injection. It took a good few minutes to explain that we were a young surf wear label and that we had been approached by a much bigger company to buy us out and that the money was a deposit. She sounded very surprised but genuinely happy for us, she ended the call by wishing us entrepreneurs luck and that she was extremely jealous of the two of us.

I got dressed in no time at all whilst texting Ben the news that we had a big pile of cash sat waiting to be spent in our bank account. I was disappointed that he was tied up grouting the family bathroom and had no chance to escape but I knew that we would have plenty of time to celebrate later that evening. The rain was still coming down in colossal proportions but I didn't care, because the phone call from Jenny had put me in such good spirits that not even the weather could tarnish my mood. I decided that I would give the travel agents a miss today. I would speak to Serena and tell her that we would go on holiday if she so wished and would let her do all of the legwork; after all, she liked nothing better than organising holidays. Instead, I decided to go to South Marston straight away. It would only take me fifteen minutes in the car and by the time I was finished the bar in the South Marston Country Club would be open, a place where I had spent many a happy night drinking the evening away. I needed to go over a few points with Julian and decided that I would send him a text of thanks once I was at the bar. The phone call from the bank had made the situation all so real and it made me realise that we really did live in a 'big brother' society. If the bank had been that quick to highlight the fact that we had received this money then surely other organisations would start to raise their eyebrows once a cool couple of a million hit the account. I knew from estate agency that if you were to sell a second property then you would get hit for capital gains tax which was something absurd like eighteen percent of your overall profit. I needed to know if this was the case. Would we have to pay such a large tax bill for selling our business? These were things that we would have to find out soon, I thought to myself, as I closed the front door behind me.

I had kept my speed to the legal limits on the way to South Marston village; the weather was still serving up heavy doses of rain and I was aware that the Wiltshire Police had their headquarters on the fringes of the village. I watched as two unmarked black BMWs raced across a roundabout with a medley of flashing blue lights going in the opposite direction. I turned left off the roundabout still watching the Police cars drive off into the distance through my mirrors. I drove past a sign signalling the village and rapidly approached a small roundabout, where, towering above the road was a gigantic sign, 'Welcome to Honda'.

I had arrived at the south entrance to the car works, not only because it didn't have large security gates outside but also because it was positioned just a few hundred metres or so from the end of the old runway. I had turned left onto the site and parked up onto a curb and turned on my hazard warning lights; the massive factories were situated about half a mile away from my position to my right hand side. The road I had stopped on appeared to veer off to the right and made its way all the way down to the large buildings. In the far off distance I could see row upon row of heavy goods vehicles with their back doors open. A much smaller road that was just wide enough for a single vehicle forked off to the left and seemed to loop inside the perimeter fence; the land in between these two roads consisted of overgrown grass and a sprinkling of mature trees. I fumbled around in my pocket looking for my cigarettes when a large lorry frightened the life out of me as it trundled past climbing up the gears. My presence didn't seem to be raising any alarms but I didn't want to push my luck too far. I lit my last remaining cigarette, put my car into first and slowly crawled along the narrow road that forked round to the left. It was the land in the centre of these two roads that I was interested in as this was roughly where the rectangular shape had been circled on the map we had found. As my car covered more of the narrow road, the long and wide test track that used to be one of the old runways came into view on my right side. Another lorry raced past, this time heading out of the site on the road I had entered on. Deciding that this smaller and much narrower track did not seem to be in use that much, I decided to pull over. I stepped out of my car and, pretending to talk on my phone in an attempt to give the impression to any prying eyes that I was lost, I walked across the road and stood on the grass verge looking carefully at the unattended ground in front of me.

The land was not level to say the least and there was no evidence to suggest that the groundsmen had paid it any attention at all over the last few years. I figured that this area would have been a low priority as all the visitors, apart from the lorries, reported in at the other entrances. The grassy square shape in front of me was not difficult to see from my position; it stood about a metre and a half above ground level and certainly did not look like a natural hill. Stood on top of this grassy mound appeared to be two weather- decayed concrete cylinders that were similar in size to a couple of car tyres stacked on top of each other. I wanted to step closer but didn't want to resemble a trespasser in any shape or form. A convoy of three lorries entered the site and steamed passed at quite some speed destined for the large factory; I instinctively crouched down so I was out of site but the lorries passed quickly and as far as I knew had paid me no attention whatsoever. Time was fast approaching eleven o'clock, only ten minutes till the bar at the Country Club opened. I decided that it would be more sensible to investigate the site early evening on Sunday as I presumed there would be less people and traffic about. That way Ben could accompany me as well. I took a photograph of the grassy hill in front of me to show Ben later on and walked back to my car. This place was definitely worth investigating further.

# Chapter 11

# Berkshire

*March 1943*

The train had a full complement of passengers as it raced through the countryside dissecting fields and roads on its journey to Swindon, but Albert Davies had not noticed that the carriage was almost bursting with fellow travellers that afternoon. Lost in his own world, he stared blankly out of the window with only his thoughts of Victoria as company. He felt an anger and bitterness growing inside of him that made him want to scream out aloud but instead he sat hunched up in his seat motionless. He felt that he had been robbed of something so precious that he was seriously starting to doubt his belief in this God awful war. He had thought

that he would at least get more than one night and day with his
Victoria. What was so special about those bloody crates that would
deny him such needed time with his wife at home?

The call from the Group Captain had come as a bitter blow
the previous evening. He had been wrong to leave the cargo with
strangers and that it was paramount that he returned to South
Marston the following day to take back possession of the crates.
Group Captain Williams had sounded sincere but also apologetic
and regretful as he instructed the Corporal to cut his leave short to
remedy the mistake he had made at the Wiltshire airfield. Davies
had tried to explain that they were in extremely safe hands but his
account of the previous day had seemed to fall upon deaf ears.
Victoria of course had not understood, although she didn't let
it show; Albert knew that the news had cut her open and left her
heartbroken. He had pleaded with the senior officer to allow him
at least one more night and day with his beloved wife but it was
clear that his last several years dedicated to the war effort accounted
for nothing. He was to leave his wife prematurely to go and baby-
sit seven wooden crates. The couple had made passionate love the
previous evening, something that Davies dearly missed when he
was away from home but something else was starting to torture him
deep down inside. Davies had awoken late in the morning at twenty
past eleven. Paying great attention not to waken his sleeping soul
mate, he had slipped out of bed, dressed, and prepared himself for
the day ahead. When it had come to leaving home, Victoria was still
tucked up in bed fast asleep, an image that the Corporal wanted to
keep in his memory for the rest of his life, but that image that was
so beautiful that Davies had decided to kiss her gently on the cheek
and had left her to enjoy her dreams. Davies hated goodbyes. It
would be months before Davies would see his wife again and he
regretted not saying goodbye, not to hold her and tell her everything
would be alright. He hoped that she would understand when she
awoke and prayed that she would forgive him.

A young Private dressed in full army uniform who sat opposite
Davies started to cry quietly as he looked at a photograph he was
holding. Davies glanced at him quickly not wanting to make a

spectacle out of the young distressed serviceman. Even to Albert Davies this private looked young, barely old enough to have left school, he thought, as he returned to gazing out of the window. Although every serviceman risked their lives in fighting this war, he knew that the army was taking the brunt of the hits and judging by the state of this soldier he knew it as well. "Is that a picture of a young lady?" asked Davies in an attempt to put the soldier in a lighter mood; it seemed to have its desired effect. The young private looked up and wiped a tear away from his face.

"It's a picture of my mother, father and myself. It's the first time I've ever been away from home." He offered Davies the picture as he spoke. Davies took the photograph and studied the young man's family. Love and happiness radiated from their faces; they were clearly very close. The Corporal was interested to learn where this Private would be serving but feared that his reaction may have distressed the already nervous soldier, especially if he was destined for some awfully dangerous hell hole. He reached into his coat inner pocket and pulled out a recently taken photograph of Victoria and handed it to the Private, who looked at it with an impressed smile and gave it back. Davies described how he had left her asleep in bed and that he felt awful as a consequence. Although he had elected to wear a casual shirt and pair of trousers, he had decided to wear the Group Captain's coat for the journey back to South Marston; the Private had noted the high rank. "Are you a pilot?" he had asked gingerly. Davies explained his role based in Gibraltar and had insisted that he would much rather be at the thick of it on the front line. The Corporal was sad to hear that the young Private was also destined for the Mediterranean because he would probably be involved in the rumoured allied attack on Sicily. Davies secretly doubted the boy's safe return.

The train was fast approaching Swindon station as Albert Davies started to think about the wooden crates. He became uncomfortable with a string of thoughts that had entered his head. What if the precious cargo was not waiting for him on his arrival? What if the person delegated to collect them did not arrive? He had been given the same security word, 'Dandelion', and could only hand over the consignment once this word was presented to him. "Dandelion," he mumbled to himself under his breath and chuckled quietly at the RAF's hierarchy's lack of imagination. The whole scenario involving these crates had been a mixed bag of emotions for Albert Davies; he had been grateful to have been given the opportunity to see his wife but felt bitter as well that his time had been cut short. He couldn't harbour a grudge over the Foreman dying suddenly of a heart attack but felt strongly that the whole task could have been handled better with a little more detailed planning. It was typical of the RAF, he thought, as he felt the train start to slow down ever so slightly. Davies gathered up his newspaper and his lunch box and sat up straight.

"Is this your stop?" asked the young Private who had now managed to stop his tears. Davies acknowledged that it was and noted anxiety in the young man's eyes; he had sat with the young soldier for the best part of an hour and still didn't know his name. Davies introduced himself; the Private's name was Fred Bunn aged sixteen. He explained after being questioned by Davies about his age that he had been bullied at school and decided that any life would be better than facing heartless bullies everyday. He lied about his age and applied for the army; after several weeks he was enrolled in the infantry, much to his parents' despair.

The brakes of the train started to take grip of the wheels and the train started to slow with more force and Davies along with a handful of other passengers rose to his feet and started to gather his belongings together. The Corporal could see that the young soldier was vulnerable and felt a certain sadness for him, so he slipped off an elastic band from his wrist and handed it to Fred Bunn. "I know this is only an elastic band and it sounds very silly but I have worn this ever since the war started and I like to think that it has kept me safe throughout the whole time, so I would like you to wear it at all times so that it may keep you safe too." Bunn looked touched and flattered; without a moment's hesitation, he slipped the band on around his wrist. The two servicemen shook hands and wished each other the best of luck. Davies realised that they would never meet again but sincerely hoped that the young man would keep out of reach of danger and that he would return home to his loving parents safely. He headed towards the end of the carriage and stepped through the train doors onto the platform. South Marston was about five miles away from Swindon station so he decided to look for a taxi. He turned back towards the train and quickly located the carriage he and Fred Bunn had shared. The train started to pull away slowly as Albert Davies caught eye contact with the Private. Davies raised his hands to salute the young Private. Fred Bunn returned the gesture instantly as he smiled from ear to ear. Davies glanced at his watch and hastily made his way towards the exit signs at the far end of the platform; he wanted to get to the airfield as quickly as possible. Corporal Albert Davies disappeared down the station stairs towards the car park; he would never reach the airfield or ever be seen again.

# Chapter 12

## Swindon

*Saturday 7ᵗʰ August 2008*

 

I had made good progress in distributing our T-shirts the previous day; although I hadn't yet counted the exact number of shirts that we had 'sold', I estimated that it would easily have been close to three hundred. Many of my friends and family had already got a cupboard full of our garments, so I had decided to spend a few hours the previous afternoon handing them out for a couple of pounds or even giving quite a few away for free. I still had a receipt book from when Boulette started trading which I had brought into work with me as Saturdays were often quiet; I planned on filling as many pages as I could with fake customers all for garments that sold at fifteen pounds each.

I loathed the thought of having to pay the tax man V.A.T for items that hadn't actually been sold but it would serve me well in creating an illusion of successful selling. I still had a box of T-shirts at the office and planned on fabricating even more sales by handing them out to anybody who walked into the office by declaring that they were misprints; hence the reason for giving them away for free. I was aware that although I personally was making a good number of house sales, many of my colleagues were struggling to tie up a sale. Much of the news recently had reported a massive slow down in the housing market due to paranoia from the mortgage companies not wanting to replicate Northern Rock's incredible demise; I would have to be careful not to rub their faces in the fact that I was selling houses and T-shirts, making considerable amounts of money in doing so.

Our company policy was never have two members of staff who could value houses working on the same Saturday, which always resulted in the fact that I would never work with Ralph at weekends. It was always a foregone conclusion that from Tuesday onwards, Ralph would book in the appointments that he didn't want to do on Saturday, safe in the knowledge that yours truly would have to do them. Having read the office diary first thing in the morning, I found that Ralph, true to form, had kindly set me up with another viewing with the Bambers, this time at a different property. Ralph had excelled himself. He had booked me in to a property that he had taken onto the market late Thursday afternoon; once again I had not seen the property before and I assured myself that there would be no shenanigans like my last encounter with the Bambers. Our office ran a key system whereby the number of the house was also the key tag number, thus helping us considerably when we had a run of multiple viewings and a pocket full of different sets of keys. Feeling considerably groggy from the previous evening, I didn't take particular care in selecting the keys to 9 Baxter Street. Ralph had stuck the appointment in at nine-thirty, probably much to his amusement which didn't leave me much time to gather my stuff and clear my head. "This takes the piss" I exclaimed to my half awake colleagues. 'What was I still doing here?' I asked myself as I contemplated my viewing with the Bambers; there would be no escape from their pathetic ridicules over our last little incident.

Driving up Baxter Street, I couldn't see any of our 'For Sale' boards so I quickly glanced at the key tag to remember the house number. I was directly outside, so I hastily shifted into reverse and tightly squeezed into a narrow space, a few cars away from a Volvo estate doing the same manoeuvre. The Bambers had arrived too. Slamming both their doors, they briskly strode over to my car, "Qu ey" squeaked Mrs. Bamber; her voice was painfully annoying to listen to. With her fake Burberry handbag, her cheap knock off D&G sunglasses and spray tan, she liked to think that she was a cut above the rest. Mr. Bamber was much more reserved than his wife, probably because he could never get a chance to speak, but he was always so negative. The Bambers had viewed properties now for some considerable time but they still had not bought; something was always not quite right. I always considered showing the Bambers a property a complete waste of time. Deep down I think they knew that they would never buy a house; they just liked looking around homes they probably couldn't afford. "Ralph said you would bring some sales particulars with photographs and measurements," said Mr. Bamber grumpily as he watched me get out of my car empty handed. "Ralph strikes again," I mumbled as I proceeded to explain that the details would be ready on Monday when the administrator came back to work. Ralph was in fine form, I thought, as I accompanied the couple through the front gate into the small garden. Ralph had entered 'Baxter Street, x3 bed £250,000' into the diary. "Two fifty!" I blurted out. "Ralph must be taking happy pills." The Bambers seemed to agree. Two hundred and fifty thousand pounds seemed a lot of money for what looked to be a complete Hell hole.

The compact garden, consisting of a tiny lawn area and path, was covered in dog shit. Items of decayed clothing spilled out of two bin bags with gapping holes in the sides; I was starting to feel embarrassed. Praying that the inside didn't resemble the front in anyway, I nervously slid the key into the lock; nothing, it wouldn't budge. The once silver lock was now nothing more than a mass of rust. "It's a new key," I explained as I desperately tried to get the thing to turn. Realising that I was fighting a losing battle, I knocked at the shabby front door in the hope that the vendor was in; it being a Saturday, I was hopeful. After what seemed like a life time, the door suddenly opened; the smell of weed struck me as a thick haze started to float through the front door into the Bambers. Stood before me was a tall, lanky, unwashed hippy character sporting dreadlocks. He looked off his head and confused to see us. I pulled a business card from my pocket and presented it to him. "I'm Edward from the Estate agents. We're here for a quick viewing." I actually hoped he would deny us access but the door opened for us to enter. The dazed and confused host scratched his head as he gestured for us to enter.

"Excuse the mess. We had a bit of a gathering last night." Piles of dirty trainers and shoes lined the hallway floor.

"It looks like the gathering is still here." I joked as I tried to avoid tripping on the countless pairs of shoes. The crusty hippy took the lead and invited us to enter the first door in the hallway.

"This is the lounge, but we are using it as another bedroom." Mrs. Bamber took a few steps through the doorway and made a sudden retreat back to the hallway; Mr. Bamber, who was obviously curious to have a glance inside, arched his head round the door frame for a few brief moments. A look of horror and disgust filled his face; I couldn't even start to imagine what horrendous sight waited for me. Taking a deep breath, I stepped forward and glanced into the front room; I couldn't help but smile when faced with two young girls dressed only in underwear as they inhaled from a homemade bong. They didn't even seem to acknowledge us as thick blue clouds of smoke gently filled the room; this had to be some kind of joke. Trying to remain as professional as one could in a situation like this, I asked if he had lived at the property for long.

"Coming up two years now. We keep on about having a tidy up but just never find the time; you know how it is." I was amazed at how unashamed this man seemed to be, when most people in their right mind would be completely embarrassed to show their home in this condition. I couldn't wait to get back to the office and tell my colleagues about this little disaster. Mrs. Bamber still looked to be in a state of shock and I feared that the following few minutes would not help her condition. "I must warn you that the kitchen has seen better days," said the hippy as we walked through the dirty hallway towards the rear of the house; I was starting to think that nothing could surprise me. I was the last to enter the kitchen as I watched Mrs. Bamber clasp her hand over her mouth.

"Please don't be sick," I whispered as I stepped through the door. Nothing could have prepared me for what I saw. I could feel last night's alcohol intake race up my throat and into my mouth; without a moment's notice sick hurled out of my mouth onto the floor. Dog shit covered the kitchen floor with scraps of ancient mouldy food; the work surfaces were lost to piles upon piles of empty beans tins and empty food sachets. The smell of stale sick and alcohol lingered in my nostrils. I had to get out of there before I added another layer of sick to this man's kitchen floor.

It was Mr. Bamber who bailed me out of this awful situation. He looked towards the hippy with a stern face. "You have been a great help, but so as not to waste any more of your time, I have to say we are looking for something a little smaller than this." I could have kissed him. Without any hesitation the three of us headed sharply towards the front door. I offered to clean up my mess, praying to God that he would not accept my offer, thankfully he declined. With my thanks and apologies, I slammed the front door and it closed behind me. Fresh air hit my lungs as I breathed in heavily to dispel any lingering smells that I had gathered; I was utterly lost for words and truly felt like murdering Ralph. I was just about to make some lame apology to the Bambers when I felt my mobile phone vibrate in my pocket. If there was any justice in this world, it would be Ralph, I thought, as I pulled my phone out of my trouser pocket and answered it. It was my colleague Jess on the other end of the line sounding very panicky. "Hammy, is everything OK? You were supposed to be at Baxter Street at nine-thirty for a viewing, you are fifteen minutes late." I was tempted to make up some story how I had been involved in some terrible car crash just to wind her up but decided I had experienced too much fun and games already this morning.

"Jess, you plonker, I am with the Bambers now, and I've already shown them around the house." I walked out onto the street so the Bambers were not in hearing distance. "Just for the record Jess, I wouldn't waste any time in trying to sell this place; it has to be one of the worst I have seen in a long time." A long silence developed from the other end of the line. "Hello, anyone there?" I was just about to hang up when Jess spoke.

"Hammy, the vendors of Baxter Street called about two minutes ago and said that you had not arrived. They are not impressed at all with our service so far." She sounded genuinely confused and worried. Looking at the Bambers, I could see that I held their full attention; I had to be careful in selecting the right words.

"Jess, what exactly does it say in the diary?" I tried to speak as quietly as possible, but I could hear the other line going in the background. "Jess don't answer that; tell me what the diary says." The other phone stopped ringing. "Thank God for that - it says, number nine Baxter Street, three bed, two hundred and fifty thousand pounds and it says it's at nine-thirty." Trying to look as cool as possible, I looked past the disgruntled couple to the shabby, black panel front door that we had just come out of.

"You say it's bad?" I had forgotten Jess was on the line. "That's odd, because Ralph was over the moon when he brought this back in. He said it was one of the best he had seen."

Stood in the middle of Baxter Street with my jaw dropped to the ground, I stared, transfixed at the rusty number six that hung on the hippy's front door. Mrs. Bamber started to click her fingers but nothing could shake me out of my state of shock. A few moments passed before my mouth started to function, "I've just done a viewing at the wrong bloody house." Simultaneously, "What?" came from both Jess and the Bambers; there was no way I could mop up this little mess. I hung up the phone to Jess and strode over to the flabbergasted wife and husband. "I'm not sure how this has happened, but I have just shown you the wrong property." Mrs. Bamber started to laugh sarcastically.

"How could even you make such a mistake?" gasped Mr. Bamber. I wanted the ground to swallow me up. I fumbled around for the key that nestled in my pocket; I pulled it out and examined the tag.

"I am such a Twat!" Shaking my head I handed the couple the key; it read '9'. I had glanced at the key tag earlier and had read it upside down. Mr. Bamber looked lost.

"But if that was the wrong house then why did that crusty hippy happily show us around his flea pit?" It was something that I could not get my head around either. Surely he would have said that his house was not up for sale, or maybe it was with another agent. I decided that the only way to make good of this situation was take the Bambers to number nine, much to my embarrassment, and then go back to number six to apologise for my blunder and for being sick over his kitchen floor.

Much to my relief, the viewing at nine Baxter Street went very well and thankfully, the vendors found it highly amusing that I had shown somebody around "smelly Simon's" house, and had thrown up in doing so. I was pleased to see that the house was well worth its asking price and the vendors looked to be a pleasure to deal with; it appeared that I had made a bad situation good, or so I thought. Jess had rung me during the viewing appointment which I couldn't answer, so she sent me a text message: 'Hammy, just 2 warn u Ralph in office and crazy x.' How the hell did Ralph find out? Just what I needed on a Saturday, I thought, as I slipped my phone back into my pocket and headed back to apologise to 'smelly Simon' at number six.

Ralph was pacing up and down the office wearing his casual clothes as I entered into the office; to say he looked enraged was an understatement. "Edward, shall we go for a coffee across the road?" spit flew out of his mouth as he spoke "and take that tie off, you have sick down it." I would have preferred to stay in the office and face my bollocking in front of Jess than have the whole world listen in, but that was Ralph; he would never administer disciplining in front of colleagues. Jess looked concerned for my fate and dared not lift her face away from her computer screen. Ralph very rarely got this mad but when he did it was certainly worth staying well out of his way. He always looked strange to me wearing casual clothes, probably because we spent so many hours suited and booted. Wearing trainers, ill fitting jeans and a plain T-shirt, he almost looked as if he had forgotten how to dress in anything but a shirt and tie. I needed to splash some water over my face and drink some water, so I quickly went to the bathroom to freshen up and gulp some water from the tap.

'Jaspers' coffee shop was your typically modern, trendy place to go at lunch time for professionals. Serving up big mugs of cappuccinos and hot chocolate for extortionate prices, it was always packed and this Saturday morning was no exception. Two elderly ladies gratefully thanked me as they left the coffee shop through the front door that I was holding open for them. I quickly headed to their empty table that was situated to the back of the shop. Ralph quickly followed and sat himself down in front of me. "What do you fancy? One of those chocca wokka whatever they are called things?" Ralph had a certain way with words that amused me; before I could answer a young waiter appeared dressed in a smart, all black uniform and took our orders nervously. I turned back to face Ralph who now seemed to be a little calmer within himself, "Hammy, you made a calamitous balls up this morning; how the hell did you make a fuck up like that?" It was killing me to find out how he knew and how so quickly. Ralph seemed to read my thoughts. "I checked the office e-mails this morning from my lap top at home as Jess often forgets." I could sense that he was starting to get pissed off again. "What was waiting for me in my in box when I checked the e-mails?"

I shook my head in bewilderment. "An e-mail?" I said trying to ease the tension.

Ralph didn't look impressed. "Yes Hammy, an e-mail from the landlord of a certain number six Baxter street wanting to know why one of our representatives had carried out a viewing at their property, and to top it all off had the audacity to puke up all over the floor." The way Ralph said it made me erupt into a big smile; it sounded so stupid and so unconceivable that this could actually happen that it just seemed comical. Ralph was clearly failing to see the funny side. Holding his super size mug tightly he looked me in the eye. "Hammy, we have been working constantly now for God knows how long. I think it's time you had a break." Ralph spoke very soft and quietly and had a great deal of care in his voice. I quickly started to wonder if I was being heavily punished.

"Are you suspending me Ralph?" I asked firmly. Ralph responded instantly.

"Good God no, I just think that you need a break. I leave in just under three weeks and then it's you in command, so you will get no time for a rest then." Ralph took a sip of his steaming hot drink and a thin white cream moustache was left on Ralph's upper lip, but I didn't tell him. Ralph leaned forward. "Why don't you take a few weeks off and go and lie on a beach somewhere hot and sun yourself? At least then you may stop making these silly fuck ups." Ralph explained that there was enough cover and that there would still be a week where the two of us would still work together. It sounded like a great idea to me. After all, I had thousands and thousands of pounds to spend, so it was agreed that I would take the following two weeks off as holiday. Splendid!

# Chapter 13

# Easyjet Flight EJ2401, Somewhere over France

*Tuesday 10<sup>th</sup> August, 2008*

It was a massive relief for me to be able to sit next to Serena and Ben, when we finally boarded the two hour delayed airbus at Gatwick. We had been waiting in line for what seemed to be an eternity, and when we were finally allowed onto the aircraft, we found that there was a no allocation seat policy; basically just grab a seat. Although I quite liked aeroplanes, I hated to fly; it was the takeoff that unsettled me the most. I had probably watched too many air crash investigation programmes on the television. It was comforting to know that if this bird did go down, my best friend and girlfriend would be sat next to me. The cabin was dimly lit with just a few passengers electing to have their reading lights on; the time was fast approaching two in the morning and many passengers were lucky enough to be asleep. With weary eyes I watched a young flight attendant who looked younger than me; I estimated she would have probably just turned twenty. She quietly walked down the isle towards the cockpit softly asking if anybody wanted tea or coffee; I had a feeling that this may have been her first flight as she appeared to be quite jumpy. A few sudden bumps of turbulence produced a faint moan from the cabin as the young stewardess held onto the back of a seat for stability. We were positioned about twelve rows back from the cockpit, so when the flight deck door opened I could clearly see the mass of blue, orange, green, yellow and red lights and the countless buttons and switches. I could see the pilot in his seat, so concluded that it was the co-pilot who had started to make a coffee in the stewardess's cubicle at the front of the cabin. Dressed in a short sleeved white shirt, black tie and trousers and sporting yellow stripes on his shoulders, he laughed with the young, attractive stewardess as he waited for the water to boil. That's the life, I thought, as I closed my eyes and tried to join Ben and Serena in the land of nod.

I had gathered up Serena and Ben and explained that I was taking two weeks holiday. If anybody could get the time off then I would pay for the three of us to go somewhere hot. With Ben being self-employed, it was easy for him to find the time, and with Serena being owed holiday, her boss allowed her to take a fortnight off with immediate effect. We found a last minute deal to Gran Canaria for ten days on the internet, so three days later we found ourselves at thirty thousand feet heading for the sun. There was still roughly three hours until we landed so I tried as hard as I could to fall asleep. Apart from the flying problem, I should have felt excited and pleased to be jetting off somewhere exotic, but something was really bugging me. My mind started to drift off to the previous few days.

Ben had surprised me two days ago on the Sunday, by sending me a text message in the morning: 'went 2 Honda last night, think I found what u were on about, recs we can get in.' We met up on the Sunday afternoon and discussed what this hill could be. Ben seemed adamant that entry was possible via one of the concrete tubes on the top. After a few pints at the South Marston Country Club that evening, we ambled through the village to the outskirts where the Honda site was located. Traffic at nine o clock on a Sunday evening was few and far between and the usual constant stream of large lorries turned into a gentle trickle. It hadn't taken us long to find the suspicious mound or hill. I was impressed to find out that Ben had left a pick axe and a small shovel in the surrounding long grass. We had each brought with us a small flashlight that would not have been visible from any great distance, but as a precaution we had turned them off when the occasional lorry had passed. With the torches in our mouths, we leant over one of the concrete cylinders; Ben used the pick axe to break up the earth and rocks that filled it whilst I used the shovel to clear out the debris. After about an hour of back breaking digging we had to stop for a rest. We guessed that we would need ropes if we did manage to break through and also first light would provide us with some much needed visibility. We figured that it would be a fairly safe bet that there would be very few people around at four thirty, or five, in the morning. We decided to leave and head back to the pub for one more pint before we went back to our homes to grab some rope and a few hours sleep; we would meet up early the next morning and try to penetrate the earth.

Suddenly my stomach felt like it was in my mouth when without any warning, the aircraft dropped altitude momentarily. The cabin started to shake from side to side as the aircraft experienced some heavy turbulence. The cabin filled with sleepy voices as people awoke from their deep sleep, but to my surprise the co-pilot was still merrily chatting and joking with the young stewardess, neither acknowledging the bumpy ride. Leaning across Ben, I could see through the window little pockets of lights in the far off distance as we passed foreign towns as they still slept. The turbulence had not woken Serena and Ben, so I decided to pull out the in-flight magazine from the back of the chair in front of me to pass the time. I could feel my eyes become heavy again as I glanced through the glossy pages, stopping briefly at the duty free section; before long I placed the magazine back in the seat in front of me paying great attention not to wake the sleeping passenger whose chair it belonged to. Much to my relief, I watched the co-pilot finish his coffee and then return to the cockpit closing the flight deck door behind him; I knew that modern aircraft could basically fly themselves, but it was reassuring to know there were two pilots behind the controls. A stewardess whom I had not noticed before briskly walked past towards the front of the aircraft and the air filled with the most wonderful smell for a few brief moments as her perfume hung in the cool air. My eyes followed her as she approached the much younger stewardess and started to help her pack away stainless steel trays in the small kitchen area; her perfume was starting to fade. I closed my eyes and tried to relax as much as I could. I started to drift away when something brought all my senses suddenly back to life. Opening one eye and inhaling deeply, I was aware of an overwhelming odour that reminded me of pond water or a wet dog smell. I glanced down to my right towards the source of the smell. In disbelief, I nudged Ben on the arm. "Mate, your wearing the same trainers from yesterday." I tried to speak as quietly as possible. Ben grunted, then faintly chuckled to himself, as he turned away to face the window.

"Get some sleep buddy." I tried to take his advice but found it difficult to concentrate on anything else apart from his trainers; it was amazing that they were still wearable, I thought, as I closed my tired eyes.

It had been Ben's trainers that were the first to enter the small, pitch black and half flooded air raid shelter early on the Monday morning, the murky waters probably saving Ben's ankles from a nasty impact with the floor. Under just enough light to see, it had taken us about half an hour to remove enough earth and stones to reveal the bottom of the cylinder. We presumed that these concrete tubes would have served as air vents during its use. Whoever had left the shelter last had nailed up thick timber planks from the inside to cover up the vents; it was a miracle that these decaying timbers had withstood such weight over the many years. It was not Ben's choice to enter the structure so rapidly and certainly not without any ropes strapped around him for safety. We had dug out half of the cylinder, exposing only half of the timber floor; it was planned that we would stand on the side with all of the earth and stones and smash through the wooden decking. It was a plan that would have worked well, if it hadn't been for the rotten wood snapping under Ben's weight moments before he intended stepping off onto relative safety. The few seconds that proceeded were unimaginable as I contemplated Ben's fate, so it was a great relief to hear his voice close by cursing himself. Impressively he had managed to fall and still keep the torch clenched in his jaw; I could easily see the reflection of the spot light on the glistening water as Ben looked down. The structure was not deep at all; it appeared that Ben could almost touch the ceiling with his arms held high. "It's up to my belt" garbled Ben from below as I carefully knelt down besides the opening. I gently dropped down the rope that was tied around the concrete tube. I had been tempted to go down myself but figured that it was unnecessary for the both of us to get soaking wet.

"Can you see anything in there apart from a big puddle of water?" I had asked. I would have hated to have gone through all of this only to find an empty concrete box. The noise of Ben wadding through the water was surprisingly loud, so I prayed that there was nobody in close proximity walking their dog or doing a security round. Eventually the water below settled and there was no sign of Bens flash light, so I arched my neck into the darkness. "Dude, you still down there?" A few moments of silence proceeded before I heard Bens voice.

"Nothing big down here buddy, just quite a few wooden boxes stacked up against the back wall."

Although it had seemed like a lifetime, in reality it had only taken me about twenty minutes to make the opening bigger by removing more dirt and smashing away at the ancient wood. Ben below had moved a heavy box to a position underneath the opening and had managed to tie the rope around it securely. With Ben pushing and me pulling, we managed eventually to clamber the box out into the fresh morning air. Realising that we would have to leave the shelter open so any Tom, Dick or Harry could come across our little discovery, we decided to lift four boxes out of the shelter; if there was anything valuable inside then it would have been foolish to have taken only the one box. I had picked Ben up early that morning in my car; if we had thought about it properly we should have taken Ben's new van. Taking an educated gamble that nobody would discover the boxes in long grass, we decided to hide them for half an hour as we headed back to pick up Ben's van that could easily accommodate the fairly large crates. Much to our relief, the boxes were sat safely where we had left them in the long grass. It didn't take us long to load the heavy boxes and Ben's tools into the van and get out of there without raising any evident suspicion.

Using a crow bar back at Ben's house, it was easy to open the boxes; the wood had absorbed a lot of moisture over the years and had put up no resistance at all. We had opened the crates together in Ben's garage and although he was not entirely sure what the contents were, there was no doubt in my mind what these crates contained.

"What are these supposed to go on?" Ben had asked as he lifted a solid looking windscreen from one of the boxes.

"You are holding a Spitfire's armoured windscreen," I replied sounding strangely intelligent; I had built many plastic Airfix Spitfire models in my youth and recognised these to be from the Mark One Spitfire. Although the glass of the windscreens had become slightly misted with the humidity of being underground, these interesting pieces of our aviation history looked to be in fine condition.

"All that time and effort for a few lousy windscreens." Ben understandably didn't see the significance of our most resent find, but it didn't take long to educate him. I sat down on the edge of his pool table that lived in his garage and cleared my throat.

"An old wives tale this well may be but you never know." Ben also sat down on the pool table and started to roll a cigarette. "Someone years ago told me that people actually spend considerable amounts of their time scouring allotments and vegetable plots for the glass bubble canopies of the Spitfire." Ben looked deeply confused. "Apparently, the old boys after the war decided that the bubble canopies served as excellent greenhouses protecting their vegetables or what have you during the colder months." Ben's screwed up face told me that he was still not grasping what I was telling him. Ben, liking his creature comforts, had an old computer wired up in his garage with access to the internet via a wireless connection. Jumping up, I proceeded to walk over to his work bench to fire up his computer. Within a few minutes I had logged into eBay and managed to navigate my way to the aviation section; typing in a simple search of 'Spitfire', I waited for the computer to present its findings. It only took a few seconds to present seventeen pages of items being sold relating to the Spitfire fighter aircraft. I glanced down the page consisting of a wide variety of instruments, buttons etc, until I stumbled across a bubble canopy with only five hours remaining till the auction ended. Feeling rather smug with myself, I stepped aside and invited Ben to have a look with his own eyes. Without any hesitation he positioned himself in front of his computer screen.

"You have to be fucking kidding me!" The item so far had attracted twenty nine bids that currently sat at two thousand and eighty three pounds.

"The good news is," I said full in the knowledge that I had his full attention, "that the canopies are far more common than these armoured windscreens, so I think these little puppies will sell like hot cakes."

It had just turned ten o'clock by the time we had taken photographs of a windscreen and placed them on eBay for a starting bid of twenty pounds, setting the auction over a ten day period with a delayed starting date so that we could get back from holiday before the auction was due to end. I had looked at several websites documenting the restoration or even rebuilds of the famous fighter aircraft, all of which seemed to struggle to replicate the complicated shape and design of the windscreen.

"Mate, if these are so valuable to plane anoraks, won't it cause a certain amount of suspicion if we go and put four up for auction at the same time?" I was pleased that Ben was so switched on. However, the second I had discovered what these boxes contained I had already formulated a response to that query. Firstly, as these were such an interesting piece of aviation history, I had decided that I wanted to keep one for myself; because I was pretty sure that Ben would not want one, we would have only three to sell. Being an estate agent, it would be very easy to come up with a viable explanation as to how we had come across them.

"All we need to say, if anyone does ask where we found them, is that I sold an old lady's bungalow a few months ago, and when she emptied her loft, these three items were hidden away up there." Ben slowly nodded his head in agreement.

"Anyone would believe that," he said as he lit his cigarette. It was quite common for people to offer me all sorts of bizarre stuff when we were selling their properties: washing machines, juke boxes and on one occasion even a clapped out old Mini Metro. It seemed that when people were downsizing, they were all too happy to offload any unwanted, heavy items onto anyone who wanted them.

It was the Captain who brought me back from my deep state of thought. "This is your Captain speaking. We will soon be bringing round the duty free trolley; on board this aircraft we take Euros as well as Pounds Stirling." I nudged Serena to see if she wanted anything but she was still fast asleep. "After the flight attendants have been through the cabin, we will shortly be commencing our decent into Gran Canaria. David Johns, your co-pilot will update you shortly prior to landing but on behalf of myself and Easyjet, I would like to thank you for travelling with us this morning and hope you have a great holiday." Both Ben and Serena started to stir as most of the passengers seemed to be coming round from their sleep; I nudged Ben who was stretching as he yawned.

"Mate, do you have a bad feeling about those windscreens?" Ben seemed to be half asleep and in no mood for a deep conversation.

"It will be fine, dude, stop worrying, you are on holiday now." I leant forward in my chair and placed my head in my hands. Ben was right; whatever was worrying me should be forgotten about till after the holiday.

# Chapter 14

# Puerto Rico, Gran Canaria

*August, 2008*

After a white knuckle taxi drive from the airport costing us an extortionate eighty Euros, we arrived at the Reception Hall of the Terrazamar Hotel. All the lights had been turned off apart from a solitary desk lamp that sat on the Reception desk.

"I hope they know we are coming," said Ben grumpily. I would have been slightly worried as well if it hadn't been for the faint smell of cigar smoke lingering in the air. Before I could ring the shiny silver bell on the desk, an older native gentleman came ambling from a back office.

"Olla." He spoke gently and I prayed he could speak English. It took about twenty minutes for our Spanish host to fumble through the English language and our booking in paperwork; there were a few moments when I feared there had been a cock up with the bookings. After we were finally given the all clear, the Receptionist gave us our room key and detailed instructions on how to find the room. "How big is this place?" I said as I struggled with my suitcase. The room number was four hundred and twenty seven.

Serena snatched the key off me. "We don't want any more mix ups with door numbers now do we?" A lift was positioned to the rear of the Reception Hall; we had been instructed to go down to Level Three. My first impressions of the Terrazamar Hotel as I stepped out of the lift were not good; it reminded me of something from the film 'The Shawshank Redemption'. Long and narrow corridors lined with doors resembled a prison; metal staircases were positioned at each end of the corridor giving off the only natural light. When we finally found our room, I was pleasantly surprised however with the generously sized two bedroom apartment, and the fantastic views from the balcony that more than made up for the dingy communal areas.

It didn't take us long to settle into a routine; the three of us didn't want a particularly active break so we opted to spend most days lazing beside the hotel's swimming pool drinking copious amounts of cocktails and San Miguel. The evening's entertainment was provided by Disco Dave and Loveable Laura, a couple aged in their mid twenties from the East End of London. With the exception of Sundays, the likeable duo provided bingo, quizzes, drinking games and general entertainment with a consistent amount of enthusiasm and energy. I had already fallen victim to Dave's games having to participate on three occasions, one of which was having to run around the entire bar and restaurant area pleading for ladies socks, glasses, underwear and cigarettes. It hadn't taken long before the English and Spanish holiday makers knew us all by our first names. Although I tried to remember theirs, I often came up with silly nicknames instead. Dave also put on a daily football match at three o'clock on the tennis courts; often it would turn out to be England v Spain. Needless to say we lost every game heavily. With ever increasing glows and aching legs, we became popular within the hotel complex, and, with Dave safe in the knowledge that myself and Ben would be fair game to participate in his childish, but fun, games we would be a constant fixture making fools of ourselves nightly on stage. During every evening, as we returned to the hotel bar from having dinner out, I would notice a man sitting at a table alone. On the very first night I had mentioned it suggesting that it was strange to see a middle aged man on holiday alone, but both Serena and Ben thought nothing odd about it at all. He looked to have Western features and I had presumed that he was English. His hair was starting to grey at the sides and his eyes had a distant look to them; I had felt sorry for him from day one.

With disappointment, we realised that Disco Dave and Lovable Laura would not be entertaining us on the Sunday evening as we returned from our meal; we had forgotten that it was their only day off. Fearing a distinct lack of business during Sunday evenings, the hotel had cleverly put on a happy hour from ten till eleven where they offered a buy one get one free deal. Needless to say, on Sunday, our table during that hour was laden with shots, lagers and cocktails. We hadn't been sitting at our table for long, before the lonely man came in and headed towards the bar to take advantage of the free drink offer. The table beside us was vacant and had an ashtray, so, since I had noticed that he smoked roll-up cigarettes, I hoped that he would sit next to us. "Hide your lighters." I quietly said to Ben and Serena who obeyed in bewilderment. Ben had just pocketed his lighter as the man pulled out a chair on the neighbouring table.

"Babe, I'm sure he doesn't want to sit with us," said Serena as I lifted myself from the table. I had enough alcohol in me to discard any nervousness or shyness that may have been experienced when approaching a complete stranger. My target had clocked me the second I approached him. I bent down next to him and asked politely if it would be possible to borrow his lighter for a moment. Without a moment's hesitation the gentleman handed me his engraved Zippo lighter.

"You help yourself," he said in a thick American Southern State accent. After lighting my Marlborough Light, I took a few seconds to read the words engraved into his lighter. 'Maj. Ken Black, USAF, Takhli, Thailand, Home of the 355th Tactical Fighter Wing'. I could see a few tables look back at me as I crouched down besides the lonesome man.

"You got an interest in Zippo lighters?" he said inquisitively as I placed the lighter back on the table. Major Ken Black instantly accepted my offer for him to join us at our table.

"It's Hammy isn't it?" He said as he placed his belongings down on our table. It didn't surprise me that he knew my name. Both Serena and Ben introduced themselves warmly and it was evident that our guest was happy to have some company. "If it wasn't for a mountain of drinks waiting to be drunk, I would offer you guys a drink." As he introduced himself, I noticed a scar down the left hand side of his face. His eyes looked to be empty, as if there was very little life behind them. "Well you guys seem to have made yourselves at home." He spoke softly and warmly. I offered Ken a cigarette from my packet but he opted to roll one himself.

Serena took a big gulp of her cocktail and cleared her throat. "That looks like a nasty scar you have there," she said. Both Ben and I looked at each other in disbelief of her bluntness. Before I could quickly muster up an apology, Ken quickly stepped in.

"It's a corker but, hay, I wouldn't be without it." He smiled as he spoke. "I get all the pretty ladies coming up me asking what happened." After the polite laugher settled, a silence descended upon the table; *surely someone is going to ask how he got the scar?* I thought, as I selected a drink to down next.

"How did you get the scar if you don't mind me asking?" If Ben hadn't have asked then I would have, but it was a question whose answer I was not prepared for.

Ken leant back in his chair and took a deep breath. "Well to cut a long story short, I got shot down in Vietnam, twice, well within hours of each other actually." All three of us leant forward simultaneously in anticipation.

"Best not tell Hammy, he gets terrified in an airbus." Ben wasn't joking but I was fascinated to learn more.

"Did you get captured?" I had watched many Vietnam War films and knew that staying in the Saigon Hilton was not the most pleasant of experiences.

"Praise the lord I was spared the North Vietnamese hospitality, but only by the skin of my teeth." Ken downed half of his pint in one. "I was flying an F-105 Thunderchief trying to bomb the Ha Gia railroad when a SAM took my left wing off."

Serena jabbed me in the arm. "And you think flying in airliners is dangerous!"

Ken chuckled to himself and continued. "The entire left hand side of the plane was blown away including all the glass surrounding me. To this day, it still amazes me how the ejector seat was still working after a mid-air impact like that."

I was surprised that Serena was interested, but it was she who continued the questioning. "How did you survive?"

Ken was clearly enjoying being able to reminisce. "Well, I found myself on the jungle floor under my parachute, pouring with blood and with an almighty headache, so needless to say I felt like shitting my pants. Thankfully the ejector seat survival pack had a distress beacon activated once the pilot ejects, allowing any helicopter rescue crews in the area to come and get you out of a whole load of bother." I could see a medley of tattoos that decorated his right upper arm; it seemed slightly strange to see a man of his age carrying so much body artwork, the most prominent being a big '100' with a small American flag underneath. Ken must have seen me admire his artwork, because, without saying a word, he lifted up the sleeve of his shirt up to his shoulder: "the '100' symbolises the number of missions I had to fly before being allowed to return from my tour of duty." It was truly a privilege to be able to talk with somebody who had lived their life to the full, but I was aware that Serena may have felt alienated from aeroplane talk. I was just about to change the subject when I caught sight of something that made me so incredibly proud.

"My God, I don't believe it!" I couldn't take my eyes off two young blonde ladies who entered the bar area and grabbed themselves a vacant table in the restaurant. I was just about to elaborate when I felt a pain burn across the back of my head; the instant Serena had clocked me looking at the attractive young ladies she had decided to tell me who was the boss.

"They are stunning, makes me wish I was thirty years younger." Ken was correct; they were stunning but that was not what had attracted my attention to them. I couldn't believe that both Ben and Serena had not noticed.

"Guys, look at the blonde with her hair up in a bun." I could sense Serena starting to get really annoyed. "Look at her T-shirt!" I gasped, trying to stop my girlfriend from exploding but, within seconds, she was grinning from ear to ear; Ben took a few more moments for the penny to drop. Although one of my least favourite designs, it was amazing to see one of our very own T-shirts being worn by somebody I didn't know, and, to see it in another country really put the icing on the cake. We had sold hundreds of garments but this was the first time I had seen one on somebody who was not either a friend or family.

"I think they deserve a drink each for that," said Ben as he jumped up to leave our table to speak to the young ladies.

Understandably Ken looked confused. "You're telling me that the T-shirt she is wearing was designed by you guys?" With content he listened to the long-winded story of how Boulette was born from my younger years; we shared a toast to 'international fame' and downed the remainders of our pints.

I was just about to head off to the toilets when Serena spoke. "What happened the second time you got shot down?" Ken looked surprised, but thoroughly delighted that Serena had listened to his story; he linked his hands together and rested his elbows on the plastic table. "I was lucky enough to have an American Huey Helicopter in the area that was escorted by two F-4 fighters. I didn't know it at the time but an F-4 had gone down two hours earlier trying to hit the same target. As lady luck had it, I had gone down right in the middle of their search zone, so they soon managed to find a clearing close by to set her down and get me onboard." My bladder was starting to expand but I didn't want to miss any of the story. I had never heard first hand what it was like to fight in the Vietnam War and I was finding it fascinating. "As soon as I got onboard, I could tell that the chopper pilots were exhausted. They had been circling the danger zone for nearly two hours taking heavy amounts of enemy fire, so it was understandable that they just wanted to get the hell out of there once I was safely onboard." I felt the urge to ask about the wellbeing of the downed F-4 pilot but realised that it probably would have been a story without a happy ending. I could sense a touch of sadness come over Ken. "The chopper had taken some serious damage but yet the pilots managed to wrestle it to within twenty miles of their base. If it hadn't been for a single pot shot from a farmer in his field we would have made it all the way back." Serena looked engrossed; she hadn't acknowledged the twenty or so pale-faced new arrivals that had just turned up in reception. Ken started to roll another cigarette. "Don't really remember much after that. I remember the whole thing filling with smoke as it spiralled its way heavily to the ground. According to the rescue crew, it had been a miracle I had survived. However, the three crew members were not so fortunate." It was difficult to know what to say next. All I could do was shake my head in amazement and sympathy for the man, and men who went through these horrendous ordeals.

Ben jovially returned to our table with a big grin across his face. "They are Swedish." he announced as he pulled up his chair. "She usually sleeps in that, mate; she bought it from our website ages ago." Ben selected a drink and took several gulps in quick procession. "They are very impressed we own the company, buddy." Ben wiped his mouth as he spoke. "Apparently, a lot of their friends have them too." I did remember sending quite a few to Sweden, but I never in my wildest dreams imagined that I would see any of them again; it was a lovely feeling and added weight to the fact that we had sold large amounts of shirts.

"You guys are going to be very wealthy I think!" Ken was correct; we were going to be very wealthy indeed. I had, of course, spoken to Serena about Boulette possibly being bought out by a bigger company but I had not mentioned the bottles of port or the amount of money Boulette on paper would sell for. I neglected to tell her about the port, not because I wanted to keep secrets from her, but in this way our story of Boulette being sold would remain as watertight as possible. "You guys send them away to be printed?" the American veteran seemed to be impressed.

"They get printed just round the corner from us in Swindon." Ben spoke with pride as Ken registered the name of our home town.

"Swindon, where have I heard that before?" Ken scratched his thinning hair. "Funny that because I've never been to England before." It was probably because somebody had told him not to visit it if he ever did venture onto our shores!

Groups of tired looking new arrivals started to dribble into the bar area, their fatigued looking faces and bodies suggesting that they had suffered severe delays as well. Our stocks of drink were starting to dwindle, so I thought it would be best to get to the bar before all the newbies did and I still needed to use the toilet.

I just slipped my trainers back on to get up when Ken shouted out excitedly: "I know Swindon!" I was now really bursting for the toilet but felt obliged to listen. "I met a chap from Swindon a few years ago in Paris at a war plane exhibition, crazy about old RAF planes if I seem to remember correctly." I hoped that Ben would not suddenly raise the subject of our discovery of Spitfire windscreens, or the bottles of port; I wanted to keep our aviation items as secret as possible. "I remember him so well because he came across like a possessed man; kept ranting on when he had drunk too much about hidden treasures left over from the war time."

Ben responded well. "Sounds like a bloody nutter; what was his name? Sounds like your Dad, Hammy." The table once again descended into light hearted laughter.

"Can't for the life of me remember his name. I keep diaries of everything so will have his name scribbled down somewhere."

At this stage my bladder was beginning to hurt. I really didn't care what this man's name was; all that mattered was visiting the little boy's room as fast as possible.

The rest of the holiday was thoroughly enjoyable with constant good weather and pleasant company. We never saw much of Ken because, during the days, as he liked to take himself off sightseeing, but we tended to spend most evenings together drinking into the early hours sharing stories with each other. We had learned that his wife had died two years ago after losing her battle with cancer; they had always holidayed in the Canaries so Ken had decided to continue the tradition. I was pleased to hear that he would get some company after we had left. An old Air Force friend had arranged to meet Ken at the hotel and they would stay together for a week before heading off their separate ways. We had exchanged telephone numbers earlier on in the holiday and we had tried to persuade Ken to come and visit England one day. Even with his assurances that he would make the trip, I seriously doubted that I would ever see Ken again. Although Ken's tales of bravery in the Vietnamese skies went some way to easing my fear of flying, it was with great sadness that on one of the last days of our holiday, we started to receive news of my worst nightmare. One evening, news started to trickle in about a Spanish airliner that had crashed on takeoff from Madrid airport. Packed with excited Spanish holiday makers destined for Gran Canaria, and in some cases the Terrazamar Hotel, the Spanair flight had suffered massive casualties earlier that day. Pockets of Spanish residents at the hotel had started to weep uncontrollably. News coming through had been limited but everybody knew that it had been an awful disaster. It had been a poignant end to an otherwise faultless holiday; although feeling saddened by the events that had unravelled on our last day, I left feeling privileged and honoured to have known and befriended Ken.

# Chapter 15

# Swindon

*Saturday 21ˢᵗ August, 2008*

Overall it had been good to return from holiday; I always missed my bed when staying away from home and I was much more comfortable in our cooler English climate. My parents had kindly volunteered to pick us up from Gatwick airport, and luckily the flight coming back had not been delayed, resulting in my parents not having to wait around for long periods of time. The terminal was cold in the early evening as we lugged our bags through arrivals to meet my parents; Mum, being so typically Mum, had bought with her three jumpers just in case we had not prepared for the cooler weather. Needless to say, I was freezing in my T-shirt and jeans and the jumper was most welcome.

Both Serena and Ben slept in the car on the way back to Swindon, but I had stayed awake to talk to my parents although I was extremely tired. After I had been updated on how the cats had been and how Clive next door had fallen off his ladder trying to fix his aerial, Mum had informed me that we had been burgled. "Burgled?" I had gasped bringing both Serena and Ben back to semi-conscienceless. After Mum had managed to calm me down, she explained that it had been very strange indeed. The intruders had entered the house by breaking the back door window in the bottom right hand corner, closest to the lock with the key inside. They had been foolish enough to leave the key there but they simply never expected that they would fall victim of a burglary; the Police had called it 'an opportunist crime'. What the Police or my parents could not work out was why nothing appeared to have been taken; after all, if they had taken the opportunity to break in, it seemed unbelievable that they would not take anything. The Police had said that it was not entirely unheard of. Quite often, they had explained, burglars entered a property but had then got disturbed or spooked by somebody or something. It was quite possible, they had said, that our burglar or burglars had been scared off by somebody coming to the door or even by one of the cats making an unexpected sound. Probably the strangest thing about the burglary so far was that the intruders appeared to have fed the cats. Mum had gone to work completely forgetting to feed the poor felines, and on her return, the cats had both their bowls half full of food. The Police had apparently shrugged it off as not important; they had suggested that perhaps the cats were making such a noise that they fed them to shut them up; I figured that they were spot on. They had advised that on my return I was to go through all of my belongings with a tooth pick and see if anything of mine had been taken; Mum had scanned over the obvious things and couldn't see anything absent. The only belongings of mine that would have been worth taking was the casement of port, I thought to myself; however I had hidden it away in a place so safe that not even the combined efforts of MI5 and MI6 could find it.

We dropped Serena off at her house first as Ben lived only a few houses away from me. I could tell that the day's travel had taken its toll on her as she kissed me goodnight on the cheek. "That was a lovely holiday, babes; thank you." With Ben wide awake, we decided that he would come back to mine to have a few bottles of beer and a joint as a nightcap and I wanted to check eBay on how our windscreens were doing and thought it only fair that Ben was there as well. It took only ten minutes or so to get back to my house and unload our bags from the back of the car; the house was in pitch blackness. A small part of me was glad that Ben was still with us, just in case our uninvited visitors had decided to come back once again. My two cats, Biggles and Toby, hardly bothered to look up as I clambered my way through the front door with bags under each arm. With the cats being their lazy, contented selves, I was satisfied that there were no intruders in the house. After turning on most of the downstairs lights, I grabbed two bottles of beer from the fridge, hugged my Mum and Dad in thanks for the lift and headed upstairs with Ben. My room appeared to be exactly how I left it, a complete and utter mess. My television, play station, stereo system and my laptop were all where they should be, on the floor. "They could have at least folded up my clothes!" I joked as I grabbed my laptop and plonked myself down on the end of my bed. Ben had made himself at home in my chair in the corner of the room; he had discovered my tin where I kept my weed and had proceeded to make a joint with its contents. I opened my bottle and took a big gulp as I waited for eBay to load up on my screen; I got up and opened the window a little and then returned to my computer.

"Holy shit, I've never seen anything like this before!" Ben jumped up and raced over to the bed spraying tobacco, weed and papers all over my floor. I swivelled the computer around so he could see the screen. Staring back at us was '304' in our inbox indicating that we had over three hundred unopened messages. The number of bids and people watching the items was just as staggering. With only nineteen hours remaining we had accumulated over ninety bids with the winning bid so far up to two thousand and twenty two pounds; we had put the three up at the same time and all three were going to sell at some astronomical price each. I realised that it would take ages to read all of the messages in the inbox but I wanted to respond to as many as possible, so I started to read a couple from the top of the list. The first couple of emails asked the same questions: 'Are there any serial marks or numbers on the frames or glass anywhere?' and 'Do you have a buy it now price?' This was going to be very boring indeed, I conceded. Ben had made his joint, lit it, taken several drags before he passed it over to me. Being careful not to drop ash all over my keyboard, I continued scanning through the emails. "This bloke has emailed me loads of times by the looks of it." I mumbled as I opened his first one. 'Please advise origins. Will want to view so please advise your location.' It was from 'Spitfirecrazy'. I wondered if all war bird enthusiasts were just as blunt and rude. Several of his following emails carried on along the same lines until I got to his seventh email. 'Your obvious lack of response clearly implies foul play. You have no such rights as to sell belongings of the Ministry of Defence; please advise your status.' Feeling slightly light-headed from my beer and weed intake, I tried my best to reply as legibly and politely as I could. I explained that I had been given them by an old lady who was grateful to get rid of them and that if he wanted to come and have a look at them then he was most welcome; I never got a response back. Strangely enough, a large percentage of the emails seemed to be questioning if I would remove the small circular mirror that was fixed to the top of the windscreen and sell it separately. I figured they must have been very hard to obtain.

After half an hour of scanning through all of the emails, it was pleasing to see that nine of them were Boulette-related. I had forgotten that I had placed several designs up for auction a couple of days before the windscreens. Out of the four T-shirts I had stuck on eBay, three had sold for over fifteen pounds each; the auction had finished four days ago and the items were well overdue to be dispatched. I quickly responded to the purchasers explaining that I had been away on holiday and that the garments would be sent First Class on Monday morning. After replying to their emails, I logged into my 'PayPal' account to see if their funds had cleared. "What the hell is my password?" I whispered to myself as the website asked me for my login details. I was well known for having a poor memory and passwords tended to be my Achilles heel, so I tried to keep most of them the same so I had less to remember but I still struggled. Because I had a lot of passwords to remember at work, I always kept a little black book with them all written down, aware that potentially this was quite a silly thing to do but I had encoded them all so to the untrained eye it just looked like rows of sentences that didn't make a lot of sense. It read something like 'Hammy don't forget to bid on eBay for that BMW motor car, ha pay your pal with little Biggles and email him your mother's maiden name'. It would always help me to remember that my eBay password was BMW motor, my PayPal password was Biggles and my email password was Clement; every time I had to use a new password I would just add it to the garble in my little black book but where was it?

Starting to panic slightly, I rose to my feet and started to look through all my trouser and jacket pockets, and, with no luck there I started to rifle around under my bed amongst the shoes and dirty clothes. Sensing more panic setting in, I started to go through my cupboard, my drawers, my work bag, the mess around Ben's little area and even the bin; although my scribblings didn't make much sense, they did have all my bank passwords and even my debit card's pin number; I had to find the notebook. I raced down the stairs to see if my parents were still awake. Fortunately, they had just finished their hot chocolate and were just about to turn in for the night. "I can't find my black book," I gasped almost out of breath as I stood on Toby's tail; he screeched and made a run for the hallway.

"Slow down and start again," said my Mum with bewilderment across her face. I took a deep breath and explained my little problem. Thinking clearly, she suggested that it may be at work if it definitely was not at home. I shook my head doubting that I would ever leave it in the office but it was a possibility that I had forgotten it just this once.

"What if the burglar was after my book and nothing else?" I asked without thinking before I spoke.

Dad proceeded to shake his head vigorously. "Impossible, they wouldn't have gone to all that trouble just for a little book full of gobbledegook. They would have taken your Mum's jewellery, our TV or keys to the Jag." It was hard not to believe my Dad, because it did make sense that there would have been other belongings missing if the burglary had gone to plan; perhaps they did get frightened off by something. I wouldn't be one hundred percent convinced until I had been through my desk at work in the morning. The following day being a Sunday, the office would be closed and it would give me more freedom to search everything if so required. After saying my goodnights to Mum and Dad, and apology strokes to Toby, I headed back upstairs to see if Ben had passed out yet.

Looking absolutely exhausted (and stoned), Ben had waited for my return with his bags gathered and coat already on. "Good job you didn't keep the bottles here." Ben's eyebrows were raised and he smiled from just one side of his mouth. I grabbed my bottle to make a toast.

"I'll drink to that, old fruit." The true location was quite safe. It had been by pure coincidence that my Nan had called me the evening of our meeting with Julian in Wanborough. She had requested the presence of her strapping young Grandson to do her a favour. My Nan lived only about twenty miles away on the outskirts of a small market town and liked to remind us regularly that it was no trouble getting to her by car. I felt guilty enough for not seeing her as much as I should and didn't have any hesitation in agreeing to help her. It wasn't in fact my Nan that needed the favour; it was her best friend Olive who lived on the street next to my Nan's and she needed some bulky boxes lifting up into her loft. Olive's husband had died last winter and her nearest family lived miles away in Scotland somewhere, so my Nan hadn't thought twice about volunteering my services; I didn't mind in the slightest. I had asked Olive very courteously if she would mind if I put a box of mine up in her loft for a short while as I just didn't have the room at home or in my car; she had agreed unreservedly saying that it would be nice to have some company when I came back and picked it up.

With Ben ready for his bed, he left my house around midnight; I too was struggling to keep my eyes open and the thought of a night's sleep in my own bed was becoming irresistible. As I wearily took my clothes off, I scanned every inch of my room praying to catch sight of my estranged notebook; I didn't hold much hope in finding it but I had to feel like I was doing everything I could to locate it. I could hear my Mum and Dad climb the stairs and walk down the landing towards their bedroom; I took my cricket bat from out of my cupboard and placed it on the floor next to my bed. "You can kiss that Mr. Burglar," I said out aloud as I turned on my bedside lamp and turned out the main light. I was just about to jump into bed when a hard object hit my window with some force, the impact loud enough surely to catch my Mum and Dad's attention.

"Mate you still awake?" Still trying to slow my heart rate down, I walked over to the window; Ben had managed to put a nice big crack in the glass.

"You tit, you just cracked my window." I could just make out Ben's silhouette and the bright yellow jumper my Mum had brought him just about visible as he stood shivering on my front lawn.

"I'll pay for your whole house to have new windows if you like Matey, but for now I just need my phone that I left on the chair." I glanced down at the chair, where I could see Ben's phone, house keys, lighter and tobacco sat together where Ben had left them. I found an old cigarette carton on my floor, filled it with Ben's belongings and dropped it out of the window. "Cheers, Matey, see you tomorrow." I closed my window and headed over to bed. It was now becoming a battle to keep my eyes open, so I pulled back my duvet and froze like a statue.

Nestling on my pillow, just underneath my duvet sat some sort of weed. I had seen them a billion times before on lawns, roadsides and even on waste grounds; I knew for certain that I had not put it there. Its green stalk and long leaves and bright yellow flowers looked to have been carefully placed in position; if it wasn't my Mum making some loving gesture, then this was getting a bit weird. Before waking my parents I decided to give Ben a quick call; he never turned off his phone and I knew that he would answer. After several rings, a very sleepy sounding Ben answered the phone. "Sorry to wake you, old fruit, just a quick one. This is going to sound very odd but I don't suppose you left a little yellow flower on my pillow?" I waited for a response but none came. "Hello, anyone there?" The line went dead. It was probably safe to assume that it wasn't my best friend who had left it there. I turned the main light on in my room and headed through the landing to my Mum and Dad's bedroom. Praying that I was not disturbing anything, I knocked firmly on their door, fearing the worst, but my Dad shouted grumpily:

"It's OK. We are awake." I sheepishly poked my head through the door.

"I'll be in my bedroom when you are ready; there's something I want you guys to see," and with that I closed the door behind me.

It was only a matter of seconds before my parents scurried into my bedroom wrapped in their dressing gowns, a look of horror on their faces suggesting that they were probably expecting something far worse than what was actually waiting for them. With my finger I pointed to my pillow, both my parents instantly walked up to my bedside to get a closer look at the out-of-place weed.

"Well I can tell you for certain Edward that it wasn't there when I changed your bed a week ago, and I certainly didn't put it there." My Mum did genuinely look to be confused and there was no way in the world that it would have been my Dad who had put it there.

"Did you change my bed before or after our break in?" I asked deep in thought.

My Mum scratched her head momentarily. "I changed your bed on the Saturday and we had our unexpected visitor on the

Tuesday." It was obvious that our intruder had left it specifically for my attention. My Mum suggested that we should report it to the Police in the morning; maybe they could lift some fingerprints off it or perhaps there had been other burglaries in the area with similarities; either way we all thought that the Police should know about it. Using my tweezers I carefully picked up the weed and placed it on my bedside table.

"What is it anyway?" I asked knowing that my parents would have the answer.

"It's a dandelion Edward" answered my mother as she turned out the light and closed my bedroom door on her way out.

## Chapter 16

# Swindon

*Monday 23rd August, 2008*

I hadn't found my black book the previous day at the office; I hoped as I walked through the office doors that somebody might be able to shed some light on its whereabouts. Being five minutes late, I was surprised to see that only Jess so far had turned up to work. "Don't you look brown, Mr. Hammy," she had commented as I placed my bag down on my desk. I never really liked leaving the office for long periods of time, as I was always afraid that I would return to a mountain of complaints and problems to sort out.

"Has something so bad happened that everybody has left the company?" I asked with some sincerity. Jess just chuckled to herself and carried on opening the post. I looked behind me to Ralph's desk; his chair didn't have a jacket over it, his computer wasn't on and there was no tea mug hiding away behind his computer screen. Hammy getting to work before Ralph was unheard of. "Ralph overslept or something?" I muttered as I bent down to turn on his computer. Jess quickly stopped me.

"That won't be necessary Hammy; have you not heard?" *Here we go again,* I thought to myself; I was supposed to be second in command yet I always seemed to be the last to hear things.

"Have I not heard what?" I started to remember why I hated returning to work after long spells away. Jess sat down on the edge of her desk, looking uncomfortable to be the one to tell me the news.

"Ralph isn't coming back, Hammy." I sat down on the edge of Ralph's desk. I had come to terms with the fact that Ralph was leaving, but was deeply saddened that it appeared I wouldn't get the chance to say goodbye. Jess walked over to Ralph's desk and put an arm around me. "It's OK, Hun; he said on Friday when he left that he would soon be in touch to arrange his leaving party." I doubted that very much. In the years that I had worked with Ralph, he only attended a handful of leaving do's, and there would have been hundreds. His trait would be to ring up about half an hour before we were all due to meet and 'play his joker card,' resulting in his absence from the evenings entertainment. Jess sensing my sadness, hugged me tighter and pointed with her free hand to my desk. "I found them on the mat this morning; there was one for everybody."

I had failed to see the little blue envelope that Jess had placed on my phone; I looked at everybody else's phones and they all had the same little blue envelope. With a little smile, I leant forward and picked up the envelope; without any delay I tore it open. Inside was a little card with a picture of a quill and bottle of ink. In silver writing were the words 'A note to say thank you.' Feeling a sense of sadness wash over me, I opened the card, and a piece of paper dropped out and fell to the floor.

"Oh, I didn't have a separate piece of paper in my card," moaned Jess as she bent down to pick it up. Tom, our trainee negotiator strode into the office, whistling merrily and loudly. Sporting a new hair cut and what looked to be a new suit; he then sat down at his desk and picked up the blue envelope that sat next to his phone. Jess handed me the folded piece of paper as the telephones started to ring. Thankfully Tom was quick to answer it and deal with the inquiry; we had trained him well. Allowing myself no more distractions, I started to read the card first.

Hammy,

Many Thanks for your years of hard work, loyalty & dedication that you gave to the company and myself. You always gave of your very best & this was much appreciated. Been a pleasure to have known & worked with you, all the very best for the future,

Love and best wishes<br>Ralph.

I read the words again. All those years of friendship and hard work were summed up in just a few words. I wasn't expecting any great piece of literature but I thought I would have been worth just a few more lines at least. "What's on that separate sheet of paper?" asked Jess inquisitively. I had almost forgotten about the note in my hand. Taking a deep breath I unfolded it and started to read it aloud.

*"Twas in 1976 it all began,*
*Wage, £25 a week, felt like a man*
*Camden flat and a moped as well*
*Subsidised rent, things were swell*
*Worked eve's in a pub to bring in extra*
*Cos commission wasn't on the boss's agenda*

*Then Knight Allen opened, new kids in town*
*Applied once but got turned down*
*Second time around they chose me*
*Used a tactic, 2 weeks trial for free*

*So that was the start of a long career.*
*A total of 29, in October this year.*

*So now its goodbye to business reviews,*
*Hard targets and cancellation blues,*
*Mystery shopper, compliance and weekly reports.*
*Will soon be forgotten, out of my thoughts*
*But certain memories will remain forever,*
*That's you, and how we've worked well together.*
*It's the colleagues I'll miss, so a sincere thank you,*
*In helping my early retirement dream come true*

*So I wish you every happiness and success in the future*
*Good time markets always return, just like 'adieu'. "*

Some of my colleagues had walked in as I read. They had not said a word, but just came in and listened quietly until I had finished. "What was all that about?" asked Jess as she took the note from my hands. "So a sincere thank you in helping my early retirement dream come true." Jess shook her head. "God knows what that means." I knew that Ralph had a tendency sometimes to speak in riddles, but I was touched that he had taken the time to write out his life story for me, even though I didn't truly understand why he was leaving or what half of his poem meant. Tom had finished his phone call and had trained his ears on our conversation.

"Maybe you made his retirement dream come true by taking onto the market all of those houses and selling most of them." Tom spoke confidently for somebody in his late teens. "I'm sure Ralph would have bagged a whole load of commission and bonuses from all the business you have brought in over the last few years." Maybe our little trainee had hit the nail on the head.

As I was sunning myself on the Friday afternoon, Ralph had told Jess that he had always intended on taking early retirement. He had told me a few weeks ago that he was going to leave and that he was not going to another estate agent; what I couldn't understand was why he had decided to leave a week or so early. Part of the reason why I agreed to go away on holiday was because I was safe in the knowledge that I would have at least a week left working with Ralph; it didn't make any sense why he couldn't have at least stayed for a day after I returned. I tried to ring Ralph on his mobile; it was no surprise that it just went through to the answer machine, for he seemed to have a phobia with technology and very rarely had his mobile phone turned on. I didn't have his home phone number or his home address, so I was at the mercy of Ralph getting in touch with us - something I wasn't sure would happen. The moment I had put the phone down, it had started to ring; unfortunately it was my area manager, not Ralph. I flopped back on my chair and listened to the dull tones of George Stephens, as he suggested that I should go to Head Office in Bristol for an afternoon session of targets, projected forecasts, profit and loss and a whole load of other intense and insanely boring subject matter. As if a trip to Bristol wasn't bad enough, I closed my eyes in disbelief when he continued to explain that as a way of streamlining the business, the company was thinking about making redundancies. What my dickhead of an area manager was saying in a roundabout way was that they wanted our office to take the hit for one redundancy and as office manager it was me who would have to decide who would walk the plank. After explaining that although I didn't want to shirk my new responsibilities, the office currently had only three people in at work, so Stephens was left with no choice but to postpone our number-crunching session for another day. The moment I had put the phone down I realised that I didn't want this anymore. Even if the deal with the port did not go down, I still had about forty five grand to last me till I found my feet again. I looked across at Tom; although only nineteen, he had a young baby of six months and although he was excellent at his job, he should be the one to go as he had only been with us a few months. However, I decided that I would be the blood the company so clearly desired; I would have been leaving soon anyway so now seemed to be the right time. I would leave it a week to give the sale of the casement time to go through, then I would hand in my notice and save somebody's career in doing so.

With still only Jess and Tom in the office, I decided to pull my mobile phone out of my pocket and scroll down to Julian's mobile number; once again I was greeted with an international ring tone. Julian was his jovial and charismatic self as we exchanged pleasantries down the phone, as always he was delighted to hear from me. "Julian, I think it's time that Boulette was sold." I didn't mind my colleagues overhearing as they would soon find out. Julian sounded ecstatic down the line.

"That's fabulous news. I suggest we meet up at a quiet country pub again close to where you gents live. During your holiday I made another purchase that I can't wait to tell you about." It was like talking to an old friend; it truly felt that we had known each other for years and I wanted to talk to him about my worries regarding the Spitfire windscreens and our selling them.   I hoped he wouldn't see it as an issue. The fact that Julian was taking a few days rest in Monaco didn't deter him from wanting to meet us as soon as possible. He told me that he would need a couple of days to get the funds in place and then he would be ready to return to England to make the exchange. After reassuring him that the casement was in very safe hands, we arranged to meet at a little pub on the outskirts of South Marston on Friday afternoon; I decided it would be then that I would hand in my notice if all things went to plan. Julian had asked if he could take the liberty of arranging for his solicitor to draw up some contractual paperwork, all Boulette documents signing over the company to the new owner. Julian had volunteered the services of one of his close solicitor friends to act on our behalf - a conflict of interest perhaps, but Julian reassured me that all they would do was ring me once the monies had been received into their bank account. They then would forward the money into our designated bank account. Once a telephone call had been made to the bank clarifying whether the money had been received, we would sign the contract concluding the transaction; Julian would then be free to receive his casement.

Jess sat at her desk, mouth wide open staring at me. "You're selling your little T-shirt Company?" I think Jess could already see the significance. Tom jumped up from his desk and perched himself on the end of my desk.

"No fucking way, you're selling your company? Who to? Quicksilver? Billabong?" It felt great to be talking about Boulette again as a success.

"I'm afraid, guys, that I won't be taking up my position as Branch Manager." Both Tom and Jess appeared to know what was coming. "I was going to tell you next week but I guess now is as good a time than any." I put the phones on hold and continued with my little speech: "As I'm sure you have worked out by now, we have been approached by a company to buy us out, but I can't say who it is yet." I feared that I would feel sorrow and regret in telling them but I felt strangely uplifted. "As a result, it means that I won't have to work again for the rest of my life." Both Jess and Tom listened dumbstruck. "I can't go into any more detail until the deal is struck, so if you could please make sure you keep this to yourselves until I hand in my notice I would greatly appreciate it." Jess folded up her arms.

"Well, it will be you buying us the leaving presents then." She winked at me then gave me the biggest of hugs. "We're going to miss you, Hammy, you lucky bastard. Remember us when you're chilling off by the pool in your ten bed mansion."

With all the excitement, I had completely forgotten about my missing little black book; after asking my colleagues if they could recall seeing it I was still no closer to finding its whereabouts. Feeling not particularly motivated to do any work, I started the tedious process of changing my passwords. I would have to do my work passwords, eBay, PayPal; everything that required a password, I would have to change.

"Hammy don't forget to bid on eBay on that BMW motor car." Jess's voice came from the store cupboard. "Were you smoking naughty substances when you wrote this Hammy?" I didn't need to ask her what she was on about. Jess stepped out of the cupboard carrying a box of envelopes in one hand, and my little black book in the other. I approached her dubiously.

Looking her straight in the eye and asked: "Do you know anything about dandelions, Jessica?" She screwed up her face then burst out laughing. "You have to save some of that wacky backy for me, Hammy." Jess had discovered my notebook mingling between the blank paper and the A4 envelopes; although I was over the moon to have it back in my safe possession, it troubled me that I had no memories of ever going in the cupboard. It was always the Admin Staff who would look after the paper and envelope stocks, so there was no reason whatsoever for me to have left my book in the cupboard. I closely examined every page to see if any pages had been torn out; the book looked to be in the same condition as I last saw it. "Must have been the cleaners," offered Jess. "Things of mine always go for walks and end up in the most strangest of places." Jess *was probably right*, I thought, as I carefully put my book in my inner suit pocket. I too had lost items for a couple of days at a time only to discover them in some obscure location. The more I thought about it, the more it made sense that it was our clumsy cleaners. There was no other explanation.

## Chapter 17

# Wraysbury village, Berkshire

*January 1961*

The late afternoon sun was starting to fade as a delicate looking pensioner aged in his mid sixties, stepped off a bus and took a deep breath of fresh air. He admired the quaint looking High Street as he pulled a folded up piece of paper from out of his pocket and straightened it; he was thankful the bus had dropped him off only a few hundred yards away from his destination. With precision, he adjusted his old military tie and commenced the short walk up the High Street to the row of small cottages positioned just opposite the church; the wind had a deathly chill and he welcomed the thought of warmth and a hot drink.

With her eighteen year old son upstairs listening to the latest Beatles release, Tori sat in her small, but cosy living room gazing at the television. She had been glued to the TV most of the afternoon as she watched a news programme featuring the inauguration of John Fitzgerald Kennedy, making him the thirty-fifth President of the United States of America. It was an irritation for Tori as she heard the knocking on the front door. "Martin, it's probably for you," she shouted as she opened the top half of her stable front door. Tori was surprised to see the well dressed man in his more mature years standing shivering at the her front door, and she felt her defences go up upon noticing his Royal Air Force tie. "Mrs. Victoria Davies?" he had asked. It was curiosity more than anything that had gifted the single mother enough courage to invite this stranger into her house; it was something that she wouldn't normally do but she sensed this was significantly important. After escorting the gentleman to an armchair, she offered him a cup of tea that was gratefully accepted; he had been travelling for some considerable time and hot refreshment was much needed.

Retired Group Captain Jack Williams sat alone listening to the words of Lennon and McCartney as Mrs. Davies made the drinks in the kitchen. He could see a collection of photographs sitting on the mantelpiece of her missing husband, some in his uniform, others taken from holidays and family gatherings. He felt a familiar sadness and guilt wash over him; it had been these deep feelings of guilt that had brought him all these miles after so many years. Tori came from the kitchen holding a tray laden with cups and a tea pot.

"It's great news, isn't it?" she said looking at the television set. "Are you a Kennedy supporter Mr.?"

The pensioner hesitated for a brief moment. "It's Jack, Jack Williams," Tori did well not to drop the tray in surprise, even after all these years the name Group Captain Jack Williams was still etched into her memory. The passing of years had mellowed the widower considerably; there had been a time after the disappearance of her husband that she would have longed to have Group Captain Jack Williams at her mercy, but thankfully for the retired man, revenge and hatred had faded and all that was left now was inconsolable emptiness. Tori settled down on the sofa and started to pour two cups of tea.

"I think it's safe to say that I didn't expect you turning up at my door." Williams could still detect feelings of bitterness in the lonely lady, but any attempt to explain his presence was lost the second a spotty teenager walked in, changed over the television channel and flung himself down on the sofa.

"Turn that rubbish off, we have guests, Martin." Tori appeared to be genuinely embarrassed. With a huff, the teenager turned off the television, gave the retired Group Captain an unfriendly glance then slammed the door behind him.

"I suspect all too well that your son knows who I am." The retired Group Captain looked down towards the floor as he spoke; Tori couldn't help but feel sorry for the frail gentleman who sat hunched up in her living room. She got up and walked over to the fire place, where she chose a framed photograph and picked it up.

"Why now after all these years, you decide to turn up at my door? It was in 1943 when I needed the Air Force and do you know what they did? They sent me a fucking telegram saying that my husband was missing." Tori threw the photograph into the fireplace resulting in thousands of tiny pieces of glass spraying all over the hearth and floor. "What is so damn important that you had to wait twenty years to come and dig up the past?"

With difficulty Williams got up and ambled over to the bay window. "It was hot, so hot you just couldn't imagine; the arrival of the unexpected Russians threw everything in pure chaos." Williams pulled back the curtain and glanced down the street. Victoria couldn't look the retired gentleman in the eyes as he spoke. "I don't know how much you knew regarding your husband's final mission but I fear that I was responsible for his demise. Sikorski, the late Polish Prime Minister descended upon the Rock with a plane full of people and eight large crates that had to be guarded at all times. This normally would have been no problem at all, but with the Russians arrival, security was stretched to its limits." Tori didn't know if she wanted to hear all of the grim details but something compelled her to keep listening, for she was all too well aware that this would be her last chance to find out at last what had happened to her beloved Albert Davies. Williams turned to face Tori. "It was I that had ordered your husband to guard the casement all day, it was I who sent him back to England with them, and it was I who ordered him back prematurely from your grasp the weekend he went missing." He headed back towards his designated armchair. "What I'm about to tell you Mrs. Davies is so Top Secret that certain groups and organisations would kill to make sure that the secret is preserved. I know that I should not tell you this but I feel that it is the least that I should do for you." Victoria sat back down as Williams continued: "It was only after the air crash that I discovered what the contents of the casement were, and more importantly, the significance of their existence." He took a sip of tea then placed the cup back down on the saucer. "I want you to know that I didn't just randomly pick anybody to protect the casement; I chose your husband because he was the best I had available to me." The single mother faintly smiled. "However, I should have realised what perils waited for your husband during his final mission; the dangers should have been staring me in the face but I just didn't think." Tori leaned forward in anticipation. "Your husband went missing because he was guarding one of the biggest secrets of that time; it was only when I phoned your husband at home that I knew the implications involved. One of the American pilots who ferried your husband and the crates back to the United Kingdom also had a crate, and he was found in a small Wiltshire village with his throat cut."

Tori gasped in horror, "so you're saying that's what happened to my poor Albie?"

The two spoke for several hours before Williams had to leave and catch the last bus, he checked that Victoria was alright after receiving such staggering news before he got up from his chair. "Before you leave, Mr. Williams, I have something that I think you should have," and she briskly walked out of the room and energetically ran upstairs for several minutes. Jack Williams was delighted that Victoria had taken the news so well; he sensed that she would now be able to move on and lay this whole saga to bed. Tori returned to the living room holding a coat, a coat bearing the rank of Group Captain of the Royal Air Force. "I think this belongs to you," she said as she handed the man the coat. "It was returned to me a week after Albert had gone missing, having been found in the station car park along with his lunch box that had his name and address written on the side."

Williams took the coat in disbelief. "I can't believe that you have kept this after all these years." Instinctively he put the coat on and Tori straightened the collar.

"I had a funny feeling that I would be given the opportunity to give it back to you personally." Jack Williams thanked Victoria for her time and hospitality; he opened the front door as Tori spoke:

"Jack, just for the record, I don't want you to harbour any guiltiness. You said that if you hadn't sent Albert to England then he might still be with us today. Well, it was his special mission that made Albert as proud as I have ever seen him, and to put it bluntly, he thought that the sun shone out of your backside. I want you to know that if you hadn't selected my husband as crate guardian then Martin upstairs would not exist, so for that I am truly thankful." Group Captain Williams smiled as he gave a brief salute before closing the front door behind him.

# Chapter 18

## Swindon

*Tuesday 24ᵗʰ August 2008*

I had spent the first two hours of the morning in crisis talks with members of my senior management. They desperately did not want me to leave and they were willing to do anything to try and persuade me to stay. They understood my position and my reasons for wanting to leave, but they could see that with Ralph and now myself leaving, they would be in an extremely difficult position. I knew that I did not want to stay in the job when I had vast amounts of money sitting in my bank account but I did feel for my panicking bosses; if there was anything that I could do to help them out then I was only too willing to do so. After all, they had been extremely good to me over the last few years. Originally I had said that I only wanted to serve a week's notice but I thought that it would be best to make sure that our deal with Julian went through hassle free, so, having sympathy for my management's predicament, I put forward an offer that was gratefully accepted. It was agreed that I would be allowed to work when I wanted to as long as important valuations were covered; the office would ring me at six-thirty every evening to tell me what valuations there were the following day, and then all there was for me to do was turn up at the office half an hour before to gather the details before going to do the valuations. I knew that once my money had safely cleared in my bank account, I wouldn't want to come to work again, but I was comforted that at least I had given my company some time to desperately try and find my replacement. As there weren't any valuations booked in for the day, I decided to spend the afternoon car shopping; the tens of thousands of pounds I had in my bank were burning a hole in my pocket and, as I soon had to hand back my beloved BMW M3 company car, there seemed to be no better time like the present to purchase a new toy.

After explaining the situation to my colleagues, I decide to go home to change out of my suit into the scruffiest clothes I could find, since I didn't want to go round the prestigious car show rooms suited and booted; I wanted to have some fun with the salesman. After ringing Ben and finding out that he was tied up with his family for the best part of the day, I decided to get changed quickly then leave for the car sales rooms straight away. I settled for an old faded T-shirt and a pair of old jeans with cuts in the knees. I didn't want to come across as a stuffy businessman; I wanted to create some sort of mysteriousness as to who I was. The previous evening I had made a short list as to what cars particularly took my fancy: amongst them were Jaguars, Audi's, Porches and of course BMW's. Swindon had all the main car dealerships; it even had Ferrari and Lamborghini sales rooms, a sign that the town was enjoying some prosperous years and doing very well for itself indeed. I decided that my first port of call would be a new outfit in town called 'the Car Shop'. I had heard that many small car dealerships were in serious danger of going out of business due to this new company's staggeringly low prices. They had acquired a large warehouse close to the town centre; the square footage was huge and could certainly accommodate several hundred cars. The nice thing about the Car Shop was that they did not limit themselves to one particular manufacturer; they had the lot and many high end spec cars as well.

Feeling slightly intimidated by the sheer size of the building, I walked through the large glass doors to the Reception Desk. A pretty teenager greeted me from behind the desk and gestured for me to go through the double doors positioned to her right, so I followed a couple in their late fifties into a futuristic style glass corridor. "Looks like something from the Starship Enterprise," said the man peering over his shoulder. I acknowledged with a nod and a smile feeling rather annoyed that he thought I looked like a trekkie. A monument of a water fountain caught my attention in a court yard through the glass panels as I approached the end of the walkway. The former occupants must have spent a fortune in building this place, I thought, as I entered a second Reception area. Within seconds a swarm of salesman pounced on the couple in front of me; instinctively, I slowed my pace and held back a little. I counted five eager salesman dressed in horrid bright yellow shirts accompanied with red ties; needless to say, the look didn't look right. It hadn't taken long for a desperate salesman to catch eye contact with me, but he seemed a little less enthusiastic, probably because of my clothes; he walked over to where I was stood.

"Hi, welcome to the Car Shop. My name is Wayne and I will be on hand during your visit this afternoon." It was obvious that this teenager was repeating a remembered script; I seriously doubted that he possessed the ability to sell a jug of water to a man on fire.

I could see many rows of polished cars all looking brand new. "I'm looking for something that's probably two doors and has a bit of poke." Wayne looked at me with a blank expression.

"A car with a bit of power?" I could see the penny drop, so without any hesitation he led me to the other side of the building.

I was almost out of breath by the time we reached Wayne's suggested car. It was clear that he had made a typical novice salesman's error; he had judged a book by its cover.

Sitting before me was a ten year old bright blue Peugeot 106 for three thousand pounds. "This little puppy you will find is a proper babe magnet, if it's in your price range that is." The cheeky little bastard! I was about to open my mouth but I managed to restrain myself; I bit my lip and slowly started to amble down a row of cars closely followed by Wayne. A gold BMW M3 caught my eye. "Those are what dreams are made of eh?" I could tell by the longing look in my irritating salesman's eyes that he had a soft spot for the M3 but I just about managed to stop myself from dangling my car keys under his nose. I peered through the passenger's window.

"It's beautiful but I'm looking for something in a different league, if you know what I mean, Wayne." He didn't look surprised in the least. Positioned opposite was a striking red Mini Cooper with white racing stripes and a big Union Jack painted on the roof; it wasn't hard to predict Wayne's next move.

"If nine thousand is in your price range then this retro piece of British car history could be yours." It annoyed me when people pigeon-holed estate agents but Wayne really was your typical second hand car salesman. A middle aged stocky man wearing a suit and a Car Shop name badge apologetically interrupted and requested to borrow the teenager for a few minutes; I was happy to have the chance to browse in peace. I was coming to the opinion that there was nothing for me when out of the corner of my eye I saw it; its beautiful lines were like a piece of art. It looked like no other car in the place. I had to inspect it close up. The couple I had followed in stood before it

"Well love, if we win the lottery then it's yours." Upon seeing me the husband smiled, "nice to dream isn't it?" At forty one thousand pounds, I didn't need to dream.

"At this price I'm taking this little beauty out for a test drive. What a bargain!" The couple looked sick with envy.

Several minutes had passed before my new friend, Wayne, came trundling back with his hands in his pockets. "Could you open this?" I asked sincerely. It was an understatement to say that little Wayne was bewildered.

"You want to have a look in the Aston Martin? I'll have to get my supervisor for that category of car," and with that he proceeded back the way he had come only moments before. I watched him walk over to an Asian man in a suit. Wayne pointed at me as they spoke and I could see the slimy supervisor laugh as he commenced to make his way over to me.

"Good afternoon, what a good choice of car," he said as he unlocked it with the remote. "We get a lot of people admiring this; please feel free to get in." I opened the door and bent over into the car; the supervisor got in and sat in the passenger seat. "Breath taking, isn't she?" I had to agree with the man. "It's an Aston Martin DB9 touchtronic; she has a 5.9 V12 engine with an automatic gear box. Usually you couldn't pick one of these up for less that sixty grand but this one does have nearly ninety thousand miles on the clock. Even so it's an absolute steal." It was like sitting in something that had just fallen out of heaven; inside was an amazing fusion of hand stitched red leather accompanied by deep walnut and silver dials, buttons and knobs. The car was painted in a metallic graphite grey and sported nineteen inch, five spoke alloy wheels; two large exhaust pipes dominated the looks from the back and the multiple light clusters dominated the front. I knew that I was going to buy the car the moment I sat in the driver's seat; I just wasn't going to tell Mr. "I never introduced myself" straight away.

"Would it be OK to start her up?" I politely inquired; the salesman seemed to be slightly irritated by my understandable request.

"I don't have time this afternoon but I will see if I can grab someone to take it for a quick spin round the block" - not the words of a man who believed he had an opportunity to sell an Aston Martin.

I had the misfortune of having Wayne accompany me on my test drive; if it hadn't been for the roaring V12 engine, I would have probably ended up throwing him out of the car. The boy just would not shut up. The list of extras onboard the car was endless: heated front and rear windows, sat nav, door mirror memory, heated front seats, Xenon headlamps, Linn Audio system, parking sensors - this list really went on forever. What was astonishing was that Wayne had managed to fill a fifteen minute drive listing every single one; I found it hard to understand how he managed to breath. It was only towards the last few minutes of my drive that Wayne decided to divert his conversation onto me.

"What other cars have you looked at then? Bet none have been as good as this." I was glad this was my first; otherwise I'm sure I would have had Wayne's detailed professional opinion on each and every one.

"This is the first I have looked at to be honest." Wayne looked disappointed.

"Being the first car you have looked at I guess you won't be buying today, but if you did decide to buy it at some stage would you use it for your work?" For the first time in our short relationship, Wayne was showing traits of a salesman; he was clearly fishing to see what I did for work and was using subtle probing questions to find out. I decided not to make it easy for him.

"Well, I don't think I will be working from next week onwards so probably not."

Wayne scratched the side of his neck. "You're losing your job and you're looking at Aston Martins? I'll be your getaway driver if you're robbing a bank!" Without looking at him, I knew that he was looking at me waiting for my response. We were getting close to the Car Shop so I decided to put little Wayne out of his misery.

"I own a very successful surf wear label that I am just about to sell up to a massive company, but, until everyone has signed on the dotted lines, I'm afraid I can't tell you who it is but I am sure that you will hear about it on the news at some point."

Wayne started to laugh. "Fucking hell mate, fair play." He started to chuckle to himself. "I can't wait to tell my boss, who thinks you're some kind of tyre kicker that is living in the land of Narnia."

As soon as the wheels came to a halt, Wayne opened his door; it was evident that he was itching to go and tell his boss that he had read me incorrectly. "I'm just going inside to take the keys back. I'll leave you with the car to have a proper look and if you want to meet me at the tables inside, then I can answer any questions you may have." Like a bolt of lightening he ran across the small forecourt and vanished inside the building. I didn't need to have a proper look around; I had already decided to buy the car. Even before I had closed the Aston's door, I noticed the Asian supervisor strolling over to where I was standing, an unsettling grin forming across his face.

"Mr. Hamilton, my name is Mo, and I must apologise for being in such a rush earlier on. They say there's a credit crunch. Not here there isn't." He proceeded to do a slow tour of the car. "I would say these are the most desired cars in the motor world." He folded his arms. "I take it you had a whale of a time driving her?" He reminded me of a puppy dog at feeding time waiting for a scrap of food to be thrown his way; only this dog I was reluctant to throw a steak to. I felt that Wayne should get the sale.

"It was much better than my M3 - put it that way - I'll just go in and see Wayne at the tables like he said." Mo rushed round from the front of the car and stood next to me.

"Anything you want to know you can ask me." My phone started to ring; I answered it straight away making Mo retreat by several steps. It was Ben phoning from his house phone, something which he very rarely did.

"Mate, are you busy?" he asked sounding a little confused.

"Just buying a DB9." I could see the jubilation in the salesman's eyes. "What's up, mate? You never call from this number; I don't even have it saved in my phone." I took a few steps further away from Mo.

"I can't find my phone, mate, so I had to call you on this line." He spoke quicker than usual. "This is going to sound really bloody weird, but can you remember when we got back from holiday and you rang me after I left your place?"

"Of course I remember, it was to ask you about that yellow weed." There was a brief silence.

"I don't suppose you left it under my duvet by any chance?" A chill shot down my spine.

"No, matey, I have it at home bagged up, because we were going to report it to the Police the next day but never got round to it. If you have one, this is getting really fucking strange." I held a finger up to Mo to tell him that I would only be another minute. "I'll be an hour or so finishing up here then I will come straight round, buddy." I was just about to hang up when Ben spoke.

"It's a dandelion, Hammy." Then the line went dead.

I turned to face my patiently waiting salesman. "Right Mo, I'll take the car if I can drive it away today and that Wayne is credited with the sale; after all it was he who sold it to me on the test drive." The Asian man seemed taken aback but he didn't take long to process my requests.

"Wayne would of course be given the sale and if you have the funds available then I can't see any reason why you shouldn't drive it away." I was taken to a small office with a desk, a couple of chairs and a computer where I was left for a few minutes whilst Mo went and grabbed a couple of cups of coffee for us. Another incoming telephone call on my mobile phone broke the silence within the office. I normally would have hung up but upon seeing that it was Julian calling, I answered it straight away.

"Hi Hammy, how are you?" It was good to hear that he sounded like he was in a jovial mood. "Just touching base with you to make sure that we are still on for Friday?" Mo walked back into the room with two steaming hot mugs.

"Definitely still on for Friday. Shall we say twelve at the Carpenters Arms in South Marston?" We confirmed the meeting and, after quickly telling him about my new purchase, I ended the phone call. Much to my frustration, I spent the following hour and a half going through paperwork. Not content with just selling me a car, Mo tried his hardest to sell me finance deals, car wax and even seat fabric protector, all of which I declined. I paid for the car with the Boulette debit card. The insurance was provided free for one week courtesy of a National insurer giving me time to find my preferred insurance; finally I was free to take my baby home. I left my company car in the car park opting to pick it up the following day with either Serena or Ben, but after seeing Ben I wanted to spend the rest of the day playing with my new toy.

I felt like Royalty driving back from town to Ben's house. I could see other fellow road users admire the Aston as I drove past them; I hadn't felt this good in years. The mood at Ben's house was somewhat more subdued, but his entire household still managed to come out and inspect my new purchase that sat on their drive.

"I think you're earning far too much money these days, Hammy." Ben's Mum had commented. It wasn't long, however, before conversation changed from flashy sports cars to mysteriously appearing dandelions, and the possible theft of Ben's brand new all singing and dancing mobile phone. Jackie, Ben's mother, evidently was not aware that I too had also found a dandelion on my pillow, and she certainly did not know about our discovery of port. I had told Ben that he had probably mislaid his phone and that it would turn up out of the blue when he least expected it. However, it didn't take me long to remember that I too had lost something when I had found the yellow plant; my little password book. With it turning up a few days later, I had not given it a second thought, but thinking about it in more detail it did seem a little too coincidental. It was Jackie who had wanted to call the Police straight away.

"We can't have people breaking into our house and doing what they want," she had said worryingly. I could see that Ben was also starting to get a little freaked out. If it hadn't been for a desire to protect his new found wealth, I think he also would have advised to call in the Police.

Having decided that they wouldn't call the Police this time, Ben's Mum, Step Dad and Sister had left me and Ben alone in his room; I then spoke openly for the first time to Ben about a growing fear that was building up inside me. "Mate, at the risk of sounding paranoid, I think something very odd is happening here, and it's all started since we found that case." Ben started to roll a much needed joint. "I have no idea what the fuck dandelions have to do with it but I think somebody is looking for something." Ben finished licking the glue on his rolling paper and looked at me wearing a confused expression. "Think about it mate, the day I found my dandelion, my password book went missing. Admittedly, it was only for a few days but it still went missing. That book had access to most of my contacts; all the other contacts are on my phone that was with me on holiday." I could see that Ben was deep in thought. "The day you find a dandelion, your mobile phone goes missing that probably does have all of your contacts in it." Ben looked unsettled. "Do you think they know about the port?" I had thought about this in great depth. "How could they? We have only told a few people and the people we have told I trust one hundred percent." Ben nodded in agreement and lit the end of his joint.

"Well, I think if something happens again then we really should tell the authorities." I couldn't agree more.

# Chapter 19

# South Marston

*Friday 27ᵗʰ August 2008*

The only thing for me to do today, apart from meeting Julian, was to go and pay my Nan's best friend, Olive, a visit. I had thought about writing her a little thank you note and giving her a box of chocolates but decided that would be too risky; I didn't want people inquiring as to why she was receiving thank you notes. Instead I opted to take a modest size bunch of flowers with no note attached; like my Nan, her memory was almost nonexistent and I was sure that within a few hours of me leaving, she would have completely forgotten who had given them to her. On the same tack, I should really have paid my Nan a visit as I would have only been in the next street, but I feared that she might tell

Olive that I popped round, if she remembered, resulting in Olive's memory being triggered and her telling all; I couldn't take the risk. I had considered taking Ben along to retrieve our treasure; after all, I wanted him to know that we were in this together, but I was slightly worried that his presence might frighten the frail old lady so I decided to fetch the casement alone.

Throughout my life it had always been easy for me to locate Olive's house; her small terraced house, for as long as I can remember, had always had a bright red door and blinding yellow windows; the combination looked ghastly. Regretting that I hadn't called her beforehand, I gave a firm knock on the front door; it would be just my luck her not being in. Fearing that she had taken herself off for the weekend as the seconds passed away, I considered checking with her neighbours to see if they knew of her whereabouts; the relief of seeing a shadowy figure approach the door could not be put into words. Upon her opening the door, I was delighted by the fact that she remembered who I was; she genuinely appeared to be uplifted by me being on her front door step. "Edward, what a wonderful surprise, and flowers, you are a true gentleman." She stepped aside and invited me to come in, out of the cold. It wasn't long before we were sitting around her gas fire in her cosy living room sipping her finest Earl Grey tea.

"Remind me Edward, what is the special occasion? Is it my birthday?" Although the demise of her memory was regretful, I was mightily relieved to see that there had been no recent improvement. I had to be careful in what I told her, because I had experienced with my Nan that if you told her something that she thought she should know, she would quickly become panicky and unsettled.

"You probably won't remember this, Olive, because I asked you when you were very busy and I did it very quickly. But last week, when I put a couple of boxes of your old belongings in your loft, I also put a box of my junk up there because I didn't have the room to store it." Thankfully, Olive's only response was to take a sip of her tea and inform me that there was ample room up there if ever I needed to store anything else. Bless her.

Without wanting to appear rude, I asked if there was anything she needed doing like changing a light bulb or even doing the washing up; just me being there apparently served as the best help she could ask for. A cobweb in the corner of her lounge had attracted my attention; I had just stood up to remove any trace when my phone rudely interrupted me.

"Answer it Edward, I'm sure it's very important." Olive was most insistent.

"Guess who?" screeched a female's voice from down the phone. The reception was not terribly good but it was still easy for me to figure out who the caller was.

"Hello Laura, can I call you back? I'm just in the middle of something," Laura, my old colleague and friend was always a pleasure to talk to, especially since it had been several months since we last spoke bumping into each other in a local supermarket. Laura quickly ended the call; she knew that I would call her back, even though she probably suspected that I was aware that she was just on the look out for hot gossip. She loved to talk about other people's failures and successes; now it was obviously my turn to be her subject matter.

Within half an hour I was all set and ready to leave Olive's house accompanied by my crate that I held tightly like a newborn baby. Olive hardly seemed to notice the crate's presence; I think she felt that my visit was purely for her benefit which was just fine by me. Having walked me to the front door, she stood and watched me carefully place the wooden box into the boot of my car. "That's a bobby dazzler of a car," she had commented. Funnily enough, she had said the same thing about my first car, a battered banger of a Vauxhall Nova. Before leaving, I walked up to Olive and for the first time in my life I gave her a gentle hug. She responded by squeezing me tightly, her unexpected strength catching me off guard a little. She waved frantically at me as I brought my V12 into life and slowly pulled away from the pavement where I was parked. I vowed to myself that, with much more free time looming, I would spend more quality time with Nan and Olive. I thought about my Nan and Olive

for most of the drive to Ben's house. It saddened me to think
that with them being at the age where tomorrow isn't guaranteed
to anyone, they wouldn't be around forever. Not even all the
money in the world could bring them back. I promised myself
that I would use my new found fortune to do good in people's
lives and stop being so self-centred.

Ben and I had arrived in the car park to the Carpenters Arms
in perfect time; Julian was just stepping out of his Bentley.
The car park had only two other cars in it but I still decided to
park my sparkling Aston next to his car. The two cars parked
together made something of a spectacle; Julian's expression on
his face suggested that he was impressed. "Wonderful choice,"
he had commented as he warmly greeted me with a handshake,
"and a lovely looking pub as well, good choice." A voice came
from close to the entrance porch at the corner of the car park:
"you haven't tasted the food yet." A petit balding man aged in
his sixties had gone unnoticed by all three of us as he smoked
a cigarette; his welcoming smile told me that he was jesting.
Accompanied by Ben and Julian I strode over to the man who
was standing next to the front door.

"Is this place open?" I instinctively asked. Julian pointed to
a large open sign that hung on the door before he swung it open.
We entered into a small porch that was laden with pamphlets
on Wiltshire attractions. It amazed me that the local area had
so much to offer; they certainly had gone unnoticed by me in
twenty something years. We proceeded through another door that
led to a dinning area; polished oak floorboards complemented
the well-used, un-laid, wooden tables and varnished half length
wall panels. Framed black and white photographs of football
and rugby teams of yesteryear lined most of the walls, the
remaining wall space being taken up with prints of the famous
Spitfire fighter aircraft. The bar area was separated from the
dining area by a large archway that looked to be riddled with
woodworm. A superb open fireplace was the centre of attention
followed closely by the well illuminated bar. There wasn't a
soul to be seen as I walked up to the bar and plonked myself

down on an idle bar stool, Ben following suit and sat down beside me. "Where's Julian gone?" he mumbled. I looked back over my shoulder to see Julian walk though the entrance door accompanied by the man we had met briefly in the car park; both men laughed as they merrily strode over and joined us at the bar. The stranger to our party stood on the customer side of the bar as he sipped from a petite cup containing coffee before he spoke: "you gents look thirsty, suppose I better serve you." I thanked the Gods that I had not spoke foul of the establishment in front of our host. We exchanged pleasantries about the pub and our cars while we waited for our two pints of lager and glass of red wine. It turned out that the man serving us was called Colin; he wasn't the landlord but in fact a casual worker who lived in a small cottage further down the village road. "If you're planning on eating gentlemen, then I would advise that you get your orders in before two tables of six arrive in a quarter of an hour or thereabouts," he warned almost apologetically. It was a little too early for me to eat anything substantial so I opted for the easy option, a bacon sandwich; Ben and Julian must have felt the same way as they ordered exactly the same. Colin wondered off into the kitchen with our orders.

"If it's ok with you chaps I would like to take a quick peak at the casement before we start proceedings," said Julian quietly.

With Ben deciding to stay at the bar with his lager so he could chat to Colin and explain our absence if need be, Julian and I went outside to the boot of my car. As the boot door opened, momentarily I thought that Julian was more interested in my car than what was sat inside it. The door reached its full height and Julian's attention was firmly back on the port. "I can't remember the last time I was this nervous," he whispered. With great respect I pulled the case closer to us.

"Feel free to examine each and every one, my friend." I fully understood his need to be one hundred per cent sure that it was the real deal. The lid to the crate was very loosely on and it proved to be no problem at all for Julian to lift it up and reveal its contents. With the holiest of respect, he gently lifted up a bottle from its compartment and held it out in front of him. He rotated the bottle over every possible angle to examine every single bit of it; he studied the initials on the bottom, then the wax seal. He repeated this process on five different bottles. "I don't need to see anymore. The condition of the wood of the crate told me straight away that it is over fifty years old and I have no doubt, these are genuine artefacts."

Meanwhile, Ben had been engaged in a deep and meaningful conversation with Colin, who had summed up the story of our T-shirt empire being sold; Colin was loving every second and lapped up all the details. "Shall I call you Mr. Billabong or Mr. Quicksilver?" he had asked Julian as we approached the bar, causing him to go a shade of red.

"Not quite in that league I'm afraid to say, but with this little investment who knows?" A much plumper man with a stern expression entered the bar from the kitchen wearing shorts and a navy blue polo shirt; I aged him around his mid fifties. He proceeded to pull himself a pint of lager and without saying a word to Colin, he ambled over to our side of the bar.

"Judging by the horsepower sat outside, you guys aren't feeling this credit crunch." Julian took a deep breath, swallowed a large gulp of wine and cleared his throat.

"With interest rates what they are at the moment and the general financial paranoia that surrounds business now, it would be fair to say that the pinch is being felt," he calmly placed his wine glass down on the bar, "but with this God awful smoking ban coupled with the economy being in such tatters, I don't need to explain to you the meaning of a credit crunch, I'm sure, kind landlord." Julian spoke with intelligence and clarity. The entrance door opened with a creak as three middle aged couples walked in together.

"Looks like somebody is doing alright for themselves in these times of turbulence." The landlord smiled before retreating behind the bar to give Colin a hand in serving the drinks." Julian turned to face me with his back to the bar.

"Seems a tad stressed," he faintly whispered. I nodded in agreement and suggested at the same volume as Julian that he may be finding these times difficult. The bar area was starting to fill with polite laughter as the newly arrived customers started to huddle around the bar. Julian grabbed his drink.

"I suggest we go and find somewhere a little more quiet and get the party started." I couldn't have put it better myself. Ben and I both jumped up and headed towards the lounge. Again the lounge area was separated from the bar by an old wooden archway; the room looked to be very comfortable with its three leather sofas and large flat screen television that hung above a deep stone fireplace. A table was positioned in a bay window on the front wall; seating was arranged with two traditional wooden chairs and a cushioned seat that lined the three sides of the bay window. We decided to ignore the sofas and perch ourselves round the table in the bay window. Thankfully the other customers had decided to stay at the bar area and not venture into the lounge, the lunchtime BBC news on the television not being enough to entice them closer.

Julian leaned back casually in his chair. "So is the world now awash with Boulette T-shirts?" he inquired interestedly. Ben enthusiastically proceeded to explain how many T-shirts he had managed to offload before remembering the Swedish girls on holiday; the remaining five minutes consisted of Julian being filled in on how beautiful these girls were who incidentally were wearing our company's T-shirts. After I had gone into details on my efforts in getting the brand out there, Julian looked to be thoroughly satisfied. "That's excellent, and it goes without saying before we start proceedings that I will only own Boulette in name, so you are free to produce more T-shirts and designs if you wish and to treat it like your own company; remember this is only a smoke screen." It was good to hear, because the previous evening I had experienced unexpected feelings of sadness in selling our little company, but it was also good to know that Julian, on paper at least, would still be involved with us, even if he had no interest in producing surfing clothing. "Bugger," Julian interrupted the brief silence, "all the paper work I have had drawn up is in my case in the car. Would you mind terribly if I excuse myself and go and get it?" It was a pleasure to listen to Julian speak, because he spoke so politely and warmly that it was like listening to a long lost grandfather or uncle; I made a mental note to myself to try and clean up my use of the English language. As Julian left the building, I caught eye contact with Colin behind the bar; he put his thumbs up and mouthed "alright?" so with our drinks dwindling on the low side I decided to amble over to the bar.

"Everything going to plan?" he inquired as he picked up a wet, clean glass and cloth and started to dry it.

"Touch wood, so far so good. He has just popped out to grab his paperwork." As if reading my mind, he started to serve another round of drinks for our table. "I was just saying to Barry that it is nice to see people make something good of their lives." I presumed that Barry was the pre occupied gentleman we had briefly met earlier.

It wasn't long before Julian, Ben and I were once again huddled around our cosy table, only this time we shared most of it with Julian's stylish silver briefcase. With dozens of sheets of paperwork all spread out over the table and in case it was difficult to find a place to put my beer down, I settled for the redundant chair next to me. Julian reached into his case and handed me a business card. "Have you instructed a solicitor to act for you?" I looked at the card before responding to Julian's question, which was from Clarence & West Solicitors in London. I glanced at Ben who shook his head, then turned back to face Julian.

"We haven't got a solicitor. Is that going to be a problem?"

"Good God no, my friends." Julian certainly sounded reassuring. "If this had been a genuine sale and purchase of a business then I would have insisted on you guys using one, but as it is, we can't have anything put into writing regarding the other subject matter for obvious reasons. You can speak to my solicitor and then you must ring your bank to confirm the monies have arrived safely." Julian handed me an A4 piece of paper with Clarence & West Solicitors written across the top; it was a contract. I shuffled closer to Ben so that we could both read the document together; I was amazed to see that it was the first page of nine.

"Do we have to read all of this?" gasped Ben, probably after seeing the page one of nine bit. I had to admit that I supported Ben's feelings and it wasn't long before Julian put our simple minds at ease. "It is always good practise to read every word before you put your name to something but it does appear to be a ludicrously large mouthful; even I was surprised when my solicitor went through it with me on Wednesday."

Colin arrived at the table carrying a tray with three bacon sandwiches and sauces, which smelt wonderful. Julian instinctively gathered up the loose paperwork, placed it into his case and then moved the case under the table out of sight. "Bon appetit," said Colin as he walked back to the bar before starting to hum the theme tune from the great escape. Ben emptied his mouth of bacon sandwich and cleared his throat before he spoke.

"Could you please just summarise the contract. I think it's fair to say that we both trust you." Julian looked touched if not a little embarrassed. "Well, to cut down my solicitor's words by about ninety percent, it states that both parties are agreeable to Knapp Enterprises, which is my organisation, to become the sole owner of Boulette Boarding." Julian briefly paused to take a bite out of his sandwich. "Pages three to eight go into greater detail regarding copyright laws, all of which can be ignored because if you decide not to do anything with the company again then it will be dead and buried; forgotten in time. The last page lays out the sums of money involved, which is of course two million pounds. Even my solicitor does not know about the purchase of port so even if I wanted to, I couldn't put anything into writing regarding that transaction; good old fashioned trust is all we have on this one I'm afraid gentlemen." Ben scratched his head; I didn't need to look at him to know that there was a question on its way.

"What if we came under investigation and it was traced back to you? What would you do if it was discovered that this deal is a decoy, a smoke screen, a folly or whatever you want to call it?" Julian's instantaneous grin told me that he appreciated the question. He leant back in his chair and momentarily savoured the moment.

"After our first get together in that delightful pub, I realized that if I was going to be appearing to be purchasing a tiny surf wear label for what is a vast amount of money, I knew that I would have to paint a very convincing picture." He smiled from ear to ear as he crouched down under the table to retrieve his briefcase before he passed me another sheet of paper. This time it was the last page of a contract, a contract binding the sale of Rip Roar surfing to Knapp Enterprises.

"You have to be kidding me, you own Rip Roar? And for how fucking much? That's a bloody bargain!"

Ben snatched the paper from me. "Seven hundred grand! Everyone will think that you have gone surfing crazy!"

Julian smiled. "But they won't think that I have just bought Hitler's lost casement of port, and, everyone who knows you won't think that you have just sold a treasure like that; they will think that you have just sold out to Rip Roar surfing.

"Ingenious." I had to hand it to Julian, if the Titanic had been this watertight, I have no doubt that not one single life would have been lost; it was one hell of an example on how to launder money.

To keep everything above board, although I loathed the thought, I knew that we would have to pay tax on our incoming monies. It pained me to ask: "so what does the tax man make out of this little deal?"

Julian frowned. "I'm afraid we can't wiggle out of this one and it will be extortionate whatever the figure. To save me making a complete hash of an explanation, I suggest we let Dillon my solicitor explain the ins and outs." With both Ben and myself in agreement, Julian commenced dialling the numbers to Clarence and West solicitors. I turned to look at Ben, his face illustrated excitement, bewilderment, disbelief and happiness, a whole cocktail of feelings, a rollercoaster of emotions, all of which I was experiencing at the bottom of my stomach. Julian must have had a special hot line to the solicitor as it didn't take long at all for Dillon to pick up; I had learnt in agency that this was something of a rarity. A couple of polite pleasantries were exchanged before Julian handed me the phone.

"Edward, it's great to speak to you. Before we kick off, I believe you would like walking through the taxation laws of this country." Dillon projected his voice confidently and professionally, something that you would expect from a high flying solicitor, but he also came across as being extremely caring and thoughtful. I quickly whipped the phone onto loud speakerphone and turned down the volume so only our ears could hear before Dillon carried on. "The good news is that you're just about to sell your company for a lot more than nine thousand and two hundred pounds; the bad news is that the government will hammer you for that fact." It started to dawn on me that I wasn't quite going to be a millionaire. "With a figure of two million, I'm afraid that after your annual allowance is taken off you're staring down the barrel of very nearly eight hundred thousand pounds which is forty per cent of your capital gains." I leant back in my chair, it was shocking to say the least, fucking daylight robbery but at the end of the day I wasn't going to turn my nose up at six hundred thousand pounds each.

"Thieving fucking bastards," gasped Ben; I was just about to add another insult to our Government when Julian spoke to his solicitor. Having asked if we could be excused for a couple of minutes, Julian put the phone on hold so Dillon couldn't hear what was being discussed.

"I had already thought about this. Having agreed a sale price of two million pounds, I am willing to pay the tax for you with a few conditions." Julian started to speak much quieter. "Here is where the trust aspect comes in; if you will allow me to send you a cheque in a few months time when the dust settles from Rip Roar, then I will pay the eight hundred thousand pounds tax bill for you. I would also suggest that I pay you in several instalments over a couple of months, so that no dodgy dealings would be suspected." Simultaneous nodding from me and my best friend told Julian that we had a deal; there would be no going back.

With Dillon now hearing our voices loud and clear it was time to get this done and dusted, I took a deep breath. "OK Dillon we are ready, what's next?"

"I'm trusting that you have read the contract word for word, so now if you and Benjamin could sign and date the contract." Julian handed Ben a silver fountain pen. It amused me how Ben's signature looked like a drunken spider that had crawled out of a pot of ink and stumbled across a sheet of paper. With Ben's name and date taking up most of the room, I just about managed to squeeze my name underneath making it vaguely legible. Julian took the Pen from me and signed his section of the contract making it a legal document.

"All signed," announced Julian to his solicitor.

"Excellent," responded Dillon, "now before I wire over the monies could I just ask everybody that they are happy and don't have any questions?" The silence that descended over the table told the legal professional to send over the money. Taking a few moments to confirm that the account details he had were present and correct, he started the proceedings. "Once the money is showing on my system as sent, could I ask you to leave it half an hour before you ring your bank to confirm that the funds have arrived into the account without any problems?" It sounded like a fair enough request to me. There were plenty of people in the pub so I couldn't see them closing for some time yet; the more drinking time the better as far as I was concerned. "OK chaps, the money has now been sent via telegraphic transfer to the Royal Bank of Scotland. I will sort out the tax payments from this end which means that you will be receiving one million and two hundred thousand pounds, not a bad day's work if I may say so gentlemen." After expressing our sincere thanks to Dillon, we ended the telephone call.

"We'll enjoy a few beverages before you gents confirm with your bank that the money is safely there, and then if I could take receipt of the crate I think that will conclude our business for today." Colin strode over to our table.

"Judging by the grins on your faces I take it that everything went smoothly?" He started to collect our plates and empty glasses; I felt a little sorry for the man, for he clearly didn't have much money, yet here he was genuinely happy that things were going well for us complete strangers. I comforted myself by thinking about the tip he would be receiving upon our departure. To celebrate, pass the time and to allow Colin a few stolen minutes putting his feet up, Julian ordered two bottles of Champagne. It was only when Colin brought the bottles over with three flutes that we discovered that he was tea-total; nevertheless he still sat down with us and toasted our successful transaction. It felt like I was sitting around a table of old school friends. It was uplifting to meet such warm and pleasant people, so I vowed to myself that I would come here more often with Serena.

With a phone call to the bank confirming that we had received every penny owing to us, we had nothing left to do apart from hand over the bottles to Julian. As we were just finishing off our drinks I carefully pulled out the map we had found of South Marston airfield from my pocket and handed it to Julian. "No need for us to keep hold of this seeing as it was found in the crate." Julian respectfully took it from me and placed it flat in his brief case. I took it upon myself to go to the bar and pay for the meal and drinks; all in all it came to seventy eight pounds, so I gave Colin the contents of my wallet which was one hundred and fifty pounds and insisted that he personally kept the change; he didn't need any persuasion in accepting it. After saying our heartfelt goodbyes, the three of us left the way we had come in. I noticed that the pub now was starting to fill and the car park had a healthy number of cars in it. Julian paced over to his car and opened the door to the boot.

"I'm sure the bottles will be safe in here if I drive with extreme caution. Fingers crossed, they will all remain in one piece." With great care I lifted the crate from my car into the boot of his Bentley., "

Thank you so much, thank you." Julian approached me with both arms held out, he embraced me with some force making me cough and almost choke. "Spend that money of yours wisely and whatever you do don't let it turn you into monsters. I have seen far too many good people lose sight of who they are just because some easy money has sailed into their port, so don't change Hammy."

I think both myself and Ben took the warning seriously. If anything, I wanted to use the fact that I was wealthy not only to my benefit, but to other people's benefit too; I wanted to make a difference to other people's lives whilst still being able to enjoy the trappings that wealth brings, guilt free.

# Chapter 20

# Swindon

*Monday 31st August 2008*

The weekend had been the best couple of days I have had in a long time; it was a good job too as my bank balance had taken a slight hammering over several days of over indulgence. On the Friday evening, family and friends of both Ben and I piled into an unsuspecting local hotel bar. With wads of notes behind the bar, our group drank merrily into the early hours of Saturday. I had taken the opportunity to invite Laura and her boyfriend to our celebratory gathering; armed with her fancy looking camera she didn't waste an opportunity to take snapshots of Ben and myself, often with a bottle of Champagne under an arm. I would have to wait till Monday to see the pictures when I bought the local newspaper - she promised me a cracking write up and assured me that she would portray me as the next Alan Sugar or Peter Jones. I relished having well doers come up to me and congratulate me on our business success; my mother was the biggest culprit hugging me copious times and announcing to the room drunkenly how proud she was of her little boy. All in all it was a great evening with everybody falling into our web of deceit. It slightly bothered me that I was lying to all of my friends and family, but it bothered me even more that it only slightly bothered me.

With a rather heavy and groggy head, I awoke early on the Saturday morning. I decided to go and visit my sister and family in Manchester for the day. I had been promising my little nephew Henry for months that I would come so it was well overdue. Ignoring the fact that I was still probably well over the drink-drive limit, I set off in the Aston on my mission of good will. On the long drive to their house, I thought about gifts for them that would benefit them the most. My nephew and niece would be easy; they would get some toys from the local toy store and a cheque for ten thousand pounds each to help with their education. My sister and brother-in-law were far more difficult. I knew from my mother that my sister was struggling for space and longed for a conservatory, so I decided that she could pick one on line and I would pay for it there and then. It wasn't until I was fifteen miles away when I finally thought of my brother-in-law's gift. I toyed with buying him a second hand Jaguar but elected in the end for a Manchester United season ticket and another one for Henry. It was wonderful to see them all again and the gifts were greatly appreciated, even though my brother-in-law and nephew would have to remain for three years on the waiting list for season tickets; I offered Manchester City season tickets but that didn't seem to go down so well. Having spent the best part of the day with them, I accepted my sister's invitation to stay the night and drive back in the morning when I would be feeling more refreshed much to my nephew and niece's joy. In the end, having visited a nearby farm to see the animals, and having been dragged around most of the shops in Manchester, it wasn't until early evening that I returned to the Costa Del Swindon.

It was a Monday morning and I felt fucked, so it was a massive relief not to have to go to work. Out of courtesy, I called the office from my bed to see if there were any valuations that they needed me to do. "Think we have everything covered Hammy apart from one," explained a man's voice that I did not recognise. "The only one where we can't get cover from another office is a valuation on Friday, but I have to warn you, it's a stonker of a manor house and I hear that you are the best man for the job." Although this strange man's words were flattering, he irritated me and I feared that I had taken an instant dislike to him. I took down all the details and promised him, on several occasions, that I would conduct a drive-by before the valuation so I could go into it with my eyes open. I wrote down the address, date and time on a yellow post-it note and stuck it onto one of my bedside drawers, as I didn't particularly care if I forgot to go but I did think it best that I made at least some effort to remember. Feeling excited about the prospect of being in the local paper, I jumped out of bed and started the daily search for clean clothes. Having just located a passable pair of jeans, I was rudely distracted by the house phone ringing. I froze for a few moments to listen whether anybody was going to answer it. The ringing stopped in good time; either my Mum or Dad must have answered the incoming call. "Elaine, it's for you, come quick," my Dad shouted from the bottom of the stairs. He sounded frantic and panicky. Simultaneously my Mum and I burst through our respective bedroom doors and raced down the stairs to where my Dad was standing. He covered the microphone of the handset with the palm of his hand. "It's your mother. She sounds in a terrible state and she is saying that Olive is dead." I dropped to my knees in utter shock. It couldn't be; I had seen her only a couple of days before and she was in fine health. I shook my head in devastation as my Mum desperately tried to calm my Nan down. The only thing to do was to go and see my grandmother to comfort her during her hour of need. I normally would not have volunteered myself for such a task but this was different; I needed to find out whether I too had a problem or not.

I had persuaded my Mum to take her car to see my Nan on the pretence that, if we needed to bring her back, she wouldn't want to ride in a low down, two seater sports car; in reality I just didn't want to bring my distinctive Aston Martin back to the area where I had been only two days previously. By all accounts my Nan was in a complete state and was not making any sense at all; I prayed that there had been a misunderstanding, an error on my Nan's behalf; maybe she wasn't dead but asleep? Upon arriving at my Nan's house, a Police car was parked outside the property which told me that there had been no mistake; Olive had died.

A lady Constable comforted the old lady as she wept into a handkerchief. My Nan hardly acknowledged my Mum and me walk in and try and speak to her. "It's been a terrible shock for Hilda," said the Policewoman with her arm around my Grandmother, "she may need just a little time to grieve." A male officer poked his head around the door, his hi visibility jacket nearly blinding me.

"Everything alright?" he whispered to his colleague. He waited for the woman officer to gently nod her head before he left the room and closed the door behind him. Without excusing myself, I jumped to my feet and left the living room in pursuit of the officer who was waiting patiently in the kitchen with his arms folded. "It's a sad one this," said the officer as I entered the kitchen and opened the back door. I pulled out a cigarette from one of my Nan's boxes that was on her work surface and lit it.

"I take it natural causes were responsible?" I asked nervously before inhaling deeply on my cigarette. The officer was aged somewhere in his mid to late thirties and looked like he had been round the block several times; his look of confusion told me that this wasn't a simple case of nature taking its course.

"Thankfully your Grandmother at the moment has only cause to believe that her best friend died of natural causes, but she did suffer quite a shock and she needs time to find ways of dealing with it." I stuck my head out of the back door and exhaled a plume of blue smoke across the small back garden.

"Something tells me that you guys suspect fowl play," I looked for the slightest reaction in the eyes of the officer as I spoke.

"Put it this way - we are not allowed to process the scene until some officials from London come up and take a look for themselves." I could sense from the officer's tone that this was not the norm.

"What is so interesting about an old age pensioner's dead body?" I inquired, trying to sound as much off the cuff as possible. The officer closed the kitchen door and moved closer to the open back door, "Even if I had them to disclose, I am not in a position to go into details but putting a finer point on it, it seems that this old lady's death was not a symptom of old age." I flicked the butt of my cigarette into the garden and closed the back door. I was aware that this Policeman was duty-bound to keep his silence but I needed to know if this was somehow related to the strange events that myself and Ben had experienced.

"I take it that it was my Nan that found her body?" The officer didn't speak, but just nodded sympathetically. "Was she disfigured in anyway? Or tortured?" My mind started to paint the most gruesome of pictures; I started to regret asking these questions.

"No, she doesn't appear to have gone through any torture or anything like that; in fact, if it helps, she looked most peaceful." I didn't understand.

Realising that I wasn't going to get any further details from the Police at this time, I decided to go back into the living room to console my mother's mother. "Nan, I don't know how this has happened but a little elf seems to have sneaked into your kitchen and stolen a cigarette from your box." I caught just the faintest of a smile from the corner of her mouth. She seemed so desperately down and I knew that I had to try anything to pick up her spirits. The Police officer stood up and asked if my Mum could join her in the hall for a few moments.

"Of course", she replied. "Will you be OK, Mum, for a few minutes?" My Nan remained in silence. I waited until the door of the living room was closed before I went and sat next to her on the sofa. I put my arm around her and was surprised that she instantly returned the gesture; at least she was responding to me, I thought, as we shared a hug together. I found it difficult to know what to say, as I hadn't really ever been in a similar situation before so was unprepared and extremely inexperienced.

"Is it me or are Police Officers getting younger these days?" I realised that talking about Olive wasn't the best subject matter, so I would wait until she raised the subject; until then I would have to talk about everything and anything.

"They make a song and dance about everything these days." I presumed my Nan was still on the subject of the Police, so I didn't interrupt. "I remember the days when they would accompany you across a busy road, step off the pavement for you, carry your shopping, but now it's all silly earpieces and futuristic looking padded black sleeveless cardigans." I paused to think for a moment: *padded black sleeveless cardigans*? "They are bullet proof vests, Nan." It was hard not to find it amusing. "I think their job has got a little tougher these days. Now they get idiots with knives and guns to contend with, so it's easy to understand why some come across stressed and moody." She held my eye contact as I spoke; I seemed to have her full attention.

"It's a dangerous world out there these days." Her voice feeble and weak. "Oh, to think everybody around here would leave their front door unlocked and folk would just wonder in; it was a community back then. Olive's best off out of this world and I hope I'm not long behind." It wasn't unusual for me to hear my Nan speak so negatively. Apparently ever since my Granddad had died some twenty odd years ago, she would often pass comment, when she was down, about joining him in heaven; I guess we just learnt to ignore it over time.

"Everything OK?" I hadn't heard my mother and the female Police Officer enter the room; my Mum sat next to my Nan's other side on the sofa. "Mum, we think that it is best if you come and stay with us for a few weeks; Edward will be home as he seems to have semi-retired so you will have plenty of company."

The Police Officer stepped forward from the door. "It may be for the best, Hilda", she said," the world can seem a very lonely place when you're on your own after such a loss like this." The old and frail lady nodded reluctantly. Without warning, she rose from the sofa.

"I suppose I will have to go and gather some belongings together, put some makeup on and do my hair." She cautiously walked to the door. "You do know don't you that if they are after me, hiding away at your house won't stop them," and with that she closed the living room door behind her.

My mother angrily jumped to her feet and approached the Officer. "Just what the hell is going on here? My Mum clearly suspects something and you lot are being strangely secretive about the body and the scene of death; you have to tell us what is going on." My mother's attack clearly caught the woman off guard, because she backed off and excused herself so she could go and get moral support from her colleague. In only a matter of seconds, she had returned with the male Officer. He sat down on the sofa and invited my Mum to join him, which she did.

"There are irregularities in this death which has cause for suspicion." He glanced back at the door to make sure my Nan had not returned. "Although there are no signs of a break in or of anything having been stolen, we believe that Olive was murdered." My Mum gasped in horror, she clasped her hands over her mouth in an effort to suffocate any noise coming out. "When we arrived at the scene everything looked, if you can say such a thing, normal. As I said, there was no sign of breaking and entering, her body had no evident signs of any cuts or bruises and she looked like she had just passed away peacefully." I felt like we were going round in circles.

"If everything seemed so normal then why were you called, and why do you think it's murder? And more importantly how did my Nan know that she had not died of natural causes?"

He looked me straight in the eyes. "When one of our Officer's examined her body closer, he discovered small round bruising on each of her temples, possibly insignificant, but at this stage we believe that it is bruising from pressure applied from fingers; I'm afraid to say it but it looks like a professional hit." This was starting to sound like some far fetched American crime drama. "But if it was one of your Officers who discovered the bruising, how did Nan know to call you?"

The door abruptly swung open under the force applied by my Grandmother. "I will need my pills which I've left down here somewhere." She started to rifle through one of her drawers. "Can't find anything these days," she mumbled as she discarded the contents of the drawer onto the floor. "Must be in the kitchen." She headed off towards the kitchen. "She never liked dandelions, couldn't stand them." She slammed the door after she had left.

"To explain that remark and answer your question about our suspicions, she found a dandelion in Olive's mouth." The Policeman spoke in just above a whisper. "It could be a possibility that she had it in her mouth before she died, but the fluid that was expelled from her mouth and throat after death would have suggested that the weed would have been pushed out, so it certainly looks to have been placed there post death." I didn't need to hear anymore, I knew from that moment on that Ben and I had a problem; and a very big problem at that. Words from the Policeman washed over my head as I entered into tunnel vision. How long could I go on before the truth came out; I had to speak to Ben, and fast. A tap on the shoulder brought me back to earth; it was my Mum.

"Edward, the Policeman is talking to you." I shook off my trance and retuned myself back to everyone else's wavelength. "I was just saying Edward that if you could try and make sure that your Grandmother does not stray too far, as we will need to take her statement when she is thinking more clearly; and I'm afraid that will apply to yourself and your mother too." Nothing unusual in that, I thought. On the other hand, what might be unusual was the appearance of an Aston Martin in these parts, so I had to concede that the chances of my car not being noticed on Friday were next to nothing. Feeling like a rabbit in the headlights of an oncoming car, I could sense panic starting to set in. I desperately felt the urge to announce that I was there on Friday but I just couldn't bring myself to do it; rationality told me that the last thing I needed right now was to be top of a murder suspect list.

I could see through the living room window a black Vauxhall Vectra come to an aggressive stop outside my Nan's house; sporadic flashing blue lights coming from each top corner of its windscreen were the only visible clue that it was a Police car. Seconds later, a black Range Rover pulled up right behind the Vectra, stopping just as abruptly as the first vehicle, only this time there were no flashing lights.

"I know I'm not supposed to know much about these things because I'm a woman, but is this normal for a death? Even for a murder it seems like overkill." In one go my Mum had summed up my feelings without me having to say a word. With the arrival of the two vehicles, the male Officer stood up and left the room. Within moments of his departure, my Nan entered carrying what appeared to be a lifetime's worth of supplies.

"There's more of them arrived," she moaned before she sat herself down in her armchair. Not for the first time, sensing an awkward silence, my phone started to beep telling me in no uncertain terms that I had just received a text message; for once I was thankful for its distraction. Straight away I pulled my phone from out of my pocket and read the text message. It was from Ben:

Hi dude, just got the paper, crazy stuff we are on the front page, you look pissed in all the photos ha, c u for beers later.

I could see through the window our friendly Policeman chatting to the new arrivals; there were two men and one woman, all three of them dressed in smart casual clothes. They didn't look like Police Officers to me in the slightest. "We will have to buy a paper on the way back Nanna because me and Ben are on the front page." Her head rose slightly with interest but she didn't inquire as to the reason why, so I decided to show her later and explain then.

The door to the living room opened to the noise of crackle from the Policeman's radio. He entered courteously, closely followed by an attractive blonde lady who had arrived in the Land Rover. She crouched down so that she was at eye level with my Mum. "Hello, Mrs. Hamilton. I'm Agent Snowdon. I think everything here is now under control." Her voice was husky as if she was recovering from a cold, very alluring, I thought to myself, as she continued. "I think what the best thing to do now is to take your mother home and give her lots of TLC. We will be round in the morning to take your statements if that is alright with you?" My Mum nodded her head instantly. I tried everything in my power to look on the surface that I was calm and taking everything in my stride, but inside there was a completely different story. 'Agent Snowdon?' I pondered; Agents were certainly not within the ranks of the Police Force, and, unless I was very much mistaken, she belonged to either M16 or MI5; I didn't know the difference and didn't care, because either way this was getting out of control.

Within twenty minutes we had gathered my Nan's stuff into the car and had fastened her safely in. We were going to make a slight detour on the way back and drive past Olive's house, but when we arrived at her road it had been cordoned off with Police blue and white tape. My Nan on the way home did not mention her best friend once. She moaned that she forgot to leave money on the side for the gardener and she moaned that she would miss her hair appointment on the Wednesday, but not once did the word Olive leave her lips. I needed to speak to her before Agent Snowdon and her crew arrived in the morning, because I had to know whether or not Olive had told her about my brief visit on Friday; otherwise I would be in danger of our stories having major discrepancies in them. I would have to wait till later to subtly interrogate her; a few strong gin and tonics would do the trick, as she loved to jibber away after a couple of her favourite tipples. I replied to Ben's text message summoning him to the pub as soon as humanly possible, saying that I needed to speak to him out of ear shot of his mother in an exercise of damage limitation; I couldn't afford for her to be freaked out as well. "I reckon there has been a run of violent break ins, which would explain why there was such a large Police presence there this morning." In normal circumstances my Mum's theory would have been plausible, but what astounded me was that my Mum seemed to have completely forgotten about the dandelion I had discovered in my bed; I was convinced that it would only be a matter of time before she put two and two together. I remained in silence, thankful of the fact that I had not told my Mum that Ben too had found a dandelion in his bed; if that had been general knowledge I would certainly have a hell of a lot of explaining to do.

# *Chapter 21*

# Swindon

*Tuesday 1ˢᵗ September 2008*

The previous evening had not gone as well as I had hoped. I had drunk far too much at the pub with Ben, and, as a consequence I had failed to have a deep and meaningful conversation with my Nan. Even my emergency meeting with my best friend had not managed to settle my nerves in any way; he had taken on board everything I had told him about the previous day's events, but he seemed to believe that it may have been some kind of coincidence about the dandelion. "Old ladies always pick flowers out of the garden, dude." He had explained. "She probably put it in her mouth so she could use her hands." I wasn't convinced at all.

The door bell rang throughout the house; its high tone did nothing to ease my hangover. I pulled the duvet cover over my head and closed my eyes, my bed feeling warm and secure; I wondered how I was going to make it through the day. Again the door bell rang, so I buried my head underneath my pillow but I could still hear the ringing in my ears; I prayed that somebody would answer the door before they pressed the bell for a third time. Even under a layer of two pillows I could still hear my Mum's voice call up the stairs. "Hammy get yourself out of bed, the Police are here." Feeling safe and protected under my duvet and pillows, I debated on whether I should tell the authorities about my presence at Olive's on Friday. If I didn't mention the fact and it came out that I was there then, I would start to look mighty suspicious. Having summoned enough energy to get me out of bed, it only took a minute or so to get myself dressed and flatten down my hair. By the time I had entered the kitchen, Agent Snowdon and her male colleague had already made themselves at home as they sipped mugs of tea round our table; my Nan sat with them seemingly enjoying the occasion. "Edward come and join us," said the old lady on seeing me enter the room. I figured that I actually had no choice so I pulled out a chair and plonked myself down. Agent Snowdon had high cheek bones and a defined jaw line, her shoulder length blonde hair looking slightly messy as if she hadn't had time to make it look perfect; I knew the feeling well. To me she looked almost too delicate and fragile to be a Police Officer, let alone a member of her Majesty's Secret Service. Her eyes were the only part of her body that told you not to mess with her; they looked aged and somewhat cold. Her male partner looked equally attractive and just as distant as Agent Snowdon, his stare firmly fixed on my Nan looking for any reactions as she answered their questions. It was a relief to see that their line of questioning went more along the lines of her being able to help them as opposed to her being a suspect in the case; either way my Nan seemed happy to comply with their thorough questioning. They wanted to know understandable information such as the last time she saw her best friend? Did she appear to be acting normal? Did she see anything or anyone out of place? Everything that you would expect them to ask and she obliged willingly. It was only after they had asked their questions to my Mum that I realised something was up. Snowdon downed her remaining tea and rose from the table. "Thank you everyone for your time. I think that is everything we need for now. If we need to ask any further questions then we will pop round at a later date." I didn't understand why she had not asked me one question even though Agent Snowdon yesterday had told me that they would want my Nan's, Mum's and my statements. Like a predator turning to its prey, she looked down at me. "I see by the calendar on your fridge that you and a Ben have an appointment with your Bank Manager at ten pm. Allow us to give you a ride; it's the least we can do." I knew that I wasn't being asked and that they were actually telling me in a very polite fashion that they wanted to speak to me away from my family members; it was blatantly obvious that these guys were smooth operators.

"Mate, get out of bed quick, I will be round in ten minutes." Without giving Ben a chance to respond, I hung up the phone and closed my front door behind me and headed towards the black Range Rover Sport. I had opened the back left hand door fully and was about to get in before Agent Snowdon called out: "Take shotgun Edward; I'm getting quite familiar with the back seat now." Not wanting to question her, I obediently opened the front passenger seat and jumped in; moments later the man got into the driver's seat. "Normal procedure is to have you in the back but on this occasion we thought you might like to ride up front, and we don't want your friend getting freaked out, he will feel more at ease with you in the passenger seat." Their psychological mind games were completely wasted on me, as I still would have been shit scared sitting in the back, and something told me that seeing his best friend sitting in the front seat, Ben would still be mightily overwhelmed. My door had barely shut before the driver started the engine and slammed the vehicle into first gear.

"It's number 6..." Snowdon didn't allow me to finish my sentence before interrupting:

"We know his address Edward, or do we call you Hammy?"

My patience was starting to run out. "Who the hell are you guys? I'm sorry to come over so aggressive but what the fuck is going on?" My little outburst made me feel a little better, if not calmer. I sensed Agent Snowdon move forward in her seat, as she spoke for the first time as if she cared for me.

"Hammy, to save me having to explain this twice would it be cool if we waited a few minutes to pick up Ben and then I will explain all." It was a fair request and one that I was agreeable to. As we were only seconds away from Ben's house, I afforded the time. Surprisingly, the driver killed the throttle and dropped the anchors about ten properties before Ben's house.

"Give him a quick call and tell him to walk down the street a little. We don't want his parents getting hysterical if it can be avoided." Once again the driver demonstrated that they knew what they were doing.

Several minutes after calling Ben, he appeared from the end of his drive, struggling to put his coat on; his messy hair told me that we had caught him off guard. He swiftly opened the back seat behind the driver and climbed in. He looked strangely composed and undeterred by the situation. "Morning all." His chirpy greeting was peculiarly uplifting. We drove for roughly twenty minutes before we pulled over in a lay-by on a quiet country road; it was evident that our meeting with the bank manager was not going to be honoured. From the moment we stopped, it seemed that Ben was intent on putting his interrogators on the back foot. "So guys, remind me which county's Police Force drives around in black Range Rover Sports?" I had to agree with my best friend that it was time for answers. The driver turned his body so he could see both Ben and myself.

"For Ben's benefit my name is Agent Deacon and this is my colleague Agent Snowdon and we are part of an intelligence team with M15. I apologise for dragging you away from your homes but we thought it best to speak to you alone." It didn't take Sherlock Holmes to understand that this had little to do with Olive's death. "To cut the bullshit we have been observing a vicious Russian terrorist organisation operating out of London and we have had them under surveillance for over eighteen months now believing that they were involved in a terrorist plot to attack London."

Ben shook his head. "Excuse me for only achieving a Grade C at GCSE in English but I am really failing to understand what this has to do with the price of fish?" Ben had a wonderful way with words when his temper was being tested.

Snowdon came to her colleague's aid. "Although we have been able to tap a handful of their phone lines, it has been next to impossible to get one of our agents into their inner circle, and believe me it has not been through lack of trying." She reached into her jacket pocket and retrieved a packet of cigarettes. "Not Marlborough Lights I'm afraid boys but you're welcome to have one." Without any hesitation, I reached over and took one and I was followed by Ben close behind me. After giving us the use of her disposable lighter, she continued to explain: "Over the past month, activity within this cell has increased significantly with no suggestions of any terrorist bomb or attack on civilian life." I wasn't liking what I was hearing, and when I glanced at Ben, the look in his eyes confirmed that we were in deep, deep water.

Agent Deacon took over from Snowdon. "A word that we have to presume is a codeword that keeps popping up is 'dandelion'. This word has only started being used in the last four weeks and we believe that you chaps are significantly involved with this word." I had been listening so intently that I had allowed my cigarette to go out. I felt like I had never needed a hit of nicotine more now than I ever had. "It was only when the Wiltshire Police Force informed us that the old lady had been found with a dandelion in her mouth that we knew this was related; it had to be. Several weeks ago we put a call out to all Police Forces in England, Scotland, Ireland and Wales instructing them that if they stumbled across any unusual event that somehow related to a dandelion then we must be informed, and what do you know, three weeks later here we are." Ben threw his half smoked cigarette out of the window and exhaled all of the smoke from his lungs before he spoke.

"Is that when you decided to pick up two mates because one of them is the grandson of Olive's best friend? Brilliant thinking; I can see how you two got to be spies." I couldn't help but smile. "You're not concerned that one of the most ferocious terrorist groups in the world who makes the Taliban look like Primary School children have you on their radar? That doesn't make you concerned one little bit?"

"It makes me fucking shit scared but I don't understand what the fuck we have to do with all of this?" My Mum had brought me up never to swear in the presence of a woman but these circumstances warranted strong language to say the least; I felt like crapping in my pants.

'No income tax, no VAT, no money back, no guarantee.' My phone started to ring to the chorus of only fools and horses. A quick glance at my mobile told me that it was my work calling. No sooner had I answered it and told the person on the other end of the line that I was in consultation with 007 and Miss Moneypenny, Snowdon had grasped the phone from me and ended the call. "If this is the first time you have encountered a dandelion within the last month then you're free to walk away," she paused as she looked at us both deep in the eyes. "That's what we thought; I suggest that it may be wise to listen to what we have to say, because, you never know, it may just save your lives." She released her seatbelt as she continued to explain. "We don't know why it is that they seem to know all about you, and actually we don't care. It would be mightily helpful if we had the whole picture but that is not the reason why we are here; we need your help." My heart was starting to beat so rapidly that it was physically making me feel sick. Ben's pale face suggested that he was is the same boat. Deacon licked his lips and swallowed.

"We believe that Olive's murder was a mere warning to you both, and if we are correct, you will also have had less sincere warnings possibly involving dandelions. We think that through Olive they wanted to illustrate that they are not afraid to kill."

"Talking of killing, you two made a killing selling your almost non-existent T-shirt Company for vast amounts of money." It genuinely spooked me as to how much they had learnt about us.

"How do you think the likes of us can help you?" asked Ben changing the subject away to something a little more comfortable. Snowdon was the first to reply.

"We believe that they will shortly contact you directly. To be frank, if they wanted you dead, then you would be six feet under by now, so, for some reason, they want you alive." Julian suddenly entered into my head, and the chilling realisation dawned on me that it must have been him behind all of this. He must have passed information on, since, apart from Lawrence and Nigel back at Champers, Julian was the only one to know about the casement. It didn't sit right though; Julian would have had more to lose than us, and it didn't add up that he could possibly be a grass. I dispelled the thought there and then. "When they contact you we want you to report back to us immediately. Whatever you are involved in, we are not interested; we just want this cell." Snowdon sounded slightly desperate. "We have enough dirt on this lot to get them sent down, but we just can't get our hands on them, so we need to use you two as bait." I was starting to wish we had never found the port.

"What makes you so sure that they will contact us?" The thought alarmed me; I wasn't prepared for anything like this.

"They probably have you under surveillance. In fact, I would be very surprised if they didn't." Snowdon sounded cold again and very businesslike. "They know your addresses, your place of work Hammy, and your Grandmother's address; they appear to have an unhealthy obsession with you two gentlemen." Ben started to chuckle nervously.

"This has got to be some sort of windup: MI5, Russian gangs; this just can't be real." I studied the faces of the agents, their expressions suggested nothing about windups or sophisticated jokes. They were deadly serious.

A slow passing Mercedes instantly put the agents on high alert. Instinctively drawing upon their vigorous training, they pulled out from concealment a handgun each. Without taking their eyes off the passing car they pushed us down into our seats.

"We must look well dodgy if that car wasn't full of Russians," but nobody responded to Ben. After a couple of moments I lifted my head up from my lap.

"How do you know we haven't committed a crime? You say you don't want to know why we seem to be in this mess yet we could be murderers for all you two know." It just didn't sit right; this was MI5, who want to know everything. I had no doubts that if they knew the truth, then they would have no hesitation in locking us up and throwing away the key. Snowdon opened her cigarette packet and pulled one out.

"Fuck it, got to die of something." She quickly lit the end and inhaled deeply. "From where I am sitting, the only detail of your lives that could possibly warrant a little closer inspection is the sale of Boulette Boarding; however, I'm sure that this drug-smuggling, arms-dealing gang isn't particularly interested in that." She took another long drag and exhaled the smoke inside the car. "It is evident from what we have learnt about them that they don't seem to harbour any particular malice against you both, but believe me these guys have a nasty habit of crucifying their opponents; and I mean literally crucify." I instinctively shook my head in terror. It was crystal clear we were sailing up the creek with a paddle nowhere to be seen, so I had to throw these people a bone; no matter how small. I prayed that Ben would go with my flow and not drop any extra unwanted details into the conversation.

"Apart from the sale of our little business there is something that we have done that is extremely out of the ordinary." Deacon turned to face me, and almost looked to be in pain from the suspense. "A few weeks ago, before we went away on holiday, we found an old underground bunker, bizarre I know, but inside were a couple of ancient Spitfire windscreens still in their boxes." They both looked to be devouring my bone. "To cut a long story short, we sold them on eBay and made some good pennies for them; you

would be amazed at how many plane weirdos there are out there."
Snowdon digested and processed my words before she spoke.

"Well I didn't see that one coming." Ben just stared blankly
out of the window. "I'm assuming that this bunker was on
Ministry of Defence property?" I didn't have time to figure out
whether I was digging my hole a little deeper.

"Sort of... well no, ...it was on the Honda factory site over on
the east side of Swindon." Snowdon looked to her colleague.

"That means absolutely nothing to me. Is it on an old airfield or
something?" Before Deacon could respond I jumped straight in.

"Turns out it was an airfield built during the Second World
War. Are we in the shit now?" Snowdon swept back her hair the
reveal her whole face, and she shook her head.

"We should report you to the MOD for theft of their property.
If that bunker was underground you can add trespassing to that
as well, but I think we can forget those minor details if you play
ball with us." Deacon decided to contribute to the conversation.

"It does not seem feasible that relics of old planes would
warrant the attention of this gang. After all, if they wanted them
so badly then all they had to do was bid for them; it must be
something else guys."

Agent Deacon started the engine and slowly pulled away.
"We will drop you back at your homes. Think you have missed
the Bank Manager I'm afraid." An uneasiness descended upon
my body, a feeling that I had not experienced before.

"Is that it? You're just going to drop us off and that's it? You
can't just drag us around the countryside and tell us that some
crazy and psychopathic Russian gang are after us, and then just
fucking drop us off back at home." My little outburst seemed to
surprise these hardened MI5 field agents.

"Hammy, as we said, if these Ruskies wanted you dead, you
would most certainly have been nailed to a wooden cross and
crucified by now." Ben looked to be utterly petrified.

"These guys religious then? If so, that's fucking twisted,
why hang them?" I hoped with all my heart that Ben could hold
himself together for just a little longer.

Snowdon continued: "they don't crucify the same way that Jesus was crucified. The Russian Mafia seem to insist on nailing people to crosses with their legs hanging straight, whereas the Romans back in Jesus' day hung people with their ankles crossed; not that that irrelevant fact will help you sleep better at night." I went to turn on the car radio before Deacon's hand swiftly intercepted my arm and pushed it back into my body.

As I sat there, I wasn't convinced that they had covered all the angles. Addressing nobody in particular I decided to offload my troubles. "Assuming that your theory is right and these Russian monkeys do contact us, what are we supposed to do? Excuse ourselves and ask to borrow their phone quickly?" Ben chuckled flippantly to himself whilst Agents Deacon and Snowdon looked deeply into each other's eyes for a second, but they didn't need long to gather their composure and respond to my ramblings; Snowdon took the lead.

"We would like to put a tracking device on that rather lovely Aston of yours and your van too, Ben. We would recommend that you put our personal mobile numbers into your speed dial in your phones. Then familiarise yourself with phoning us from your pocket; that way, if shit hits the fan, you have some small chance of contacting us smartly and discreetly." Both Ben and I agreed to have tracking devices fitted to our vehicles. That apparently could be done in a matter of seconds. Once again the agents assured us that death wasn't something that we had to fear; for the moment anyway. They dropped the both of us back at my parent's house, and then they were gone without a so much of a goodbye or good luck.

Naturally my Mum, Dad and Gran were eager to get all the gory details from our time with the agents, they were somewhat surprised to hear that we had not quite managed to honour our appointment with the Bank Manager. Having taken the opportunity to consume half a cup of tea around the kitchen table with my family and my best friend, I decided to feed them the same story that I had fed the agents. Taking at least half an hour, I explained in detail how the two of us had located the bunker and had discovered, and sold several Spitfire windscreens. As expected, my Mum was horrified and quickly started to doubt her method of bringing up children; my Dad, on the other hand, seemed to be more enthusiastic. "You two reprobates found Spit windscreens? Worth a small fortune I imagine gents?" He then proceeded to tell a story how one of his old school friends had found an old Spitfire seat and had managed to get several hundred pounds for it by placing an advert in the local paper. Although I did mention the existence of the crazy Russian gang, the details were so diluted that in the end I made them sound like a loveable, charitable organisation on a humanitarian mission from the Far East; either way they didn't particularly appear to be disturbed or alarmed. Understandably what everybody wanted to know was whether Olive's death had anything to do with my and Ben's shenanigans, so I spared no detail in explaining that these events were in no way connected and that everybody could sleep easy; my words soothed everybody, apart from my dearest mother. I had also elected to avoid the subject of dandelions. With my mother possibly still aware that I had discovered one in my bed, I figured that if she became privy to the knowledge that dandelions were the back bone of their investigation, this information could have quite easily sent her over the edge of sanity.

# Chapter 22

# Swindon

*Tuesday 2ⁿᵈ September 2008*

It was fair to say that since the departure of Ralph from Knight Allen Estate Agents, and coupled with my rapid exit from the company, many of our competitors were starting to take advantage of Knight Allen's sudden weaknesses. Other smaller companies who historically couldn't touch us were now starting to turn the screws on us; Knight Allen's property stock was diminishing rapidly as other agents took advantage of the low staff levels taking vital business away from our books onto theirs; all in all it was a sorry state of affairs. Understandably, the few staff that were in the office when I walked in wearing scruffy casual clothes were over the moon to see me; it was most obvious that morale had hit rock bottom. Justin jumped up from his chair the moment he got off the phone. "Hay Hammy, great to see you my friend. I take it you have decided to come back and save us?" He shook my hand firmly and affectionately. I didn't recognise two members of the team, one an extremely attractive dark haired young girl and an older man dressed exquisitely in a tailored suit. The new faced man quickly introduced himself as Steve, the Acting Branch Manager.

"I think we have spoken on the phone before, Hammy." He was correct. I had taken an instant disliking of him before on the telephone as well as now. He walked over to his desk and started to fumble around in his top draw. "I know all the info is here somewhere." I discreetly turned to face Justin, who silently and subtly did the wanker sign with his right hand.

"Here it is. Funny you should come in today, Hamster, 'cos we have taken a phone call from the vendors of the big Manor House you are valuing on Friday. They wanted to know if there was any chance that you may be able to do it earlier?" He handed me the property information form, which I studied to see if I recognised any of the names, which I didn't.

"Don't you fancy doing it yourself then Steve?" He ever so slightly blushed as he contemplated his response.

"I would love to value something on this scale but your reputation precedes you, Hamster, and if there is more chance of you winning the business, then I am happy to take a back seat." *I bet you are*, I thought to myself, as I handed him back the paperwork.

"No worries, if you ring them and tell them that I can do it tomorrow morning at ten, then that will give me enough time to pop in beforehand and gather all my stuff together."

Knowing that I had to be as subtle as subtle can be, I was curious to find out if I had had any unusual visitors or telephone calls since I had been away from the office. If these Russians were so efficient and thorough, then it would have made perfect sense for them to have tried to approach me at my place at work. "Apart from Angelina Jolie, has there been anybody inquiring after me or anybody wondering what I was up to or how I was doing?" Justin started to laugh out loud.

"Oh yes, how could we forget? There has been nobody asking after you apart from your beloved Mr. Stephens, who comes in every single fucking day with his stupid walking stick and asks after you." That was good to hear, and nice to know that I had made an impression on somebody over all those years of hard graft.

"What about Ralph? Has anybody heard from him recently?" Everyone shook their heads simultaneously. I found it almost unbelievable that Ralph had not been in touch, because I knew that he was not the type of person to be able to switch off from work so quickly and readily; something wasn't sitting right with me. I studied the faces of my colleagues, who didn't appear to be hiding anything; I would have certainly have been able to tell on Justin's face as he was far too honest.

Steve perched himself on the edge of a desk that was closest to me. He was slightly overweight and his shirt was on the tad small side; his exposed belly button was not the greatest of sights. "So Hamster, you're rolling in it by all accounts. How much did you pocket from selling Bou whatever?" This man's bluntness somewhat surprised me, as I didn't know him from Adam yet here he was addressing me as if we were best buddies.

"Firstly if I could just mention, my name is Hammy, not Hamster, and secondly it's not really any of your business how much I am worth." He folded his arms and his relaxed smirk told me that he wasn't really taking onboard anything I was saying. "What I will tell you is that it's made me enough pennies to rag around in an Aston and to put me in a position to look for a couple of decent properties. It's a shame, judging by what stock you currently have on display, that I have to keep on looking." I knew that it was a shot below the belt, and I didn't want to direct any Mickey taking towards anyone else apart from the Acting Branch Manager. I wouldn't have to deal with him for much longer so I really didn't care what insults were directed his way. It was alarming that in the space of a week my office had been stripped bare of all its best and most sellable properties,

properties that myself and Ralph had worked tirelessly on to get them onto our books. As certain properties popped into my head, I found it hard to resist asking what had happened to them. However, deep down I knew that I didn't need to ask; they had either been poached by other agents or come off the market completely, an ego booster to say the least. I could think of at least twenty properties that were absent from the window displays, all of my vendors that had bought into me and not particularly the company that I worked for, clearly had vanished from the scene the moment I had.

At that particular moment in time the thought of setting my own Estate Agency had crossed my mind on more than one occasion. After all, I now had the funds that meant I would be able to sleep well at bed times. I chuckled to myself as the thought popped into my head again as I stood opposite Steve. I promised myself that if I ever did get my arse into gear, then I would poach the best of Steve's staff, the best of my former colleagues; that would include Ralph if he ever bothered to return any of my calls. "So how long have you been with the company, Steve?" I asked knowing full well from his appearance that he hadn't been with them for long. With a company policy of only allowing pastel coloured shirts, Steve's terrible bright mustard coloured shirt told me that he had not yet received a Royal bollocking from the Area Manager yet for not complying with the strict dress code. Knight Allen also frowned heavily upon any shoe that was not made from highly polished black leather, something which I fought long and hard against as I preferred to wear highly polished brown leather shoes. I argued that if brown shoes were good enough for the English rugby team when they met the Queen after their historic World Cup win, then it was good enough for Knight Allen, but apparently not. My employer simply would not budge, so I was reduced to having to keep a pair of black shoes sitting in reserve in my desk bottom drawer just in case we were sprung a surprise visit by our hierarchy.

"I'm new to agency actually. I was based in the Bristol office for the last three weeks prior to coming here." I had forgotten that I had asked Steve a question; I awkwardly attempted to portray that I was interested in what he was saying. Knowing that I didn't have to be at work against my will I decided to pop a few doors down the street to Champers. Hopefully Lawrence and Nigel would both be there.

I was not surprised to see that the shop had a good number of customers browsing the many different varieties of alcohol on offer, and it was a relief to hear both the owners laughing away behind the shop counter; it didn't take long for the laughter to stop. "Edward, it's great to see you again. I suspected that you might be on a beach by now in some corner of the globe." Lawrence's words made me awash with paranoia. *How could he be so unsubtle?* I thought, as I made my way through the seemingly deaf customers to the counter. "We saw your and Ben's picture in the paper getting very intoxicated in some swank bar, so you sold your company did you Hammy?" Nigel winked at me; I knew exactly what he was getting at.

"I just came in to thank you for putting me in contact with Julian; as I am sure you can imagine the meetings went very well." Nigel and Lawrence glanced at each other.

"Meetings?" They both said simultaneously. "Things must have gone well!" Lawrence looked over my shoulder. "I'll just serve this customer, quickly." A fat elderly lady slammed two bottles of red wine down on the counter.

"Your prices are extortionate," she hackled. I closed my eyes and shook my head. It didn't take a crystal ball to figure out what Lawrence was thinking, and I prayed that he would keep his quick wit to himself.

"Our prices are very competitive when it comes to quality spirits and fine wines. Sure, you can go to a supermarket and buy some thoroughly horrible vinegar resemblance for a matter of pennies, but I'm afraid you have to pay a little more for quality." Here it came: "just for your information people pay thousands," Lawrence looked me in the eye, "tens of thousands, and hundreds of thousands for a truly exquisite tipple." She reluctantly handed over a ten pound note. Lawrence wrapped the bottles in paper and handed her a penny change. "You see, you can even get change madam from ten pounds." She bundled the bottles of wine under her arm and started to mumble to herself as she left the shop. I decided to browse a few shelves to occupy myself until such a time as the shop was less busy. I could hear that Lawrence and Nigel were in no mood for their usual chit chat with their faithful customers. Instead, they appeared to be serving them and getting them turned around and out as fast as possible.

After I had picked up and examined a dozen or so bottles of whiskey, the shop had emptied itself of customers and Lawrence walked around from his position and perched himself on the customer side of the counter. "By all means tell me to sod off, but did you really sell your company or was it some truly spectacular money laundering scam?" Nigel walked round to join him.

"That's right", he said, "when we saw you in the paper with a rather generous write up on your success I instantly thought: you clever fucking bastard!" Even though Nigel was from the upper classes, he used swear words like they were going out of fashion.

Lawrence rubbed his hands together. "You can trust us, Hammy. We did put you in touch with Julian in the first place, and we won't breathe a word; I promise." I knew that Lawrence was telling the truth, and he was also correct in the fact that I could trust him. He simply would have nothing to gain in telling anybody about it. Having thought about it for a couple of seconds, I concluded that it would actually benefit me from them knowing the entire story; I would miss out details about Olive, dandelions and MI5 but, apart from that, they would know everything.

Having told them in great depth how we had met Julian in the first place, and then the second time clinching the deal, I decided that it would make perfect sense to ask them if they had seen anything out of the ordinary. It seemed to be logical that if a gang of some description was after our blood, then it had something to do with the port we had found. If they were using their heads they would have worked out that the one place we would go in Swindon with extremely rare booze would be Champers. I scanned the shop until I was satisfied that no customers had crept in unnoticed. "Since I showed you the bottle of port, have you had any unusual visitors or any one particularly out of the ordinary ask any weird questions?"

Both the men in front of me raised their eyebrows. "Are you having problems?" asked Nigel protectively. I really didn't know what to say; I wanted to tell them absolutely everything, the truth and nothing but the truth, but something was holding me back.

"Thinking about it, you do look like a man with big worries on his shoulders, a problem shared and all of that mumbo jumbo." Lawrence was right; I did feel the desperate urge to lighten my load and after all these two men, apart from Ben, were probably the only people in the world I could talk to and have them fully understand my precarious predicament.

With Nigel agreeing to switch the open sign to closed in the window for ten minutes, I was free to pour my heart out. They listened intently as I went into the tiniest detail; I explained how we had been whisked away by MI5 field agents and how they were in pursuit of a fearless Russian gang; I even told them about the dandelions. "That's bloody creepy." Gasped Nigel. "I had an awful feeling that your discovery would bring with it some difficult situations, but this is just off the scale. The answer to your question is no; we have not had any criminal types sniffing around, or that I know of anyway." Nigel started to look a little uncomfortable. "If there is a lunatic gang running around after your casement, who's to say they won't turn up here and trash the place looking for any clues. It makes perfect sense; I would if I was looking for something that specific." It was undeniable that Nigel had a point, and it was something that had already crossed my mind.

"Maybe they have already been here? Maybe they took a discreet look around and realised there was nothing here for them," I said lamely trying to ease his fears. He scratched his head and looked worried but calm all the same.

"Have you spoken to Julian about any of this?" At least Nigel was thinking straight.

"He isn't aware of anything; he is living in blissful ignorance. I had thought about telling him of course, but what do you say? Julian, by the way there is possibly a Russian gang after your head that has a tendency of hanging its opponents." Lawrence swore under his breath before the front door started to shake in its frame, and a loud tapping followed. I turned around to face the front door; it was Jess my former colleague. I couldn't help but smile. I could see her straining to look through the window.

"Hammy you twat, I'm late for an appointment and you have the bloody shop shut again, what is it with you?" Lawrence leaned back and just about managed to reach a packet of Marlboro Lights.

"Shove these through the letter box, Edward, and tell her she can have them for gratis." With a skip in my step, I strode over to the front door, but Jess shook her head as she pushed open the letter box with the tips of her fingers.

"It could only be you, Hammy!" Being careful not to slam my fingers on the stiff flap, I shoved the packet of cigarettes through the letter box into Jess's grateful hands.

Nigel made sure himself that Jess had properly gone by peering out of the window as far down the street as he could see, and then turned the closed sign to open in a mild attack of paranoia. "It's probably best that we don't do anything out of the ordinary for a little while." He bent down and started to tie his shoelace; even though it was already done up. "It's odd that these agents don't seem to want to learn more about the sale of your T-shirt Company, or why you and Ben don't appear to be murder suspects in that poor old ladies murder case." He laboured as he stood up and straightened his back. "What also seems peculiar is the fact that MI5 can't nail these mother fuckers. More to the point they are willing to use, well shall we say non-secret-agent material, to set a trap for them. Surely if they have all of this undeniable evidence against them, there must have been windows of opportunities where they could have gone in and busted their arses, so why use you two to catch them?" There was no doubt in my mind that Snowdon and Deacon worked for MI5, because they had been expected by the Police at my

Nan's house and when they arrived they mingled happily with the Police Officers.

"We are simply fish bait but God knows how these crazy Russians have us on their radar and how those MI5 spooks know this."

Nigel looked petrified, as he tip toed over to where I was standing and whispered into my ear: "are you wearing a wire?"

I quickly shook my head. "No that's the thing. If they asked me to wear a wire or listening device, then if this gang does get hold of me they are certainly going to want to talk about port before they kill me."

Lawrence scratched his chin deep in thought. "I know this may sound obvious but how do you know that they are after you for the port? You may have ripped a gang member off by selling them a dodgy house or something. You never know, you might have shagged one of their daughters!" Lawrence couldn't help but chuckle to himself.

"It has to be because of that port, because we found the dandelions in our beds not long after the discovery, and of course, Olive died with a dandelion in her mouth very soon after I had collected the port from her house; they have to be after the port but I just can't understand how the hell they know we had it."

Lawrence and Nigel looked at each other uncomfortably; Nigel was the first to speak: "you must believe us, Hammy, when we say that we have not told a living soul, apart from Julian of course."

Lawrence took over: "and it goes without saying that Julian would not say a word to anybody, and I'm pretty sure that would include his wife and family; besides he would have far too much to lose if he did start talking to anybody." It was really starting to get to me how these villains got to know about mine and Ben's existences, and it went without saying that Ben would not have told a living soul and it was obvious the wine shop owners had not said a thing to anybody; as far as I was aware that was all the people who knew about the casement of port.

I promised to keep Lawrence and Nigel informed of every development, no matter how small, as they were clearly genuinely worried about everybody's wellbeing. Having left the shop after saying my goodbyes to the owners, I decided that I would delay going back into the office until the morning; it was too nice a day to be stuck inside talking to estate agents.

# Chapter 23

# North Wiltshire

*Wednesday 3rd September 2008*

I had done miraculously well to collect everything I needed from the office, negotiate my way through heavy traffic and to find the place on time, well within five minutes which was close enough for me. It was only once I stepped out of my car that I realised the shear beauty and size of the Manor House before me; it was truly magnificent. Finding the property had been hard enough with it being located at the end of a long, sweeping gravel drive that was accessed via two imposing gothic, iron gates. The slate roof had an unusually shallow pitch that went nearly as low as the ground floor windows, the first floor windows being set in the roof itself and protruding out a couple of feet with small apexes above them. The property was host to two exceptionally high brick chimneys, one on the gable end of the house and one that dissected the middle of the roof. There was no sign of any cars parked on the drive; I presumed that the Bentleys and Jaguars would be locked away safely in some multiple garages round the back somewhere.

I made sure that my tie was straight and I had no fluff on my suit before I banged on the heavy panelled front door I was excited to see this property, even if I didn't have the foggiest idea as to what asking price I would put on it yet. I waited for about thirty seconds before I knocked again, only much harder this time. I was just about to pull out my phone, take a discreet photo of the front of the house and quickly fire it back to the office so they could help on the valuing, when the front door opened abruptly. "Mrs. Taylor?" I respectfully inquired. In the doorway in front of me stood an overweight woman aged in her early sixties. It was evident that she had fallen out of the ugly tree at birth and banged her head on every single branch on the way down; she was one of the most scariest woman I ever had the misfortune of meeting. She wore a black and white stripy top that did nothing for her already unpleasant figure and her hair was manly short; it amazed me that she was a Mrs.

"You're late," she snapped in a common accent as she opened the door fully for me to enter. I figured that she must be the cleaner or cook or something along those lines. My wariness of the unwelcome host soon passed the moment I stepped into the Entrance Hall which was elegant to say the least; the wall to which the stairs were attached had exposed brick work that gave it a rustic charm, whilst the perfect plasterwork on the remaining walls was a reminder as to what decade we were in. Shining silver fittings on the door handles, light switches and power sockets worked wonderfully with the polished wooden floorboards and stained black beams on the ceiling. It was hard not to stare at two matching sized paintings that hung on the wall facing the stairs, surrounded in lavish gold frames and depicting scenes from bloody and gruesome battles from our forgotten past. "You're not here to gawp at the artwork," she hissed, as she opened one of the several doors that led off the hallway. "Go inside and make yourself right at home, and Mr. Smith will be with you shortly."

I was ushered into a large drawing room that let in no sunlight whatsoever. There were four, full length bay windows with wooden shutters that were closed; the only light came from a number of wall lights dotted around the room sporadically giving off a dim glow. What struck me foremost was the furniture, or lack of it, should I say? For a room this large, I was amazed to see that it contained only a brown leather arm chair and a small mahogany side table with a glass and a bottle of water on top of it. The walls were bare with no artwork or family photographs. Even the large mantelpiece above the sizable stone fireplace had no clutter or ornaments. *Mrs. Taylor's got an easy job cleaning this place*, I mused to myself. I elected not to sit in the appealing armchair; instead I opted to stand casually by the empty fireplace; after all there were no paintings to pretend to admire. After what in reality was seconds, but felt more like hours, an extremely tall man marched into the room. His charcoal grey suit and black shirt made him look like an extra from the Godfather trilogy; he introduced himself as Mr. Smith and shook my hand with some strength. Although he spoke impeccable English, and he may have been an Oxford or Cambridge graduate, there was something foreign about his accent, something so faint it was next to impossible to detect where he came from. He started to shake the mobile phone he was holding. "Bloody things; always die when you need them the most." He put the phone down on the table next to the bottle of water and empty glass. "Would you be so kind to excuse me for a brief moment?" Before I could answer, he paced over to the door he had entered through. "Mrs. Taylor, do you have your mobile phone on you?" He shouted ensuring she would definitely have heard him no matter where she was in the house. He waited a few moments before her voice came echoing through the room.

"No I left it at home." As if annoyed by her response, he slammed the door closed behind him.

"I'm sorry to ask you this but would it be possible to borrow your phone? Our landline has been cut off as we are moving out over the next couple of days." That explained the distinct lack of furniture, I thought, as I pulled my phone out from my pocket and handed it to him. He took it from me and glanced at it quickly. "Very nice. I hope you don't mind but I have asked another estate agent to come round with us. As I'm sure you can imagine, it will take some time giving you the guided tour so I thought it best to get two valuations at the same time. Unlike you, however, they are late so I'm just going to give their office a quick call and see where the hell they have got to." That was music to my ears. It wasn't terribly unusual for people to get a couple of valuations done at the same time, and although I normally didn't like it, on this occasion I would be grateful of a professional second opinion on the value of the property and I was happy that the opposition was late. He excused himself and left the room closing the door behind him, so I decided to take advantage of the comfy leather seat that was sitting in the middle of the room invitingly.

I waited, and waited, and then waited some more, and I couldn't believe the cheek of this other agent being this late; I couldn't wait to find out who it was. Trying to fight the boredom that was setting in, I decided to do a lap of the generously sized room pressing on every wooden panel that I passed. I was aware that some manor houses built in the same era as this one sometimes had small, hidden passageways and tunnels built into the walls that were often concealed behind wooden panelling. They would serve as an exit from the house often to nearby vicarages. I had learnt on one occasion about a colleague finding a passageway that was used by smugglers to secretly enter the property when the house was under surveillance by local authorities. I of course didn't find anything but it certainly helped to pass some of the time; it also stopped my mind from wondering what was going on, for a few minutes anyway. I glanced at my watch; I had been at the property for nearly twenty-five minutes and all I had seen was the Entrance Hall and the bare Drawing Room. Deciding that I would go and see how Mr. Smith was getting on in tracking down the absent estate agent, I turned the handle of the door through which he had departed and pushed; it didn't budge, and it was apparent that I had been locked in the room. Feeling a little uncomfortable under the collar I shouted out: "hello, is anyone there? I seem to be locked in." I waited for a reply; any kind of response would have done but nothing came. Not wanting to look impatient or make a fool out of myself, I decided to sit back down in the armchair and wait; it was unthinkable that they had forgotten about me in such a short space of time so I conceded that the best course of action was to sit and wait patiently. I wouldn't have to wait long before I was in human company again.

Unlike before, when the door had been locked, I could hear the key in the lock slowly turn followed by the handle turning; I thanked the Gods that I had not been forgotten. I watched as the door slowly opened and in walked Mr. Smith. He nodded his head and spoke in a broad eastern accent. "Hammy; sorry for your wait." Alarm bells started to ring straight away, and I could feel my heart pounding so hard in my chest that I actually thought that it was going to break my skin. Questions started to race through my head; *how in God's name did he know that I was called Hammy?* And more worryingly, at long last I was able to place his accent; he was unmistakeably Russian. Knowing that I was deep in the shit, I couldn't help but admire how he had managed to get me into a dark and locked room, miles away from anywhere with no mobile phone; fucking genius. Mr. Smith, or whatever his real name was, pulled out a packet of foreign cigarettes. "Not Marlborough Lights, I am afraid my friend, but it's a smoke all the same." He held out the packet for me to take one; even though I was desperate for a nicotine hit, I shook my head. I wasn't in any mood for taking any handouts from my kidnapper. "Very well, Hammy, your choice. Now without any further delay, I would like to introduce you to a friend of mine, and funnily enough a friend of yours too." My mind started to race, there was little doubt that I was moments away from being introduced to some torturer who was going to take great delight in taking out my eyeballs and feeding them to me with tomato ketchup. Like waiting for a penalty kick by my beloved Swindon Town football club, I hung on the edge of my seat in anticipation, waiting for somebody to show themselves in the doorway; once again I wasn't made to wait for long.

"You have got to be fucking kidding me; this has got to be some kind of fucked up joke." My words didn't seem to reach the figure standing in the doorway. Even though the man's outline in front of me was deep in shadow, there was no mistaking who stood in front of me cowering behind the shadows.

"Hammy it's wonderful to see you again. You appear to have lost weight. Is being a millionaire not suiting you then?" I was dumbstruck, I knew what words I wanted to say and what order they should come out in but I had apparently lost the ability to talk. The blackened figure stepped forwards a couple of paces, closed and locked the door behind him; for the first time I was aware of other people lurking in the shadows in the Entrance Hall. "Sorry about luring you into this little trap but I really didn't know how else to get you alone." He pulled out of his breast pocket a pair of glasses and put them on so they just rested on the end of his nose. "You see, Hammy, we painted such a glamorous picture of this glorious house that nobody will be expecting you back for at least three hours." Ralph was right, valuations on properties this size could take all afternoon and Ralph, my former friend and boss, knew this all to well.

"Ralph, excuse me for not thinking straight but I really haven't got a clue as to what the fuck is going on here. Are you planning on telling me?" Ralph smirked and nodded; he calmly walked over to the fireplace and leant on the chimney breast.

"Where do I start?" He took a deep breath and exhaled slowly through his nose. "A long time ago, many years before you and I were born, a secret plan was devised that could have, should have in fact, changed history. Millions of lives that were lost during the Second World War could have been avoided, and they would have been avoided if it hadn't been for a series of events that simply ruined everything." It wasn't helping that Ralph was not getting to the point straight away; a history lesson was the last thing I needed right now. "Edward, you are an educated man, so I have no doubt that you are aware how the Second World War started." He looked deep into my eyes for the slightest of responses. Thanks to Lawrence and Nigel I had some clue as to where Ralph was going with this, but I didn't let on in anyway.

"If my faded memory of history lessons at school serve me correct, the war started because Hitler invaded Poland."

Ralph nodded his head enthusiastically. "Good, good, that's the bit I needed you to know. Good old public schools eh?" He paced from the fireplace to one of the blocked up windows. "Did you know, Hammy, that Sikorski was the Polish Prime Minister at that time?" I shook my head blankly, even though I knew all too well that he was the man in charge at the time. "Well you see, Hammy, he died in a horrific plane crash off the coast of Gibraltar, a tragic event that also claimed the life of his daughter, a plane crash that was, and still is, the source of much speculation and many a conspiracy theory." I started to wish that I had accepted Mr. Smith's offer of a smoke.

"I don't understand, Ralph, what the hell has this got to do with me?" Ralph started to laugh inappropriately aloud.

"Edward, do you plan on playing the idiot all night?" I wanted to stand up but realised that I had nowhere to go.

"Do you want to throw me a clue, Ralph, or shall I sit here all night guessing what you are on about?"

Mr. Smith stepped forward; I could tell by the expression on his face that he was losing patience rapidly. "After the crash, the finger of blame was quickly pointed at Russia." Mr. Smith spoke passionately and from the heart. "It was those Russians who did it - reported all of the British and Polish newspapers - after all, there was a Russian aircraft at the airfield in Gibraltar the day Sikorski's plane went down so it must have been them. I say "rubbish." The British were so quick to the point the finger that they must have been hiding something." I scratched my head in bewilderment, but before I could open my mouth, Mr. Smith continued. "After the investigation of the plane crash, whispers started to filter through to Moscow that Sikorski had sold Russia out for immunity from invasion by Nazi Germany." I couldn't listen to any more, what did this have to do with me? Or more in particular what did it have to with our discovery of the port? I requested a cigarette which Mr. Smith thankfully obliged with before he continued. "We know for a fact that Sikorski signed a peace pact with Stalin, and the Polish Prime Minister quickly formed an alliance with the Russian leader whereby he learnt all of the Russian's secret plans for dealing with a rapidly strengthening Germany. The moment it became undeniable that Germany was building up its forces on the Polish borders, Sikorski acted, and acted with much haste."

Ralph stepped forwards to continue my lesson in history. "A casement of vintage port was put together and sent to Hitler as a peace offering, a gesture if you like, to say don't invade us, we are your friends; I'm sure you can imagine what that casement of port looked like, Edward. Anyway, after a handful of Polish officials were captured and held prisoner under Nazi rule they started to talk, and talk uncontrollably. Word started to reach Russia that the casement of port wasn't just a pathetic attempt to put a smile on Hitler's face." Ralph peered over the top of his glasses, "are you following all of this, Hammy?" I instantly nodded obediently. "After what must have been some uncomfortable questioning by Hitler's soldiers, it was soon learnt that the crate sent to Hitler didn't just contain port but in fact something of indescribable significance." Even though I was all too aware that I was head deep in trouble, I couldn't help but hang on every word that was coming out of Ralph's mouth; it truly was fascinating, if not immensely scary. Ralph kept me waiting in suspense for several painstakingly long seconds before he continued. "Believe it or not but Sikorski had the bottles containing the port specially hand crafted such that they were designed to crack open at the seams when hit in the right place with very little force. The crafty bugger had the bottles commissioned so that inside every single bottle were engravings containing details of dates and places of when and where the Russians planned to attack the Nazi war machine hitting them when they least expected it." I scratched my head vacantly.

"This is all very interesting but could you remind me why I am here? And while you are at it, you could tell me why the Russians appear to be keen on the idea of getting their hands on this casement."

Mr. Smith sighed impatiently. "Don't you see, Edward? It is written in the history books that Russia took Sikorski's life when in reality we were his first ally; it was us who were betrayed by him yet the British still insist that we were the ones who plotted his death. We Russians have long memories, they seem to forget that it was the British who also signed a pact with Poland stating that if Poland was to be invaded then that would bring the British Empire into the war. We believe strongly that the British know a lot more than they are letting on, and used us as a very convenient scapegoat. After all, we know that the British spy, Kim Philby was in Gibraltar at the time and he had been working previously as an assassin behind enemy lines." I still didn't understand. I had been following word for word but things were still no clearer. "A Polish prisoner one night after extreme torture told their capturers that it was an idea born from the British Government. There was quiet unrest in the British camp that Churchill had signed this peace treaty with Poland; it was truly an act of good faith but yet an impractical one. The British were hardly prepared for war, as they were still trying to pick up the pieces from the First World War; it wasn't a secret that they were not fully combat ready for yet another war."

Ralph stepped forwards from out of the shadows cast by the dark bay window. "Give this man another cigarette, Mr. Smith." Ralph walked over to my chair and crouched down in front of me. "It becomes blatantly obvious, Edward, once you start putting the pieces together. The British you see, Hammy, were so sure that the Germans were going to invade Poland in a matter of weeks that they hatched a last minute plan to try and buy them some much needed time." I raised my eyebrows to Ralph to show him that I still wasn't sure of the point of all of this, he proceeded to explain. "Churchill's Government knew that the Russians had a ferocious army that far outnumbered the Nazi army, even though they had outdated tanks, aircraft and machinery. At some point during the Nazi war campaign, the British Government figured that the Nazis would have to fight battles on both the Eastern and Western fronts. In August 1939, Hitler and Russia signed a treaty of non-aggression, which incidentally was meant to last for ten years. However, it was widely believed that both countries merely used the treaty to build up their forces before blowing the living shit out of each other. It wasn't a well kept secret that Hitler despised Communism and in particular Stalin, the Russian leader. Hitler believed the Russians to be sub-human; he desperately wanted their land for farming and genuinely believed that the Germans could do a better job of farming the Soviet land than the Russians. Churchill knew that attacks on both Poland and Russia were a forgone conclusion. What he desperately needed to do was make sure that the first attack was on the well prepared Russian army. Churchill was aware that if the Nazis were to attack Moscow and possibly Leningrad first, then Hitler's advancing armies would encounter a resistance so strong that they would have ended up losing large percentages of their army and machinery, giving the allied forces much needed time to build up their attack force. This mysterious casement of port Edward was the one thing that could have stopped Hitler from bringing Britain into the war so prematurely."

Apart from a couple of things, everything was starting to become clearer. Nigel and Lawrence had told me in great detail how Sikorski had sent Hitler the casement of port, and how the Polish Prime Minister had made such a schoolboy error on the emblem of the Third Reich on each and every bottle of port. It all started to make sense; if Hitler hadn't have been so offended with the errors on the wax seals, then maybe he wouldn't have returned them in such haste. Even I could concede that if Hitler had read and understood the Soviet plans to hit Germany where it hurt, then it was perfectly feasible that Hitler would have postponed his plans to invade Poland and concentrate more in blitzing major Russian cities. Mr. Smith started to explain in great detail how the Poles had made such a grave error on the presentation of the bottles; like an actor, I pretended to be amazed at the story that was unfolding in front of me. Feeling my leg muscles starting to cramp, I stood up to get some blood pumping around my legs again; I walked to a window and turned to face my captors.

"I can understand why Mr. Smith here is so keen to make the acquaintance of these bottles of port, but you Ralph, for the life of me, I can't figure out why you seem to be so deeply involved in the Russian quest for justice." Ralph smiled as he listened to each and every word come out of my mouth. Whatever his story was, I knew that it was going to be good.

"It was 1961 when the Royal Air Force finally banged on my Grandmother's door, and before then the family had no clue as to the disappearance of my Grandfather, Albert Davies. You see, Edward, long before I was born, the Russians were already in hot pursuit of this casement. It took them some years to track me down, but once they did they spared no detail in telling me the story of this missing port. Correctly, they figured that I had an interest in tracking this casement down; after all, it had cost my grandfather his life and he was never found. With substantial financial backing from the Kremlin, I came to Wiltshire many years ago in the search for this treasure; I couldn't thank the Lord enough once I discovered that it had been discovered right underneath my very own nose."

I shook my head in utter disbelief. "I don't understand, Ralph. What makes you so convinced I have anything to do with this?" Ralph Davies smirked to himself as he pondered his response. "I take my hat off to you Edward. I'm sure that you created an illusion that even MI5 could even feasibly buy; it was almost one hundred percent watertight." It astonished me to see Ralph pull out a box of cigarettes, get one out and light it; I had always thought that Ralph was opposed to smoking. Smoke poured out of Ralph's mouth as he spoke. "Do you want me to tell you where you went wrong?" Ralph looked me deep into the eyes. "The first time I noted that something was untoward was when Jess came running back into the office in a huff because you had managed to get the wine shop shut. It was not long after that, that you declared the sale of your, well let's face it, mediocre T-shirt company for vast quantities of money. At that time I was in high alert but I wasn't one hundred percent sure." I watched as Ralph finished his cigarette, I was fascinated to learn how he had finally realised that it was me who had discovered the port. I waited before Ralph had stubbed his cigarette out on the floor before I decided to question my former friend.

"Nothing that you have told me today, Ralph, would convince anybody that I had something to do with this. Picture it Ralph, would a court room believe you when you have told them those instances of coincidence; you would get laughed out of court, my friend." Ralph looked to be getting a little annoyed, even though he appeared to be holding his composure well. He walked over to where I was stood and placed a firm hand on my shoulder. "You fucked up Hammy, you and your best friend, fucked up big style." I couldn't bare the suspense; I had to know how we had gone wrong, even though we had been so careful.

"e-Bay Hammy. You got too greedy, just too God damn greedy." I carefully watched as he lifted from one of his inner pockets a note pad computer. He spent a few moments tapping away before he revealed to me what was on the screen. "Since when, Edward, have you had an interest in wartime aviation?" Staring back at me from the small LCD screen was a page from eBay, a page that Ralph had saved. It showed the bidding history of one of the Spitfire bullet proof windscreens I had placed up for auction before we had gone away on holiday. "The ironic thing about all of this Edward is that you probably would have gotten away with all of it if it hadn't been for those windscreens. It was quite simply, Hammy, a tiny, but silly error in judgement all the same." There was no point in me putting up any resistance at this stage. Something had niggled me on the flight to our holiday destination about those windscreens; deep down I knew that I had fucked up somewhere down the line. Ralph could clearly see the confusion written all across my face. "Don't beat yourself up about it Edward; your efforts in laundering the sale of the port were most admirable. I wouldn't have had the foggiest idea unless you had put the windscreens on the world's biggest auction site. Even then I may not have known, but you insisted on listing these items under your T-shirt Company's name, Boulette Boarding. You wouldn't have known this but I regularly checked websites such as eBay for new items listed linked to the Second World War, and more specifically Spitfire items. You see Edward, many years ago when I started my quest to find the port, my first place to look was South Marston airfield. You see, years ago, when a retired Group Captain of the Royal Air Force had visited my Grandmother, he informed her that my Grandfather had flown to the little known airfield with the crates so I made sure that that airfield was the first place I looked. I must congratulate you Edward for finding the underground hanger. After all, when I found it, the airfield was still in operation and the hanger was easy to find." Ralph's account of events was informative and chilling but something didn't make sense.

"If you knew what was down there then why didn't you take the windscreens?" Ralph enjoyed the question.

"I decided that it would be more beneficial to my cause to leave the boxes where I had found them. I knew that if I learnt that somebody had found them someday then there was more than a good chance that they also knew something about the casement of port, and you didn't let me down Edward." I shook my head and laughed in defeat; not even my gift of the gab could paint an innocent light on this little situation.

Loud knocking on the door echoed through the room. I was glad for a few stolen seconds to gather my thoughts and composure. It took Mr. Smith only a matter of seconds to reach the door and open it. It wasn't a relief to see a stern faced Mrs. Taylor stood imposingly in the doorway. "All sorted, they have been dealt with," she said as she looked me straight in the eyes. She was calculating and cold and sent the shivers right through my already petrified body.

"Thank you Linda," said Ralph before he closed and locked the door with her still stood in the doorway. Ralph took a few steps away from the closed door. "It appears that your options are quickly being eradicated, young Edward. Maybe now is the time to start telling your story before you start to lose vital body parts." Ralph's words cut me like a knife cutting through soft tissue. I had worked my pants off for Ralph and this was the thanks I got; there was no doubt in my mind that Ralph would have been willing to have me murdered if I didn't tell him what he wanted to hear. I had to admit to myself that there was no place for me to hide; it was more than apparent that they had enough evidence to hang me. My life now clearly depended on telling them what they wanted to hear.

"Even if I did have these bottles of port, what's the point in me telling you where they are? Because once you have them safely in your hands, we all know that I am dog food." For the first time in the afternoon, Ralph looked considerate and caring.

"If you can introduce us to that casement then you have our assurances that you and your family will live happily ever after." He scratched his head deep in thought. "Once we have the bottles we can draw a line under this little situation. Olive's demise was not my finest hour, I have to admit, but let it serve as a sincere warning to you, Ben's and your families that they will not be safe until we have those bottles safely in our possession."

Thinking fast on your feet was a criterion for becoming a truly great estate agent. It was a talent that I would have to use to its full potential to see tomorrow in. "I don't quite know how to say this but I have sold three bottles already."

Ralph and Mr. Smith looked at each other for what seemed like an eternity. Mr. Smith turned to me, looking a little flustered. "You have only sold three bottles?" There was surprise in his voice. He was correct to suspect that I had sold the entire casement; it was a lie that if need be I would have to take to my grave. I started to realise that they didn't hold all of the best playing cards. They couldn't kill me unless they knew where the box of port was; it was information that I was not going to give up lightly.

"I will go and fetch the crate, alone, and bring it back to you both. There is no way I can retrieve the three bottles that have already been sold, since they are now gone for good." The two men looked at each other in silence; their faces were emotionless and deadly cold. Mr. Smith was the first to respond.

"Edward, you are telling us that you still have in your safe possession seventeen bottles?" I quickly nodded my head.

"That's correct, I do, which I am willing to hand over to you guys on two conditions." Once again the two men glanced over at each other, only this time it was only for a few fractions of a second. Ralph cleared his throat.

"Edward, I have already said that you have our guarantee that you, your best friend's and your families can walk away and forget any of this ever happened, what is the second condition?" I wiped a streak of sweat away from my forehead with the sleeve of my shirt.

"Whatever money we made from those three bottles is ours to keep, and I want you to guarantee that you won't be going after the missing three bottles." Mr. Smith stepped closer to me.

"You have heard the story today, and you know that all my Nation wants is material proof that this casement actually existed; the complete complement of bottles would have been ideal but seventeen bottles will be perfectly sufficient." My relief in hearing Mr. Smith's words was extremely short lived, because it took only a matter of seconds for the realisation to set in that I actually didn't have any bottles at my disposal; I would have to deal with that later, my first priority was to get the hell out of here in one piece.

Ralph handed me from out of his jacket pocket a cheap mobile phone. "You won't be needing yours anymore, and this phone will only receive incoming phone calls and text messages. We will text you a postcode tomorrow morning, and then you will be expected to get to the rendezvous by the time the text message will state." Ralph took off his glasses, folded them and placed them carefully in his shirt chest pocket. "By all means you can bring Ben along for the ride, but if you bring anybody else with you then let me promise you that we will find you, and your families. Do you understand me clearly Edward?" I was in no position to enter into a debate, as it was blindingly obvious that these men were deadly serious; I would have to do exactly what they said, well nearly everything they said.

Ralph unlocked the door and opened it. "I think that concludes our business for today." He gestured with an outstretched arm for me to leave the room. I wouldn't need a second invitation to leave; like a rat up a drain pipe, I was out that door. "Remember Hammy, if you bring anyone apart from Benjamin then your family name probably won't live on." Sadly I knew that Ralph was not joking.

# Chapter 24

# North Wiltshire

*Wednesday 3rd September 2008*

During my rather hair raising meeting with Mr. Smith and my former boss, I was blissfully unaware that Special Agents Harris, Flynn, Simpson and Woods were sitting in hiding in close proximity to the Manor House. Harris and Flynn occupied a black BMW that was discreetly parked only a few yards away from the imposing front gates, while Simpson and Woods waited patiently in a black Range Rover behind the property surrounded by heavy layers of foliage from surrounding trees. The two vehicles had tailed my car all the way to the house following a hidden tracking device that had been placed underneath my car;

now all they could do was to wait for further orders or for any developments occurring from the rustic manor.

Harris had reported back to base on several occasions insisting that they were wasting their time here, as it was clear to him that I was on a routine valuation at a boring old house. Simpson who was positioned behind the property was far more enthusiastic and vigilant; he could see regular movements of cars going in and out of the grounds and sensed that this was no ordinary Estate Agent's valuation. At one point during the stakeout, Simpson had requested permission to leave his vehicle and go and have a closer look; his request fell on deaf ears, and he was instructed to stay in his car at all times. David Simpson, a father to three young girls radioed in. "I can see four males and a rather plump old woman leave the house through a back door. Would you like me to intercept?" Once again Agent Snowdon's voice came crackling over the radio.

"Negative Black Widow, you are to stay still and keep everything peeled." Snowdon could hear Simpson's frustration over the radio.

"You have to let me take a look. We have been following these bastards for months now and they could be here right underneath my nose." Once again, Snowdon hesitantly refused Simpson's understandable request.

It is believed that it was Simpson's car that was hit first, a hit that could only have been carried out by professionals. A single bullet had entered through the passenger window, entered the side of Agent Wood's head and then travelled in and out of Simpson's neck. Blood had covered nearly the entire cream leather interior of the car; it was a scene of ruthless carnage. With identical characteristics, the black BMW came under attack next, with exactly the same outcome: both agents executed. Forensic experts had spent hours covering every single inch of the two vehicles. Their findings were most disturbing. It became widely accepted that these four agents would have known very little about the attacks they had encountered, and it was becoming obvious that a decoy would have had to have been used in order for strangers to have got so close to the cars. The initial findings suggested that a decoy was used to approach the vehicles from the drivers side, a decoy that on the surface would not have posed any threat whatsoever to the agents inside. Then, once the occupants' attention was firmly fixed on the driver's side of the car, a highly skilled and trained gunman took his shot from the passenger side of the cars. It was an attack that had knocked the MI5 team sideways. Not one agent had experienced anything like this before; with two spent bullets and four dead agents, Snowdon had to concede that they were dealing with a different class of criminal.

It went without saying that once the alarm was raised by a frail old man walking his dog, the Manor House swarmed with Police Officers and members of MI5. The house had been stormed by armed response officers within fifteen minutes of the old man stumbling across one of the dead agent's cars; under the orders to shoot to kill, the armed agents found it hard to conceal their disappointment upon finding an empty house. It had come as no surprise that the property had been vacated in supersonic time, and MI5 had learnt that this gang was super organised and they realised that they would have some task ahead of them if they wanted to catch them. Although she had no hard facts to back up her suspicions, Snowdon knew that I was still alive; these criminals clearly had no problem with murder and would have taken advantage on numerous occasions to put a hole in the back of my head if they had wanted me dead. Snowdon was uncomfortable with the fact that there would be no second chances. They would have to nail these mother fuckers next time and without any more loss of life.

# Chapter 25

# Swindon

*Wednesday 3rd September 2008*

From leaving Ralph and Mr. Smith at the Manor House, it had taken a fleet of Police cars carrying no nonsense armed Police Officers only ten minutes to intercept my car on its way home. Causing a massive spectacle, people gathered on the pavements to watch me get manhandled into the back of a marked Police car; I put up no resistance whatsoever, even though I was made to look like a major criminal. I watched from the back seat as people took photos from their phones of the scene unfolding in front of them. "Rot in jail," some kind citizen had shouted from the top of their voice at me; I couldn't help but stick up two fingers to him. On any other day, I would have been so scared that I wouldn't have been able to fight back my tears. Today though, I was almost happy for the safety and professionalism of our massively unappreciated Police Force. I counted a total of four Police cars that had been used to make sure that I went no further; the small crowd that had quickly formed must have thought that my Aston must have been doing some crazy speeds to warrant such Police presence.

I was taken to the main Police Station in Swindon with the convoy having its sirens blaring out, stopping for nothing, not even red traffic lights; they had raced me through Swindon's streets seemingly having no care for anybody else. I was whisked through a gated entrance and through a back door as if my feet had not touched the ground. Skipping the front desk procedure, I was rushed through a door and up some stairs to the first floor of this extremely new and modern Police Station. Unbeknown to me, Agents Snowdon and Deacon, accompanied by a uniformed Police Officer, were waiting. Feeling a little worse for wear, I stumbled through the door of the windowless interrogation room.

"Hammy take a seat. We have some serious talking to do." I could tell that Agent Snowdon was exhausted, as her voice was weak almost as if she was living on the fumes of her batteries; she was not disguising the fact well that the last few hours had knocked her for six. I sat down on the hard and uncomfortable chair; the faces surrounding me looked glum as if they hadn't slept for at least a couple of days.

Deacon turned to the uniformed Police Officer. "Could you bring it in?" Obediently the stockily-built Policeman left the room. It was apparent that the MI5 agents were in no mood for polite small talk as they sat in silence until whatever Deacon had requested would arrive. The deadly silence was not to last long as a tap came from the door and in came the Police Officer carrying a large wooden crate. With extreme care he placed it on the middle of the table and retreated to his spot in the corner of the room; adrenalin was pumping through my body so quickly that I physically felt sick.

"Good, that was the response I was looking for." Snowdon hadn't taken her eyes off me the whole time the crate had been in the room. "You see Edward, we are MI5, and it is our job to gather intelligence; it is what we do." She rose from the table and walked over to the wall with her back facing me. "Did you honestly think that you could hide something of this scale from us? Take a look inside the box Hammy; I think you will be surprised." Nothing at this stage would have surprised me, and I knew all too well what the box was supposed to symbolise. I reservedly lifted the lid and peered in, and much to my amazement, the crate was laid out in exactly the same way as the casement we had found. Twenty bottles each in their own compartment, five rows of four; from a glance they even looked spookily similar.

"May I?" I asked as I carefully lifted out a bottle from its cosy compartment.

"To save the bullshit Mr. Hamilton, we know all about the bottles of port." Snowdon turned to face me. "As you know, the bottle that you are holding is frightfully similar to the ones that you sold to Julian Knapp." I did well not to drop the bottle; the kitchen was starting to get far too hot for my liking. "If you examine them carefully then you will discover that they are not one hundred percent the same, but let's face it, they are bloody brilliant seeing as they were made in only two days." To be perfectly honest I couldn't tell any difference at all; whoever knocked these up seriously deserved promotion. I turned the bottle to inspect the bottom of the bottle. These were fantastic fakes as the AH engraved on the bottom was a perfect match; even the wax seals on the neck of the bottles were outstanding replicas. I reunited the bottle with its compartment and looked up to the agents.

"You guys know about Julian?" Snowdon had a hint of annoyance in her expression; she left Agent Deacon, who looked a whole lot calmer to explain.

"In a word Hammy, yes. We know about Julian Knapp, and we know all about the hoax business deal that disguised the sale of the crate of port you found." There really was nowhere for me to go from this junction in time, I could have sat there all night denying the existence of any port but it was evident that everybody else knew the truth. Agent Snowdon walked over to the Police Officer and discreetly nodded. Then he handed her some folded up paperwork and left the room. Snowdon tossed the papers onto the table.

"If you would be so kind as to read that then sign it." I dubiously picked up the paperwork and unfolded it; 'The Official Secrets Act' was plastered across the top of the document.

"What the fuck?" I was told once again to read it and sign it. Having read, and not particularly understood it, I signed my name on the second page of the paperwork. "Something tells me that I am going to be here for a long time." For the first time in my acquaintance with the Agent she showed a little humour with a slight, but gorgeous smirk.

"Now that the formalities are done with, Hammy, we can put you in the picture." She sat back down in her chair at the table. "To cut a very long story short, we know Julian Knapp very well. In fact he is one of us; well, at least he is on our payroll. Everything that we told you before about this Russian gang is one hundred per cent true. We had been investigating them for months regarding other crimes and are now, as we were then, desperate to catch them." If I hadn't have been shitting bricks then I may have found some comic value in this. After all, it seemed to be a day of pure bloody coincidences, but instead I was left feeling alone and utterly out of my depth. "What we didn't tell you, Edward, is that the second we intercepted the word 'dandelion' we were aware instantly of what we were dealing with; no surprises there, seeing as it was our Government that made up the password in the first place." I was disgusted with myself when it dawned on me that my biggest fear was the fact that I almost certainly was going to lose the money I had received. Deacon appeared to be on my wavelength.

"One of the reasons why we made you sign the Official Secrets Act is that you can keep the money." I was hearing the words come out of his mouth loud and clearly but I couldn't comprehend what he had just said. "As a condition of you helping us nail these mother fuckers, you will be able to keep the money, and most importantly keep up the tall tale of you and Ben selling your company for all that money." I shook my head in utter disbelief; surely I hadn't walked into two traps during the last couple of weeks. That appeared to be Snowdon's queue to go ahead and tell me how wonderful they were.

"We became aware that the port had been discovered once we encountered the word "dandelion" being used on a regular basis; what we didn't know was how the hell to find you. It would be nice to claim credit that we thought about contacting Nigel and Lawrence being that they owned a highly regarded wine shop; however we didn't cover that base, but it was a pure fluke that the two wine shop owners were acquaintances of Julian Knapp."

"So you're saying that if I hadn't have taken the port to Champers then this horrid situation would not have arisen?"

Snowdon chuckled to herself. "I'm afraid not. That link between the three gentlemen has probably saved your life, and I'm sure you would rather MI5 stood by your side when facing these lunatics than you and Ben being there all on your lonesomes." I had to admit that there was no denying the fact that I was mightily happy to have these guys batting on my side. "I hope you don't mind us using Julian as bait for you guys to firmly bite on." Deacon sounded almost apologetic. "I'm sure that you're not going to complain about being able to keep all of the money, like we are not going to complain about been given the perfect opportunity to get these sons of bitches."

After informing Snowdon and Deacon that I had been given a phone to await further instructions, it was decided that it was in mine and Ben's interest to spend the night enjoying free accommodation at the Police Force's expense; in other words both me and Ben were to spend the night in a cell together for our, and our families safety. I had eventually conceded that it was more than likely that this gang had my home under surveillance, and the last thing I wanted to do was give them any temptation to raid my house in the dead of the night intending on getting their grubby hands on the crate of port. Whilst Ben was being fetched from whatever he was doing, I was instructed to relax and call for attention if I needed anything; I figured it was a small price to pay for allowing nearly a million pounds to stay safely in my bank account.

# Chapter 26

# Berkshire

*Thursday 4ᵗʰ September 2008*

I awoke fairly early in the morning with a bitter chill on my legs and back. The wafer thin blue blanket was doing nothing to keep my body warmth in let alone cover my entire hunched up body. With blurry vision, I could see a figure asleep under a similar blue blanket on a bench bed on the opposite side of the cell. "Mate is that you?" I quietly whispered; a grunt could be heard from underneath the cover that told me my best friend had joined me at some point during the night. I managed to slip in and out of sleep for several hours until a loud bleeping bought all my senses racing back to life; it was a noise that was alien to me, yet I knew all to well what it signified.

"You get that phone from a museum, dude?" Clearly the annoying high pitched tone had brought Ben back to the land of the living. Knowing that Ben was blissfully unaware as to why I would have an archaic Nokia mobile phone in my possession, I decided to let Ben doze for a bit longer. It was inevitable that the two of us were in for one hell of a bad day so I decided to let him get as much rest as he could. Without making hardly any movement or sound, I reservedly opened the text message in the inbox.

'Go to Coopers LTD for 10:00pm on the dot, New Greenham Park just outside Thatcham, Berkshire. RG19 6HW. Park outside and take crate inside with you. They will be expecting you. Remember Edward, only you and Ben, or suffer the consequences.'

I sat up on my hard bed for the night leaning my back against the cold brick wall; the dire situation that I had got myself into was now starting to sink in. Not for the first time in twenty four hours, I started to fear for mine and Ben's lives. My dark thoughts started to freak me out somewhat. I was in desperate need for some comforting; I needed encouragement, and I needed somebody to tell me that it was all going to alright. Making as little noise as I could, I leant over and quietly pressed the panic button on the wall of our cell.

It was a welcome sight to say the least as I watched Agent Snowdon carefully enter the cell carrying two steaming hot mugs of coffee and an overnight wash bag. "I thought you chaps may like a cuppa to wake up to." Her hair was all over the place and she certainly did not look like she had had a good night's sleep. "Do I take it that the fact you have rung the bell means that they have been in contact with you?" She parked her bottom on the end of my bed and yawned uncontrollably. Even though her blonde hair looked liked she had brushed it with a firework, she looked innocently beautiful; her lack of makeup seemed to enhance her looks and her sleep-deprived body and face looked more inviting, more welcoming. Without saying a word, I handed her my newly acquired ancient phone so she could read the message. She studied it for several moments before she spoke. "We need to act and act quickly, as we only have a little over two hours to get your butts to Thatcham." Being completely engrossed as the situation unfolded in front of me, it hadn't even crossed my mind to look at the time. Quickly I glanced at my watch and Snowdon was right; it was two minutes to eight. "Ok, you wake up sleeping beauty over there and I will gather everyone up. Be ready in five minutes as I will get somebody to fetch you and accompany the two of you to the briefing room." Her deodorant lingered in the air long after she had slammed the thick metal door closed; Ben seemed to have been completely oblivious to her morning wakeup call. He was still hunched up in a ball under his blanket; he had not moved the entire time Snowdon had been in the cell.

"Dude you alive?" Amidst a chorus of rumbling and grunting, the seemingly lifeless body in the corner of the cell rose like some religious miracle.

"Fucking hell this bed is uncomfortable; I think I would rather have slept on a bed of nails than this." It was encouraging to see that Ben still had some humour left as I knew it would be most welcome later on. I got up and handed him a mug of coffee. Having quickly rifled through the wash bag, I pulled out one of the toothbrushes and toothpaste and started to brush my teeth in the complimentary sink provided. With the fresh taste of mint in my mouth, I proceeded to explain to Ben the current situation, including as to why I had the old Nokia phone in my possession. Without any further delay, he jumped out of his bed and quickly started to brush his teeth and straighten his hair; within a few minutes we were sitting in silence at the end of our beds waiting to be collected.

A timid tap came from the door followed by it opening slowly. "If you are ready, then they are waiting for you in the briefing room, so if you would like to follow me?" The youthful female's voice sounded relatively young, but the open door was blocking my view of the doorway. Necking back the remainder of my coffee, I got up and wiped my mouth with my sleeve.

Our escort seemed a little flustered. She barely looked old enough to have qualified for the Force, but it was evident in her eyes that she was all to aware that this was a big occasion. Sensing that she felt sorry for us and feared for our safety and our wellbeing, I gave her a big grin as I walked passed her into the clinical corridor; Ben smartly followed close behind. We obediently followed her as she guided us through a mass of mazes; we passed what must have been hundreds of doors that aligned the identical looking hallways. Uniformed Police Officers stopped to look at us as we passed them; word had obviously spread around the station of MI5's presence and of the undercover operation that was in progress.

Feeling the long guided walk on my legs, we finally arrived at the briefing room; the female escort knocked on the door and opened it cautiously. Ben and I were invited into a large and bright meeting room with a huge oval table in the centre. Amidst the countless strange faces, I was thankful to recognise Snowdon and Deacon chatting to each other in the far corner of the room. At least twenty men and woman dressed in a mixture of both smart business dress and intimidating black Police uniforms quietly mingled with each other. The uniformed officers of which I counted ten, reminded me of New Zealand All Black rugby players. They wore tight black T-shirts with the wording Police on the arms. Above the T-shirts were thick black vests with all sorts of radios and wiring fixed on; I remained thankful that these guys were batting for my side. A deadly silence descended upon the room once mine and Ben's presences were known. "I'm scared, mate," Ben whispered under his breath, but I had no time to reply. A young, well groomed man dressed in a stylish grey suit paced over to us.

"Edward, Ben, it's great to have you on board, please come this way." We were chaperoned over to the table and given chairs to sit down on. Amongst other things, the crate that Snowdon had shown me the day before was sitting in the centre of the glass table. It wasn't the crate that had caught Ben's attention.

"Mate, I hope those aren't for us." It took a few milliseconds to register what he was on about; once I did, a chill shot down my spine. Sitting next to the crate was what looked like two navy blue bullet proof vests.

"OK, if I could have every ones' attention. Could somebody get the blinds and everybody else please take your seats." I didn't need to look up to see whose voice it was; I would recognise Snowdon's voice anywhere. She pulled down a gigantic white projector screen. "As I'm sure you guys are aware, we don't have much time so I will say all this just the once." Having turned on the projector a large illuminated map of Berkshire plastered itself across the screen. On the right hand side of the map was the town called Newbury, and on the left hand edge of the map was Reading. Just to the left of Newbury was a much smaller town called Thatcham, which had been circled; roughly about a mile South East of Thatcham was another circle over the name Brimpton. "We know that Edward and Ben here have been summoned to an Industrial Estate to the South East of Thatcham here." She pointed to a circle with a long teaching stick. "We know that we can't be seen to be tailing these guys so we have to try and get one step ahead of them." She paused to take a gulp of water from a nearby bottle. "It is not likely that they will hang around inside the Coopers Ltd building for long, as they will want to be like the SAS, in and out of there before anyone notices." A couple of the men chuckled under their breaths. "We have been studying the immediate area all night; experience tells us that they will be looking for a way to get a lightning quick and unseen getaway. The obvious choice is by car, but they will suspect that we will be following them and they will see the motorway as far too risky." She pointed to a second circle that must have only been two miles away from the Industrial Estate. "This is Brimpton airfield. Although it has a grass runway and only several resident light aircraft, it is one of only a handful of active airfields in Berkshire; as I'm sure you will all agree, it provides a perfect way to slip away undetected." She strode over to the table and picked up several sheets of paperwork before returning to her position at the projector screen. "Starting from this morning, 'the Bathroom Place,' which is a shop next to Coopers Ltd, has four new members of staff working there; these agents will be able to keep a much needed close eye on next door. We have SAS sharp shooters and armed response at Brimpton airfield posing as aircraft mechanics." She turned to face Ben and me. "Your rather lovely Aston will have a tracking device fitted but we can't risk you guys carrying one, as they may be on the look out. I promise you that at any point in this plan you will always have us watching close behind you; you may not see us but we will be there for you." She paced over to the table and gave Deacon his cue to continue.

Agent Deacon rose from the table and cleared his throat; he picked up one of the vests on the table. "However today pans out, it is compulsory that you wear these at all times." He leant over on the table and looked us in the eyes. "I can't stress this enough guys, when you're back here on the debriefing I want to see that you're still wearing them. Understood?" Both myself and Ben started to nod frantically.

"If they might see a wire then why won't they see this vest?" I winked at Ben, as it was an astute question and warranted acknowledgment. I shouldn't have doubted that Deacon had all the bases covered; he pulled out from under the table two brand new fashionable snowboarding jackets and tossed one each over to us. "You wear these over the vests. Today is overcast with drizzle, so they won't think twice about you wearing these, and if all goes to plan we will be on top of them before they even think about what clothes you have on your backs." He swiftly diverted his attention to the wooden crate on the table. "I take it everyone here has signed the Official Secrets Act?" Heads nodded around the table in synchronisation. "Going from the bottles that Julian Knapp acquired, these are the best replicas we could produce in the timescales we had to play with; believe me they are bloody good." He respectfully lifted a bottle out of its box. "We don't plan on giving the targets long to inspect them before we pounce on them, and they certainly should hold up for an initial brief inspection." Snowdon stood up to interrupt.

"Your safety depends on them not smelling a rat with this casement. They must know that it exists and is authentic otherwise they won't walk into our trap." Snowdon's tiredness was starting to show, as she was now getting snappy and impatient. "If there are no further questions then we better saddle up and rock 'n roll. Remember, you two, we are with you every step of the way."

Wearing the bullet proof vest and my trendy new snowboarding coat, my sports car interior felt like it had shrunk a few sizes, as I started up the cold engine amongst a small crowd of well wishers within the Police courtyard. Officers gave us the thumbs up and wished us both the very best of luck; it felt more like we were leaving for a six month tour of Afghanistan than a days work in Berkshire. We had been told to leave the Police complex as safely, but as quickly as possible. The Police Station was on a busy road with very few places to stop nearby; although the probability of being followed was minimal they didn't want to leave anything to chance. Feeling like a schoolboy again, and a little like James Bond, I opened up the throttle and weaved my way down the narrow exit road and through the open barrier onto the A420. With little over an hour to get to my destination, and being under instruction by the Police to get there as quickly as possible, I decided to full throttle it pretty much the whole way there. I obediently followed my Sat Nav down the M4 motorway until I got to Junction Thirteen, with an average speed of one hundred and twenty six miles per hour; the chances of anyone following was next to nothing. Screaming off the Motorway and onto the A34 dual carriageway, Ben clocked a marked Police car heading in the opposite direction to us. The moment I saw it, the driver turned on its sirens and flashing blue lights. Its brake lights came on under a cloud of burning rubber as the car drastically slowed to make an emergency U turn in the road. I watched in my rear view mirror as the Police car headed our way for a couple of seconds with blazing blue lights and flashing headlights. Then, as if instructed to by a higher command, the flashing stopped and the car appeared to be slowing down. "This is fucking crazy," gasped my excited passenger. "Not even the Motorway Police will stop us; it's like we are invincible."

With five minutes to spare, the satellite navigation system directed us to the main entrance at New Greenham Park. A large oval glass building surrounded by tall flagpoles served as a gatehouse and its full length, blue tinted windows, gave a very futuristic impression of this modern business park; it shocked me as to how big this place was. "Mate, this is nothing like I expected; it's massive. I was expecting some shabby, rundown industrial unit." As we drove through the vast estate following the arrows on my Sat Nav, I prayed that MI5 and the Police were seriously on the ball; with the sheer size of this place, it was easy to see how they could lose sight of us. Like Ben, I was expecting a small cluster of industrial buildings from the seventies; I started to get a whole lot more worried. Having passed what must have been over fifty high specification industrial properties of all different shapes and colours, the Sat Nav told me to stop outside a sprinkling of much older buildings. "This is the place," sighed Ben as he pointed to a large sign on the front of the building, 'Coopers Ltd.'

The building standing in front of us appeared to be made of corrugated iron; it was painted in royal blue and resembled something more like a former military building than its modern surrounding neighbours. The building was two stories high; it had a canopied Visitor's Entrance and a much bigger Goods Entrance next to it that could certainly accommodate a big van or small lorry. The ageing building enjoyed the benefit of a large concrete car park that was positioned to the front; it appeared to share the car park with its direct neighbour, the Bathroom Place. We easily managed to find a vacant parking space close to the Main Entrance of Coopers Ltd. Before we stepped out of the car, I scanned the area looking for any signs of undercover officers, but there was nobody to be seen. "Good luck my friend," I said as I pulled myself out of the car and slammed the door closed behind. Ben quickly followed. Aware that there may have been prying eyes on us from the Coopers building, I made no hesitation in grabbing the wooden crate from the boot of my car and proceeded to walk briskly over to the Visitor's Entrance.

"Something doesn't feel right," mumbled Ben as I opened the front door.

"Too late now my friend," I said as I walked into the cool Reception Area. A man in his mid thirties stood behind a counter, and he instantly looked up when he heard the front door open. As calmly as I could muster my strength, I confidently walked up to the front desk. "I think we are expected. We were told to come here." For a few brief moments, the man looked to be confused, and he looked me over from head to toe then caught sight of what I was holding and the penny dropped.

"Mr. Hamilton and Mr. Lewis?" We both nodded nervously. "That's correct. We have been expecting you both." He turned to the back wall and unhooked a set of keys from a loop that was screwed to the wall. He lifted up a section of the counter. "If you would like to bring that box with you and follow me?" Asking no questions, we followed him past the front desk and through a door that led into a large warehouse area, where ten or so employees of the company were working hard in boxing up goods and loading them onto white transit vans. The Receptionist turned to face us; he tossed Ben a set of keys. "I'm told that you have to take that white Transit over there through the back exit with your cargo onboard." He rifled through his pockets and pulled out a Tom-Tom Satellite Navigation System. "Your final destination has already been programmed into it, so all you have to do is turn it on and follow the directions." He handed it to Ben. My heart started to sink rapidly, and the man must have seen horror written across my face. "It's OK, Transits aren't that bad and your car will be perfectly safe here until you return."

Ben chuckled to himself. "Yeah, that's if we ever do return." In my moment of terror, I suspected that Ben had failed to understand the implications of taking the Transit out through the back entrance; we were seriously fucked.

"I'll get the back door opened up for you." And with that, the Receptionist left us and headed towards the rear of the building.

"Ben mate, Ralph and those bastards are cleverer than those spooks think; if that Sat Nav doesn't take us on a south easterly heading we are proper screwed." Ben's face painted a thousand words; he clearly didn't understand. Speaking as quietly as I could, I tried to let him in on the bigger picture. "Dude, the tracking device is buried somewhere in my car, we don't have one on us and the last thing they will be looking for is a white Transit van slipping out the back way. We don't even know if they are watching the back exit, as all eyes are probably on my car at the front."

Ben swept his hand quickly through his hair. "Oh shit." Before Ben had started the engine of the maturing Transit van, he had already christened it Trevor. Before he owned his classy new van, Ben had owned a rust bucket just like this one. Even though it poured out thick black clouds of smoke and had holes in it so big that you could fit your fist through them, he missed it and jumped at the opportunity of driving a similar machine. His enjoyment time of being reacquainted with a ten year old white van was soon cut short; heavy rain had not helped the fact that it had taken my best friend and the Tom-Tom nearly a quarter of an hour to get out of the Business Park. Visibility had slowly declined as we got lost amongst the similar looking roads and entrance gates. I was slowly giving up hope that we would be noticed sneaking out of the complex.

Having finally managed to escape from the Business Park, it was only a matter of minutes that I realised we were heading in the opposite direction from Brimpton airfield. "One thing is for certain mate; we aren't going to that airfield where half of MI5 and the Police Force are camped out." I secretly had hoped that I was wrong. Maybe we would hit a ring road and circle our way back round in that direction. Ben's words made it dawn on me that the Russians had stitched us up like a kipper. By the time the rain had declined, we had already skipped passed the outskirts of Thatcham and were being instructed to join the B4009 in two miles time. The van ground to a halt as we hit traffic lights. The harder I tried to think of a cunning plan, my head became foggier, so I looked out the window for inspiration but my mind became cloudier and cloudier; I turned to the one thing that could make me think straight, a Marlborough Light. The small yellow flame from my lighter was just about to devour the end of my cigarette when I was thrown back into the Ford's seat. The engine revved and before I knew what was happening the van had mounted the grassy verge in the middle of the road. Violently I was thrown around the cab as Ben speeded towards the red lighted traffic lights, with two wheels on the grass verge and two wheels on the road; we must have looked like one hell of a sight. My instincts were screaming at me to shout out and demand from Ben an explanation as to what he was playing at, but twenty something years of being his best friend told me to trust him and remain quiet. Pinned to my seat, I looked on in bewilderment as Ben overtook the queue of waiting vehicles with only inches to spare on my side; I started to laugh uncontrollably when I saw what was waiting at the front of the queue.

In my whole entire life I had never been so pleased to see a Volvo Estate Police car; it hadn't yet sunk in as to how quickly Ben had thought to perform his little act of genius. I would have loved to have been a fly on a wall in the Police car. You can imagine the confusion and surprise when they looked into their mirrors and saw a rusty old transit racing towards them tilted at a fifteen degree angle. The traffic lights were still glowing red when Ben manoeuvred the van alongside the Police car and pulled up just in front of it. The second the van stopped the Police car's sirens sounded out. The traffic lights turned green as I watched through the passenger side mirror a very pissed off looking Police Officer get out of his car; he talked into his radio as he approached Ben's side of the van. Ben wound down the window. "'Morning, Officer, how you doing?" asked Ben triumphantly. The Policeman didn't look amused to say the least.

"Turn off the engine." Ben turned off the engine. "Is this your vehicle sir?" wearing a smug smile Ben shook his head. "No, it's not mine and to be quite honest I don't know whose it is. As far as I am aware I don't have any insurance and for the life of me I haven't got a clue where my driving licence is." *Yep, that will do the trick, Mate,* I thought to myself.

"Please come with me, Sir." Before I knew it, I was sitting in the cab of the Transit alone watching Ben get manhandled into the back of the Volvo. I didn't mind sitting there in the slightest, holding up the traffic for ten minutes. I kept my fingers crossed that Ben had bought MI5 enough time to readjust their plan of action.

Much quicker than I had anticipated, Ben returned to the van and clambered into the cab. "Lovely jubley" and with that he started the engine and pulled away. Excitedly he explained in detail what had happened during his brief encounter with the Police. "The moment I got into car I was asked what our names were by the driver of the Police car. You could tell he was about to throw all of his toys out of the pram any moment." Holding the steering wheel with one hand, he used the other to pull out one of my cigarettes from its box on the dash board. I quickly held out my lighter for him so he would continue with his account. "Anyway, where was I?" He wound down the window a little and exhaled a plume of blue smoke out the window. "The Policeman on the passenger side, the dick who came to the van, radioed through our names, the van's licence plate, colour, make, and model and best of all where we were." I couldn't help but smile at Ben; the boy had done good. "I even managed to interrupt, when he was on the radio to say that we would be heading up the B4009 dual carriageway northbound. To say he looked a bit miffed would be an understatement." He passed me the half smoked cigarette. "Anyway, when the radio message came back that he was to let me go instantly, I thought he was going to start crying." Ben started to laugh. "They both looked at each other in utter disbelief when they were strictly told not to follow the van. They didn't know what to say so I said my cheerios and left."

Although Ben's stunt with the Police car was ingenious, I knew that we were far from out of the woods yet. The fact that they knew what road we were on and what direction we were heading was merely a piss in the ocean; we had no idea where the hell we were going so I was sure they didn't have a bloody clue either.

Always keeping an eye out for possible following cars, friends or foes, we travelled up the B4009 for roughly half an hour; the traffic was fairly light so we covered some good ground. Amongst the countless road signs we passed of alien sounding places, we passed several for 'the living rainforest'; my imagination didn't need long to conjure up horrible visions of dying in the middle of thick woodland to be heard and seen by nobody. Before we got the chance to discover what the living rain forest was, our Sat Nav instructed us to turn off the main road and take a much quieter village road. We drove through thick forestry on a small and narrow lane before the landscape opened up in front of us; we had come to a quiet t-junction in the road. The Tom-Tom told us to turn left; with no traffic on the roads Ben swung the van out and proceeded in an easterly direction. I looked out through Ben's side window; there was only thick woodland to be seen. Then I glanced out of my door window and saw open fields. We passed a sign post telling us that a place called Hampstead Norreys was somewhere behind us before the Tom-Tom started to tell us that we had arrived at our destination on our left hand side. "That's weird," said Ben as he strained to see past me through the passenger window. "All there is here is a bunch of fields." He pulled over the van so that he could get a better look. He was right; at first glimpse all it appeared to be was agricultural land that was being used by the local farmer. The farm land was quite vast and sheltered by a canvas of trees that surrounded the recently ploughed fields whose perimeters seemed to have a decaying road that ran all around the sides of the land. Something instantly struck me as being odd about the scenery that surrounded us; a straight and narrow white patch ran straight through two of the fields.

"I don't believe it!" It suddenly had dawned on me what the white patches and the surrounding broken up roadway was. "We have been led to another bloody airfield, buddy." Ben looked confused, so once again he took in the landscape through the side window.

"Mate, I'm not being funny but I don't see any aircraft, runways or any buildings; all I see are lots of cows." I pointed to the long and narrow white patch that dissected two of the fields.

"I would bet that this used to be an old wartime airfield. Look at that long white stretch in the soil."

Ben leaned over me to get a closer look. "And?"

I started to feel like a boring old wartime historian. "That long white stretch I reckon used to be a runway; the whiteness you see now is the chalk left over in the soil when they dug up the tarmac and returned the land to agricultural use. I pointed to the breaking up boundary road that could just about be seen through the hedgerows. South Marston had the same road; it's a perimeter track used for taxing aircraft and patrol vehicles."

Ben appeared to be amused. "You and your bloody airfields!" Without saying another word, he slammed the Transit into first gear and carefully pulled off the road and through an open gate leading onto the farm land. The wheels spun in the mud spraying up dirt all over the side of the van. Still without saying a word, Ben slammed on the brakes and cut the throttle. "Buddy did you see that?" His voice sounded panicky and unlike the normal laid back Ben that I knew so well. I hadn't seen anything suspicious; before I opened my mouth, I scanned the horizon to see if there was anything staring back at me that was out of the ordinary. From the furthest corner of the open space I saw what had caught Ben's attention. "There it is again. Did you see that, dude?" The flash of car headlights in the distance had been unmistakable; we had certainly been spotted arriving at the destination. "Let's hope that old cracked up road isn't too far gone so that we can get the van through to the other side." Without waiting for my response, Ben slowly started to roll the Transit forward. Puddles of rain from a recent downpour lay on the broken tarmac making it extremely difficult to ascertain where the big holes and cracks were in the road; cautiously Ben kept the van moving. The thin narrow road we were driving on was at best a mixture of overgrown weeds, a mass of mud and irregular patches of old tarmac and it was evident that not even the farmer used it to get from A to B. We passed a pair of large concrete blocks that had what appeared to be iron handles attached to the top of them. The van just about managed to squeeze between the two. Several metres down the track from the concrete blocks, Ben stopped the van for a few moments. He pointed past me to my side. "I think you're right, Mate. Look through there." Hidden amongst thick foliage from surrounding trees I could just about make out a moss-covered long and narrow building. The grey and green structure stood only a few meters from the ground and had most evidently been neglected for many years. Set back off the road, Ben had done well to spot it. Ben slowly put the wheels into motion again. "Definitely an old airfield mate. That would have been a bunker or even weapons store," Ben nodded to himself.

Having passed several more camouflaged abandoned buildings, the road was becoming impassable in parts; overgrown vegetation was so dense that even a tractor would have had a hard time getting through so we decided to ditch the van and make up the rest of the ground on foot carrying the crate of port in turns. Having decided to cut straight across the middle of the fields as opposed to driving all the way around, it only took us quite a few minutes of heavy walking before our reception party became a lot more visible. I could now make out the outline of six darkly dressed figures, a Jaguar and a Mercedes Benz, but after we took several more steps another machine came into our view. Stood about twenty meters away from the waiting people, hidden away in a concealed corner of the field was a Jet Ranger helicopter. Eagle-eyed Ben was the first to spot it. "Snowdon was spot on: these bastards are going to escape by air, and ironically from an airfield." Although Snowdon had been good, I feared that this gang had got the better of her; she may well have been looking for an airfield close by but what were the chances of this place even showing up on a map? All she would know would be that it was just farming land. I had to concede that this time we were really alone. As we got within about thirty metres from the sinister-looking men, the helicopter blades started to turn slowly.

"Stop right there, Hammy." I recognised the voice to be Ralph's. Obediently we both stopped dead in our tracks and Ben, who was carrying the crate, very slowly bent down and placed it on the ground; like some criminals under the Police's spot light, we both raised our arms to the air. Cautiously the six men, including Ralph, walked up to our position.

"You can put your hands down chaps. You are not under arrest." Mr. Smith's words did nothing to calm my nerves. Mr. Smith and Ralph approached the wooden crate. "If you two could step back a little and remain perfectly still, I would very much appreciate it." Hanging on every word that came out of Mr. Smith's mouth, we stepped back three or four steps and remained still.

Mr. Smith got down on his knees and opened the crate; with the utmost respect he lifted one of the seventeen bottles out from its compartment and studied every intricate detail on the glass of the bottle. Saying absolutely nothing, he carefully handed it to one of his associates; they exchanged a few brief words in Russian before the man handed it to Ralph. Concentrating entirely on the cork and the neck of the bottle, Ralph studied the object for what seemed to be a lifetime; eventually he nodded his head.

"The cork is infested with maggots; it has got into the liquid making it undrinkable but it does give us a genuine sign that these bottles are old; these are not forgeries," he said as he bent down to put the bottle back in its compartment. Feeling a massive weight lift off my shoulders, I turned to face Ben whose relief was written all across his face. I turned back to face the sinister-looking men, and was just about to ask if our business here was concluded when my ears filled with an alien noise. Before my brain could process the unfamiliar sound, I caught out of the corner of my right eye Ben moving suddenly and awkwardly. Instantly I turned to face him, another loud dull thud hit my ears, and blood from Ben's upper leg spraying out in front of him like a champagne bottle opening; he fell lifelessly to the floor. My heart felt like it had stopped and I was so petrified that I had become paralysed to the spot where I was standing. I ordered my body to move, to run, but it had frozen rigid. I could feel my knees go weak. I was about to let them fold and allow myself to collapse to the ground when a force so great hit me straight in the back that it threw me forwards; the shear velocity of the blow felt like a speeding train had collided with me square on from behind. In a complete paralysed state I tried to call out but my lungs appeared to have failed me. Another dull thud hit my body, only this time I could feel pain; pain like I had never felt before. Feeling my head go light and my vision blurry, I remember hitting the ground hard, face first, I thanked the Lord that I was still conscious and I looked up with colourless vision as if I was looking through the heat coming off a desert.

A scene of chaos unfolded in front of my very eyes, Ralph had dived to the floor only to be hit in his stomach; blood rushed out turning his white shirt a deep claret colour, and his lifeless body hit the ground. "Snaypery snaypery," screamed out Mr. Smith. Although I knew not one word of Russian, I was able to figure out what he was frantically yelling: "Sniper, sniper." Instinctively, he grabbed the crate of port and ran behind his colleagues towards the helicopter loading it after them as quickly as he could. Mr. Smith tried to jump in afterwards as the helicopter started to lift but at that moment two bullets in close succession impacted into his back and he fell forwards. The blades of the helicopter started to turn more rapidly as it lifted off the ground leaving Mr. Smith lying face down on the ground.

I could just about hear the swirl of the rotors as the helicopter rapidly took to the sky but then there was an almighty bang and the helicopter gyrated wildly descending towards the ground which it hit hard exploding in an expanding fireball. I could feel the heat on my face as I passed out.

# Chapter 27

# Zihuatanejo, Mexico

*Today*

*"You remember the name of the town don't you?"*

My bottle of San Miguel is now nearly empty. I of course can, and will, order another one, but this bottle is the most important one of the day. Like the bottle I had yesterday, and the day before, and the day before that, and in fact every single day for the last seven months, I will toast the health of Agent Emma Snowdon with every bottle. Once again, I watch as the early evening sun sets behind the brilliant blue sea water; without a cloud in the sky it is easy to forget one's troubles and past events, but today, like all the other days, my mind is still very much on Snowdon.

During that Thursday in September of last year, I remember vividly the empty and lonely feeling I had experienced when the realisation had dawned that we had managed to lose Snowdon and her MI5 team. She had carried out her job admirably. Even though we had managed to lose her, there is simply no denying the fact that she was seriously on the ball. She had correctly guessed that the Russians would be aiming to retreat to an airfield, although it turned out that she had picked the wrong one. However, unbeknown to me she had majestically covered every single angle.

It had taken the four undercover agents working at the Bathroom Place no more than six minutes to realise that something was up, and instantly a message came through to Snowdon's team that something was wrong. Whilst being in constant contact with the team posing as mechanics at Brimpton airfield, Snowdon had waited no more than three minutes before she put her back up plan into motion. She was unhappy with the intelligence that had been supplied to her during the initial planning stages of the mission. It hadn't sat right with her that there were only two active airfields in a county the size of Berkshire; it was information that had formed the backbone of this operation. Brimpton was the obvious choice, the choice of scholars and academics; after all it was only two miles away from the initial rendezvous at Coopers Ltd. The other logical option was the remaining active airfield, White Waltham, which was home to the West London Aero Club. This for Snowdon was not an option, as it was the other side of Reading and as close to London as Junction 8/9 of the M4; it would have been a suicidal and quite frankly comical attempt in evading the cream of the crop of the intelligence service. She had considered other ways and means of escape for this evidently intelligent gang, but she kept coming back to air; they would have to fly out. Snowdon's field of expertise was identity theft and fraud; she knew nothing about airfields of yesteryear or of Berkshire as a place; however it turns out that she knew some people who did.

Upon realising that she and her team were barking up the wrong tree, she instantly scrambled a Police helicopter and instructed it to pick her up; it would become her mobile operational control centre. Then she made a phone call, a phone call that within three minutes would launch two RAF Puma helicopters of 33 Squadron from nearby RAF Benson. Capable of a top speed of one hundred and sixty three miles per hour, these choppers from the Frontline Support Helicopter base were more than capable of covering all of the ground and quickly. The crew onboard these helicopters had a superior knowledge of used and disused airfields in the area, with each chopper having a highly trained four-man Assault Team from "A" Sabre Squadron, Special Air Service, armed with sniper rifles with laser sighting, laser target markers and laser-guided rocket-propelled grenades. They were in a perfect position to cover all eventualities.

The first Puma to get airborne headed straight for a place called Theale, a disused wartime airfield that is now half submerged by water. Theale, being only seven or eight miles away from Coopers Ltd, quickly became the first choice to put under surveillance. The second Royal Air Force helicopter to take to the skies, using the knowledge that we had last been seen heading towards the B4009, aimed his nose straight for Hampstead Norreys. Snowdon's Police helicopter would track our van flying behind us and maintaining contact without getting too close. She would issue the orders to all the other parties in the operation.

Hampstead Norreys airfield has been well known to the RAF ever since those dark days during the Second World War. Although now used for its rightful purpose as agricultural land, the RAF Benson boys still occasionally used it for training exercises such as 'touch and goes' and troop deployments (apologies if the farmer didn't know!) The pilot of the second Puma circled Hampstead Norreys first at some distance so they couldn't even be heard let alone be seen. Not one hundred percent satisfied that it was all clear; he put the chopper down on high ground roughly about a kilometre away from the field. Giving the onboard marksman enough time to scan every inch of the former airfield through his powerful sniper scope, they were quickly able to establish that Hampstead Norreys was in fact the intended rendezvous. Snowdon then reported that the van was about to arrive. With armed response units at least fifteen minutes away from the meeting place, Snowdon gave the Puma the all clear to carry out their plan alone as previously briefed. Calling upon every aspect of his rigorous training, the SAS Sniper calmly and coolly had picked off his targets one by one.

It turns out that the most vital initial target was Ralph followed very closely by myself and Benjamin. It hadn't occurred to me at the time why Deacon was so adamant that we had to wear our vests at all times; it of course now makes perfect sense knowing that he always planned to get Ralph, then me and Ben, shot with a high powered sniper rifle. That way, our prime assassin, once the crate had been handed over, would be eliminated and we would appear to have met the same fate, protecting our lives from the remaining Russians; after all there would be no point in sending people to kill us for revenge if we were already dead. To make the whole thing look believable, and to make us no longer a threat, MI5 decided that it would be far more convenient to protect us if we were dead and buried.

However, it was paramount firstly that the crate had to be destroyed, and destroyed with a small audience and secondly that at least one of the Russians who had verified the authenticity of the port bottles should survive and be able to give a first hand account of their existence and destruction . That is why the SAS team, using a laser target marker and a rocket-propelled grenade that followed the beam, took out the Jet Ranger helicopter making sure that the crate had been loaded and Mr. Smith had been injured at the last minute in a way that would convince the helicopter crew that there was no point in being heroic and stopping to pick him up. After all, Mr. Smith was a big player in this gang and MI5 needed to make at least one arrest out of this. He also had examined the bottles and would be able to report back to his masters that they existed. Immediately after the shooting, the Puma had flown over and landed within metres of where the three of us lay in pools of our own blood, drifting in and out of consciousness; there was nothing they could do for Ralph. Ben and I were loaded onto the Puma and airlifted to the John Radcliffe Hospital in Oxford. Two heavily-armed SAS Commandos from the chopper stayed with Mr. Smith until the other Puma and the authorities arrived. I don't remember the helicopter flight or arriving at the hospital, but for the few brief moments that I was conscious, I was able to work out that Ben was in a serious condition. At that exact moment in time, I didn't know what had hit me, let alone who had pulled the trigger; the only thing I was bothered about was staying alive. When I was finally privy to the truth, my anger couldn't be put into words. How could Snowdon have taken such a risky gamble, a gamble that could easily have taken my life and most probably Ben's too? It took a considerable amount of time to realise that actually Snowdon didn't need to have gone to all that bother; after all it would have worked out in her favour having the two of us dead. All she had to do was to wait for one of the Russians to put a bullet in the middle of our heads, which incidentally, she informed me was a forgone certainty.

It has now been many months since those events that altered our lives so much and only now can I laugh at the irony of the whole situation. It was myself and Ben who thought we were the clever ones, it was us who were laying red herrings and decoys to disguise the truth. It was us and only us who were in full control of our very own destinies. In reality we were overconfident and that was definitely not the case; we had, in fact, managed to walk into not only one trap, but two. Credit where it is due, the Russians did show signs of brilliance at times; they had outthought and outmanoeuvred MI5 on several occasions but it was always MI5, and Snowdon in particular, who were that one step ahead of the game. MI5 had built up substantial knowledge on the Russian gang; they had been following them for months and as a result were learning how to second guess them. As soon as the casement of port popped up on the radar, the battle field changed and all of a sudden they had inherited two pieces of live bait. Orders had come through from the very top of the British Government that, with immediate effect, the Russians were to become a secondary objective and the acquirement of Sikorski's crate was to become an absolute priority. Snowdon headed up the task force whose sole aim was to get their hands on the crate, no matter what the cost. It was all too apparent that the Russians were convinced that this casement existed, so she knew that she would have to pull something spectacular out of the hat in order for all parties to walk away happy. All in all, it would be fair to say that she achieved this. The British were happy, because they have the port safely back in their hands, even if it did cost them two million pounds. The Russians wouldn't have been disappointed; despite losing most of their team in the helicopter crash, the remainder of the team had managed to escape the clutches of MI5, but more importantly they had proved to themselves that the casement actually did exist; they are, of course, blissfully unaware that the British still have possession of it. I wonder why they need it?! And last but not least that leaves me and Ben. We were supposed to grab the money and live till we are old and grey safe in the knowledge that no revenge attacks will be carried out against us; Snowdon nearly, but not quite, managed that.

I constantly find myself asking the question: if I could go back in time and change anything, would I? It would be true to say that I miss the use of my right arm; writing this book with just the one hand admittedly is a pain in the backside to say the least. I'm surrounded by wonderful people in heavenly surroundings. I can't remember the last time I saw rain, and traffic wardens are now just a fragment of my imagination. But yet my life is missing something. I dearly miss my Mum and Dad, who decided not to set up a new life for themselves here in Mexico, although they do spend most of their lives in the villa I bought for them in the south of France. I miss my cats Biggles and Toby and I worry that they don't understand why I have suddenly gone. They are never far away from my thoughts; I pray that Mum and Dad are giving them both oodles of strokes and biscuit treats. I miss my sister, her husband, Andrew, and my nephew and niece, Henry and Sophie; my fingers are constantly crossed that someday they will take up my offer of staying with me for as long as they like. I miss the heartache of seeing my Swindon Town go 2-0 up at half time only to throw it away in the second half. I would pay hundreds of pounds just to get a decent joint of beef with a dollop of proper horseradish source, to watch Clarkson on Top Gear again, to have an energy supplier salesman knock on my door and try to convert my gas and electrical business to their firm. I miss England and all the people who live there, even if they do moan and groan that the country isn't what it used to be; I say bugger off to another country if it's that bad and you will soon see how wonderful the green green grass of home is.

As for Ben, well he misses the use of his right leg but as I sit here watching him surrounded by young natives playing football on the beach with his false leg, I count my blessings that things could have turned out a whole lot worse. He is fortunate that his mother, stepfather, Howard, and his one and only sister Emma saw the merits of setting up home in Mexico, even though they are here on the pretence that they are looking after two best friends who lost limbs serving in Afghanistan. Life here is good and the money we have in the bank serves us as kings, the small estate agency we have patched together is doing just fine. So will we return to the United Kingdom someday? It is a move that will be seriously considered once the current Government stop making a hash of everything and Boris Johnson is the Conservative Prime Minister. When Swindon makes it to the premiership again and when the nation becomes once again proud to be British; until then, it's another San Miguel por favor. Cheers!

Lightning Source UK Ltd.
Milton Keynes UK
19 May 2010

154405UK00001B/282/P